Gloria's Birthday

GLORIA'S BIRTHDAY

Norma Levinson

C

CENTURY

LONDON SYDNEY AUCKLAND JOHANNESBURG

Copyright © Norma Levinson 1989

All rights reserved
First published in Great Britain in 1989 by
Century Hutchinson Ltd
Brookmount House, 62–65 Chandos Place
London WC2N 4NW

Century Hutchinson South Africa (Pty) Ltd
PO Box 337, Bergvlei 2012, South Africa

Century Hutchinson Australia Pty Ltd
20 Alfred Street, Milsons Point, Sydney, NSW 2061
Australia

Century Hutchinson New Zealand Ltd
PO Box 40–086, Glenfield, Auckland 10
New Zealand

British Library Cataloguing in Publication Data
Levinson, Norma
  Gloria's birthday.
  I. Title
  823′.914 [F]

ISBN 0-7126-3440-1

Printed in Great Britain by
Mackays of Chatham PLC, Chatham, Kent

For my parents, Judah and Miriam, with love

I thank my friends Doreen West and Gaby Marks for their help and advice.

Contents

1

The Other Three

'Time is a great healer,' said Professor Gottleib.

I watched the second hand jerk halfway round the huge wooden clock on the wall above his head. The ticking made a noise like the cracking of a whip. 'What an original idea! However did you cotton on to it?' I sneered. His face didn't change; his eyes remained expressionless.

'Edges blur; the pain diminishes. A scab forms over the injury, if you give it a chance and refrain from poking at it.'

'Spare me your platitudes, please! You sound like my mother who used to say the same things to me in so many words. I'd run into the house, screaming my head off with a bloody knee, and she'd talk to me in baby language while she cleaned it up, kissed it better and fixed a big, fancy bandage on it. Then she'd pop a sweet into my mouth, tell me what a brave girl I was and encourage me to run out to play again, knowing I'd soon forget about it. I must remind you that I'm not six years old any more.'

'And did you forget about it?'

'Invariably.'

'Did she also tell you to stop crying?'

'Yes. However did you guess?'

'And you stopped?'

I didn't bother to answer. I closed my eyes and heaved a sigh to register my irritation and boredom.

'You don't cry now, do you? Why is that?'

'I haven't busted my knee recently.'

'Why *me*! Why did it have to happen to *me*!' His voice rose, high; whining, as if mimicking me.

'I never said that! You're the one who talks in clichés!'

'What have you got against them?'

'They're trite and by definition are overused.'

'And self-evidently true. But of course, you expend a great deal of your energy in avoiding the truth.'

'Are you trying to make me angry?'

'I don't have to try. You can't hear or see or think about anything else but your anger. Isn't that so?'

'Professor Gottlieb,' I said, 'I am grateful to you for speaking up in court on my behalf, and because of the court's ruling, I have to see you. But I don't have to listen to you.'

'I'm afraid you do,' he said. 'I am very much afraid that you do – unless you prefer the alternative. Why *are* you so angry?'

'Have *you* ever lost a child?'

'Would you feel less angry if I had? If you knew that *my* lovely young daughter was dead?'

'You are extremely offensive.'

'Never mind about that. Answer the question.'

'I'm not a monster.'

'I'm not interested in moral judgements about yourself. Well?'

'How can I answer your damned questions,' I shouted, 'when you start off with false assumptions on purpose to provoke me? Of course I wouldn't be glad if your daughter was killed!'

'Glad? I didn't ask you whether you'd be glad.'

'I thought that's what you meant.'

He shook his head slowly. I longed to strike him.

'I asked whether you'd feel less angry.'

'How can I if I'm not angry to start with?'

'Would you feel comforted, then?'

'No.'

'You are not the only woman to have lost a child,' he said.

'You don't say!'

'It feels like that to you?'

I shrugged, stared at the clock, then checked my watch. He took no notice.

'During the Siege of Leningrad, do you know how many women lost their children?'

I bent my head, closed my eyes and tried not to hear.

'All those mothers – about your age – starving and frozen, scraping around in the bloody snow, searching for the remains of their dead sons. Most of them were already widows, of course. Some lost as many as three or four children. In one way, they were more fortunate than you.'

'What do you mean?' Scenes from the old newsreels crowded my vision, unbidden and unwanted, refusing to go away.

'At least they were not alone in their grief. They were able to share it fully with one another, and share the fight for life and dignity too. There was no time for despair. And there was an enemy against whom they could vent their combined anger. That always helps. Revenge and hatred are far more efficacious emotions than forgiveness and love. There was a marked drop in the numbers of mental breakdowns among the civilian population during the war. Mind you, the hospitals for nervous diseases were bulging at the seams by the following year.'

'If you're trying to tell me that feelings of revenge offer only temporary relief, I'll settle for that.'

'You did settle for it. It doesn't seem to have worked for you. Why is that?'

'How should I know? If you must pepper me with questions, ask a few that have answers.'

'I'd like to see you and your husband together tomorrow. Does that meet with your approval?'

'No. Frank's a very private man, and all this prying and probing distresses and embarrasses him. Anyway, he'll be at work. Someone's got to earn a living.'

'But of course it doesn't distress or embarrass you, does it? He'll be here tomorrow evening.'

'So what does it matter whether I approve or not?'

'What about your parents? Would you mind if they came to one of our talks?'

'Yes I would! I'd mind very much! I won't have them dragged into all this nonsense!'

11

'Nonsense? Perhaps. They have other grandchildren after all, haven't they?'

'Yes. My brother has five children.'

'But you had just the one? Why?'

'We couldn't have any more. I'd appreciate it if you wouldn't bring this up with my husband when you see him.'

'Why is that?'

'Why, why, why! I don't *know* why! Can't I say *anything* without you asking *why* all the time? Don't I have a right to a little privacy?'

'To a little; certainly. Do you like it here?'

'Yes. I like it.'

'Good.' Irony was wasted on him. He really was one of the vilest men I'd ever met, and if our sessions were anything to go by, he was worse than a total failure at his job. 'Would you prefer staying in the hospital to going home?'

I was so taken aback that I just sat and stared at him. 'But I can't go home,' I quavered.

'Would you answer my question, please.'

'I'm used to the hospital.' I wiped my sweaty hands against my skirt, then took the cigarette that Professor Gottleib offered me. He watched it shaking as he proffered a light. 'I'm not ready. The routine suits me and I help out the nurses,' I said in a gabble.

'I know. I've seen you. The patients and staff will miss you when you leave. But there's a world outside, waiting for you to find your way in it again. And all the people who love you and who loved Gloria are waiting there, to help you.' His voice sounded gentle, kind; but I knew better than to trust him. He could turn cold and hostile at the blink of an eye.

'I'm afraid,' I said.

'Of what?'

'I don't know. Those people . . . those people you mentioned.'

'Your friends; your family; your husband?'

'Yes. They've become strangers to me.'

12

'And you're afraid of strangers?'

'Of course not!' I snapped. 'You know what I mean.'

'Tell me what you mean.'

'I can't!' I shouted.

'Try. You don't have to feel ashamed.'

'Ashamed? What do you mean – feel ashamed? Why should I?'

'Let's start with your friends – your best friends. What are their names?'

'Doreen and Laurie Westwood. They've been marvellous to us since . . .'

'And do they have children?'

'Yes. Twins. Adam and Tim. They were at school with Gloria.'

'And how do you feel about the twins?'

'When they were youngsters they practically lived in our house. I'm extremely fond of them.'

'And are you jealous?'

'Of whom?'

'Your friends. They have two children and you don't have any. Is that fair?'

The blood rushed to my head. I stood up and walked unsteadily round the room. I felt frightened; ill.

'I won't listen to you any longer.'

'We've been through all this. Well?'

'You want me to tell you I'm jealous of my best friends and that I resent the fact that their kids are alive! I don't understand your spiteful, hypothetical questions! You can't manipulate me into telling you lies about myself!'

'Would they be lies?'

'YES!'

'Then you are most unusual. Do you consider yourself unusual?'

'No. I mean yes.'

'Do you feel guilty when you think of your friends and their children? Do you feel so guilty that you can't tolerate the thoughts you have about people you care for, and so they become strangers? Isn't that possible?' He was shouting; screaming at me. I covered my ears.

13

'Stop shouting!'

'I haven't raised my voice, Beattie. I'll play the tape back to you.'

'No! I don't want to hear it!'

'Why have your parents become strangers to you?'

'I don't know. I just feel uncomfortable with them.'

'Is it because you reject their comfort? The kiss, the cuddle, the bandage, won't heal *this* injury. You're not their little girl any more, but a middle-aged woman, and you can't go running to them with it. They might try to make it better and that can't be. And if you did cry, perhaps you wouldn't be able to stop. They'd feel helpless and useless. So you push them away. One has to be ruthless, eh, Beattie? You mustn't distress them by exposing your anguish. Why, they might treat it like a broken knee, instead of a broken heart.'

'I'm sorry to have to tell you that you're talking absolute nonsense.'

'I'm waiting to be corrected,' said Professor Gottleib.

I sat down and twiddled my hair round my fingers, doubled it over and made a knot in it, then another one. He watched me carefully.

'I haven't got any easy answers,' I said. 'I only know that you're wrong about practically everything and you assume you're right. I find it very upsetting.'

'Your husband – is he a stranger?'

'Yes. Everybody is, but it's nothing to do with them. It's me. I don't know who I am any more.'

'We're talking about your husband,' said Professor Gottleib coldly. 'Not you. Gloria was his daughter too. Do you think about that?'

'Yes.'

'How is he feeling?'

'Wretched, heart-broken, grief-stricken. I've got a lot of adjectives up my sleeve. I keep a thesaurus there. But I think your next patient is waiting outside. Our time was up five minutes ago.'

'There is no one waiting and I have plenty of time. Continue, please.'

'. . . Miserable, desolate.' I busied myself tearing the knots out of my hair.

'And how is he coping? Do you think about that, too?'

'Of course!' I said irritably. 'Frank has great courage and strength and purpose. If he's dogged by bitterness and despair and dread and all the other horrible feelings which assail him, he doesn't succumb. He engages himself in his work; his research. He has more resources to draw upon than I . . . than most people, and tries to discipline himself so that he can go on from day to day. He's wonderful!' The sound of my voice embarrassed me. I had to get up again and take a turn around the room. I stood in front of one of Professor Gottleib's ghastly abstract pictures on the wall, and pretended to study it.

'He's wonderful?' He actually seemed to be mocking both Frank and me. 'He's so wonderful, so disciplined, so brave and strong that he doesn't really suffer much, does he? Perhaps he's even able to put the loss of his daughter right to the back of his mind and even think of other things; his work, the pleasures life still has to offer, making love with his wife, as if nothing had changed! He's terrible, isn't he? Unfeeling, selfish, hard! You can't go back to live with a man like that, can you? Can you? He might want to hold you in his arms to comfort you, but what if he wants to go beyond comfort and descend into passion? That must not be! But worse than that, desire may stir in you. Passion may dissolve *your* grief, and Gloria's death might be forgotten, however fleetingly. You don't admire Frank for his courage and fortitude, do you, Beatrice Dwek? You despise him for his weakness and infidelity to your daughter's memory! I advise you not to try to leave this room. You are here because you committed a crime and I dislike having to remind you that you are not a free agent. You must comply with the treatment here.'

'And listen to your outrageous remarks!' I screamed. 'And answer your horrible questions? What if I refuse?'

'You know the alternative as well as I do. We both

heard and understood the judgement. Would you like me to remind you of it?'

'No,' I said. 'No!'

'We fumble in the dark; grope our way through its labyrinths looking for the light, and it's strange and frightening because we don't know how to get to it. But if we give up and stop striving, the light won't find *us*. All *I'm* trying to do, is explore the possible paths using my experience, and hope I can persuade you to struggle along with me. You'll find your way out, but not by crouching in a corner scratching at the same stone wall with your eyes closed against the alternatives. I'm not pretending to you that it's easy or comfortable. It's rough going, and now and then I have to shove you through difficulties and confusion, when what you really want to do is to stay put where it's safe, even though it's as black as hell.'

I'd never heard Professor Gottleib speak like this before. His manner caught me off guard. 'From where I am, I seem to be beset with stone walls. I don't believe there is a light for me to find. I feel I've lost my reason for escaping from this horrible dark void.' A lump boiled in my throat, half choking me. 'I need help,' I croaked, surprised out of my life at what I was saying, and the sound of a voice that didn't belong to me.

He took no notice. Instead he extracted a folder from the sheaf on the desk, opened it and began to write. The noise of the ticking clock filled the room. They'd be serving the lunch on Ward 3 and I was usually there to give a hand.

'I'd better be going now.'

Without looking up from his writing, or pausing for a moment, he flapped his left hand at me, indicating that I should stay where I was. Since I had nothing better to do, I closed my eyes and went over in my mind what he had said about Frank which had made me almost faint with rage. He had misjudged us both, of course! Frank, unfeeling, selfish, hard! How dare he make such assertions about what I was thinking and feeling; and about a man he hardly knew! If there was anyone who fitted that

16

description, it was him! He was also incredibly arrogant, sitting here, scribbling, keeping me waiting, so that he could feed his lust for power!

'What are the three most important, most difficult words for one vulnerable human being to say to another, when that human being is unsure of a sympathetic response?'

I opened my eyes to find him looking at me intently, his chin resting on his clasped hands.

'I love you.' I could feel myself blushing. God! He must be able to see my face turning deep crimson, but of course he hadn't the grace to look away. The wretch was obviously misinterpreting my answer; assuming that I had romantic designs on him!

'What about "I need help"? You're going to make it, Beattie! I'll stake my reputation on that!'

'I hope you value your reputation,' I said, wondering what the hell was happening to me. My facial muscles seemed out of control.

He smiled. It was the first time I'd ever seen his face register anything but cold indifference. It transformed him.

'You have a beautiful smile, Beattie,' said Professor Gottleib. He was probably a little mad, and no wonder. 'You admit you need help. From whom?'

'From you.' I actually detested him, and was saying things I didn't mean. He shook his head. I looked down at my lap.

'You need someone better qualified. Could you suggest someone?'

'I don't know any psychiatrists. I certainly don't know anyone with a longer string of letters after his name than you. Are you telling me that I'm too far gone for you to help?' I could feel my heart pounding in my throat.

'Yes. Something like that. What generally happens when patients are discharged from hospital because they can no longer be helped by the doctor in its environment?'

'They go home – to die, I suppose.' I tried to sound

17

nonchalant; instead, the words came out like a yodeller in training.

'To die – or to recover. You don't need this hospital any more. It's time to go home, Beattie. Home, to the person most qualified to help you.'

'Frank?'

'Yes. Frank. I've written down my recommendation and conditions for your release, which should be within the next ten days.'

'Would you enlighten me as to the conditions?'

'I was just about to. You must attend the weekly group therapy sessions and I shall want to see you at my clinic at monthly intervals. You will also be required to start work within a week of your discharge.'

'I can't go back to work! You know damn well I can't!'

He tried to steamroller me, raising his voice as if he was daft or deaf to what I was saying.

'If this is a condition of my release, then I'll just have to stay here!' There was no point in attempting to engage in a sensible discussion with him. I let him rant on by himself.

'I'm the Honorary Medical Officer of The Haven – a small home in North London for the aged and infirm. I was at the annual committee meeting last night and took the opportunity of recommending you for a job there; cleaning, a little cooking, serving the meals and helping out generally in dressing and taking care of the residents.'

'This random idea doesn't appeal to me at all. I've no experience in dealing with a bunch of old people and have neither the disposition nor the desire to do so.'

'Why?'

'Mixing with old sick people will just increase my depression. It wouldn't be fair on them anyway,' I added, pleased that I'd thought of something to say which would extricate me. 'After all, they'll need cheering up and I'm the last person to fulfil that need.'

'Have you considered that *you* may need "cheering up", as you say?'

I laughed scornfully. 'Well, you're suggesting the right place – a real fun palace!'

'What do you think the cliché, "cheering up", means?'

'I don't know. I've forgotten.'

'Adjusting energy. Turning its power away from self-absorption to the outside. The Haven is a small residential home and no more than twelve elderly people are cared for there at any one time. Each has survived loneliness, grief, ill health, neglect and loss, and perhaps someone like you may learn the meaning of "cheering up" about which you are, at present, ignorant. As it happens, this job is for a general help. No one expects you to develop relationships. I've spoken to the matron, who is willing to employ you on a month's trial, starting on March first.'

'Thank you for having the courtesy to consult me first.' He looked at me blandly. 'What's this matron like? Does she know my history.'

'She's a compassionate, humorous, charming woman and knows only that you're a patient of mine.'

'She sounds too good to be true. I dislike her already. Anyway, how do you know I'm not still dangerous?'

'You are extremely dangerous – particularly when you smile.'

This cold fish was actually flirting with me! I couldn't believe my ears! He could probably be struck off the register of psychiatrists or whatever one called their roll of honour, for behaving skittishly with a patient. I looked at him sharply, mortified that he might notice the peculiar pleasure it gave me.

'But,' he continued, 'if you're referring to possible violent attacks on frail old people – I don't think we need concern ourselves unduly. What do you say? Will you give it some thought, and perhaps discuss the idea with Frank tomorrow evening?'

Frank. My Frank, all alone, waiting for me to get well; to come home. Visiting me in this horrible place, week after week. Holding me when I screamed and raved, his face white, his hands and voice shaking, trying to comfort me; to talk about Gloria. 'You are extremely dangerous –

19

particularly when you smile.' How long had it been since I'd smiled at Frank?

'I want to go home, Professor Gottleib,' I said.

'I'm going to miss you, Beatrice Dwek,' said Professor Gottleib. He stood up, walked round the desk and took both my hands in his, drawing me to my feet.

'I'll miss you too,' I said, smiling.

'Don't forget those three little words – say them as often as possible to each other. Frank needs to hear them – and to say them. He's been without you for a very long time. What are they?'

'I need help,' I said, clearly; fearlessly. The cassette in his recorder clicked to a full stop.

'I was thinking of the other three. What are *they*?'

'The other three?' I asked, pretending to be puzzled. Revenge – something else – was very sweet. I watched, confidently; unwaveringly, as he averted his eyes.

'I love you,' said Professor Gottleib.

2

Page Nought

It was already quite dark when Frank brought me home.
I sat in the car, twisting my hair into knots, while he
pulled my suitcase and plastic carrier bag out of the boot.
I knew Mrs Colley, our neighbour, was watching us
through the window but at least our friends and parents
weren't crowding the pavement, smiles ripping their faces,
waiting to welcome me. I watched him push the gate
open, walk up the slushy front steps, unlock the door,
turn on the light in the passage and dump the case next
to the hall-stand. He looked so lonely.

'Come on.'

He helped me out of the car for I was stiff and frozen
with cold and fear, then put his arm round me and pushed
me gently into the house, closing the door behind us.
Our house. Our home, so familiar to me yet suddenly so
strange. He tried to take off my jacket, but I folded my
arms, shivering.

'In a minute, Frank. I'm cold.' My hands and feet were
icy, yet my forehead was wet with perspiration. I was ill;
very ill, and it was irresponsible of the doctors to have
discharged me from hospital. 'It's like an igloo in here.'

'Turn on the fire while I put the kettle on.'

I fumbled for the light switch in the living room, not
knowing quite where it was, and looked around me. The
sideboard was crammed with cards and vases of flowers.
I lit the gas fire and knelt on the rug, warming my hands,
listening to Frank moving about in the kitchen. He came
in, carrying the tray laden with tea things and put it on
the coffee table, drew the curtains across and turned on
the lamps. Then he bent down and pulled me to my feet.

I wrapped my arms round him while he stroked my back and hair.

'I'm so glad to be home, sweetheart,' I lied, hiding my face in his shoulder.

'You don't have to say that, Beattie. I know how scared and strange you feel. But *I'm* glad; if only you knew how glad! The house has been so dreary and empty without you.'

'Will it ever be anything else but dreary and empty?'

'That's up to us. We've got to try and help each other. Have you seen all the cards?'

'I'll look at them later. Let's have tea. You pour. My hands keep shaking.'

'Your mum and dad want to come over tomorrow. Is that all right?'

'No! It is *not* all right. I told you I didn't want to see anyone just yet. If you told them yes, you'll just have to phone and tell them no. How many days are there in February?'

'Twenty-eight this year.' He looked at me apprehensively. 'Why?'

'Don't say "why". That word makes me sick,' I shouted. 'Why, why, why! That's all I've had these last three months, and now *you're* starting off with it! All I want to know is how many days I've got left before I have to go to that damned old folk's home!' I swallowed the hot tea, and watched him slyly. He looked worn out and utterly wretched.

'I'm just going upstairs for a moment,' I told him.

'I'll get supper ready. I bought some salt beef for a treat – and picked up three mystery salads from the deli.'

'I'm not hungry. You can put my share in your sandwiches for tomorrow.' I crawled up the stairs like an old woman and went into our bedroom.

Frank had obviously cleaned and tidied up when he heard I was coming home. He usually left all the mess for me. There were yet more flowers on my bedside table, and the bed was actually made. He'd found the frilly pillowcases and cover, thinking, no doubt, that I'd be

22

touched by his thoughtfulness. I felt merely irritated. I had no intention of sleeping in this bed, anyway.

I went into Gloria's room which she'd had since she was a little girl. When she and Dave got married and moved to Brighton, we put her divan in the boxroom. I'd forgotten about the sponge mattress leaning against the wall in here, and seeing it surprised me. We bought it for ourselves when we were first married, and later, Frank used to drag it down to the back garden on a summer Sunday. All the kids in the neighbourhood had jumped and somersaulted on that old mattress. 'Gloria! Gloria! Ask your dad to bring out the mattress. Go on!' Then Dave and Gloria slept on it whenever they came to visit.

Frank came up with two clinking glasses. 'We should get rid of that old thing. It must be going mouldy inside,' I said.

He went over and examined it. 'It's as fresh as a daisy. Let's hang on to it for a while. It's handy for visitors and Paula had a marvellous time on it that last weekend. We had a marvellous time on it, too, come to think of it.' He took my hand.

I moved away from him to look at the books on the shelf. *Anne of Green Gables, Jane Eyre, Daddy Longlegs, Little Women, Good Wives.* I picked up *Good Wives* and looked again at what Gloria had written on the fly-leaf: 'Page Nought. This is the best book I have ever read in my life and Pages 251 to 260 are the most Unbearable Pages. I will love this book until the day I die. Gloria Dwek aged 11.'

'What visitors? Anyway, Paula won't remember the mattress.'

'Then we'll have to remind her. They want to bring her over next weekend.'

'*They?*'

'I mean, Dave wants to bring her.'

'Did I or did I not tell you that I want to be left alone?'

'Don't you want to see our granddaughter?'

'No. I do not.' I pushed past him and went into the bathroom. 'I'm going to have a shower,' I called. 'By the way, Gloria's dead. You keep forgetting. I'll be sleeping in the boxroom tonight. I've got used to having a bed to myself.'

I heard him going downstairs as I ran the hot water, and stood staring at the mirror. The ugliness of the face there repelled yet fascinated me: a hard, lifeless, hideous mask pressed on to features that resembled mine, denying them animation and vitality. I don't know how long I stood there, mesmerized by the dull, unblinking eyes and the stiff, cruel mouth, hateful and vindictive. I moved, zombie-like, under the shower and turned the face against the powerful jet of water. I wrapped myself in the towel and sat on the side of the bath, wondering what to do next, wishing I was back in hospital, serving the evening drinks. I went into our bedroom to look for a nightie.

Frank was lying on top of the quilt, the corner of *Good Wives* digging into his temple, fast asleep. I hadn't heard him come upstairs. I rescued the book which was open at Page Nought, then turned to Page 251, remembering how I had passed her bedroom door and heard her weeping.

'What's the matter, Gloria?' Her eyes were red and swollen like ping-pong balls, a sodden handkerchief held against her face.

'Beth just died. Why did it have to be Beth? She was so good and kind and Jo loved her so much.'

'It's a story, darling. Only a made-up story,' I said stupidly, unsuccessfully stifling a giggle.

'It's not funny, Mother. I know it's a story, but it seems so real. It makes me sad, because it could easily be true. I wish people you love didn't have to die.'

'We all wish that. But if the person we love is old and tired and suffering, it would be cruel and selfish to want them to stay alive for ever. And if people didn't die, there'd be no room in the world for the following generations.'

'Why did Beth have to die so young, though? Even if she believed she was going to heaven, I bet she would much rather have stayed here with Marmee and her father

24

and sisters. Nothing will ever be the same again, now she's dead. Jo will be miserable for the rest of her life.'

'Nothing will ever be the same, but that doesn't mean she's going to grieve for ever. You wait till you read this chapter, here – "Under the Umbrella" – and then the next book, *Jo's Boys*. Life goes on, Gloria. It's got to. You struggle on and in time the pain and anguish fades. You ask Dad. When Grandma Dwek died, Dad was fifteen and Uncle Charlie was only four. They adored her. It was terrible for them and Grandpa. But within three years Grandpa remarried and they've been very happy. It wasn't easy for anyone at first, especially poor Edna, but look how Dad and all of us love her! That doesn't mean he's forgotten his real mother. He just had to get used to being without her – and gradually he did.'

'Why do you call Grandma Edna poor? Was *she* miserable?'

'Oh, yes – sometimes. Imagine what it's like, trying to cope with four lads – *and* their mother's mother – who don't necessarily want you around, just because their father does! She was some special lady!'

'She still is!' said Gloria. 'I'm glad Grandpa fell in love with her and that she's my grandma.'

'So am I. Let's turn your light off now. It's nearly tomorrow and *Good Wives* won't run away.'

I read the Unbearable Pages over and over, then looked down at Frank. I wiped his face with my towel and held his hand while he roused himself.

'You've been crying in your sleep, Frank. Have you been reading the Unbearable Pages?'

'Just Page Nought.'

I bent to kiss him.

'Where've you been?' he asked. 'Thank goodness you woke me up. I was having one hell of a nightmare. You kept saying you were staying in the boxroom until February thirtieth.'

'And did I say I didn't want to see Mum and Dad and Paula?'

'What are you? A mind-reader? This is very spooky. Go on.'

'And I didn't want any salt beef?'

'That was the really chilling part of it.'

'I had the same horrible nightmare, sweetheart.'

'And what woke *you* up?' he asked, smiling.

'I came in here, sleepwalking, and stumbled on you. Oh, Frank, I'm so glad to be home and awake!'

'Don't go away again, Beattie,' said Frank, holding me. 'Promise!'

'I promise.'

I looked in my drawer for a nightie while he went down to get the supper. I'd forgotten all about the notebook which I'd bought and put here months ago. It was bound in flowered cloth, the pages held by spiral rings so that it opened out flat, as if welcoming the owner to make a start.

'What have you got there?' said Frank, putting the tray on the bed.

'Gloria's birthday present. She wanted to write the stories down about the people she worked with. I thought it was the nicest notebook I'd ever seen, so I bought it and put it in the drawer until . . .'

'You write in it, Beattie. It belongs to you, now.'

'What shall I write about?'

'What about the people *you're* going to work with at The Haven?'

'Are you trying to give me another relapse? It's bad enough that I've got to go there, let alone write about the dreaded experience.'

'It might not be as dreadful as you think. We'll leave the book open on your table, here, and when you're ready, you'll find plenty to write about. A word here; a word there – and before you look round you'll have written two words!'

'You're over-ambitious. I won't even make it to Page Nought.'

'You've got to finish the book before you can write Page Nought,' said Frank.

3
Page One

On 28 February I telephoned Matron to ask her what time I should present myself and she suggested ten o'clock, which would be a good time for her to chat to me, explain my duties and show me round. She sounded as if she'd just woken up and not in the least like the brisk and efficient martinet I envisaged. Nevertheless, I wished there were twenty-nine days in February. Frank and I drove over that evening to make sure I knew where The Haven was and to have a look at the outside. It was down one of those posh, tree-lined avenues in North Finchley, about two hundred yards from the busy shopping centre on the main road, set among well-kept, large houses, each with their own driveways, lamps on the gates and well-kept front lawns. The Haven looked like a poor, neglected relation. It was only a twenty-minute drive from our house, which was in a much more humble area of North London. However, with rush-hour traffic, I'd probably have to set out at the crack of dawn.

At ten o'clock the next morning I rang the front doorbell, shaking like a leaf. A grim-faced nurse of about thirty-five admitted me.

'Hello,' I said. 'I'm Mrs Dwek. I've an appointment with Matron.'

'Who?'

'Mrs Dwek. Mrs Beatrice Dwek.'

'She never said anything to me about an appointment. You'd better wait here and I'll try to find her.' She pointed to a bench in the hall.

'Nurse! Nurse!' Someone was calling from a room nearby.

'Will you *wait!*' she yelled. 'I've only got one pair of

hands! Matron has a visitor, and I have to go and find her!'

'I don't mind waiting, Nurse,' I said.

She ignored me and disappeared.

'Nurse! Help! *Help*!'

I jumped up and ran through a door off the hall where the voice was coming from. It was a large, tiled washroom with pegs and radiators and heated, laden towel racks, three basins and three spacious cubicles with the doors open. An old lady with one arm sat comfortably on one of the toilets. She pressed a button on the wall and it flushed with a terrific whoosh, then grasped the rail next to her.

'Can I help you?' I asked. 'Nurse has gone to find Matron.'

'Who are *you*?' She looked at me suspiciously.

'I'm the new Help. My name's Beattie.'

'Beattie, Shmeatie,' she sneered. 'So what are you standing there for? Pull me up, then, you lump!'

I put my arms round her and lifted her to her feet. She was as light and as bony as a little bird. 'Do you need . . .'

'You think I'm helpless? You think I don't know how to manage myself? Go and turn on the hot tap and bring my flannel and towel to the sink. Not those! They belong to the Old Maid. The pink ones!'

I turned my back respectfully and did as I was told.

The toilet lid banged down with a crash and she came tottering out. 'Bring the stool here.'

I placed it where she directed, next to the sink, and watched nervously as she sat down and with great care began washing herself with her one hand.

'You're all the same; lazy, useless lumps,' she said, squeezing the flannel with admirable skill.

'I hope no one here is the same as you,' I snapped.

'What did you say, Street Woman?'

'You heard, you old devil!' She cackled so merrily and infectiously that I felt my face splitting in two.

'My name is Sarah Yanofsky.'

'My name is Beatrice Dwek, but most people call me

28

Beattie. Not Lump; not Street Woman; not Shmeattie. BEATTIE!' I bellowed.

'Pass me that pink toothbrush, Shmeattie. I want to clean my teeth.' She put the plug in the basin, ran cold water and swilled her dentures.

'I'd like to wash your mouth out with weed-killer, but soap might do the trick. Here. Here's a pretty little red piece. It will fit nicely in that trap of yours, now it's not full of teeth!'

She rocked with laughter. I really liked Sarah Yanofsky. I could hear someone walking quickly along the hall, and passed Sarah her toothbrush. She was scrubbing away when the nurse came in.

'And what's going on here?' she said irritably.

'What does it look like, Meshugana Hunt?' said Sarah. 'A honeymoon?'

'I can't understand a word you're saying when you haven't got your teeth in.'

I understood perfectly. My mother was brought up in the East End when it was almost entirely a Jewish neighbourhood and could speak Yiddish quite well. I'd learnt a few of the more racy insults from her. Meshugana Hunt, or Mad Dog, was a fairly mild one.

'She said she's cleaning her teeth.'

Sarah slipped them into her mouth. 'Beattie said she'll take me to Woolworth's this afternoon.'

'Matron may have other ideas. You shouldn't make arrangements with the residents without first consulting her. She'd like to see you now. If you go upstairs, you'll find her flat on the top landing.'

It was like an oven in the house. I was wearing winter clothes, and hadn't thought to wear a blouse under my jumper. Obviously the place had to be kept very warm for the old people. I hung my coat and scarf on the hall-stand and plodded up two long flights of broad, linoleum-covered stairs until I reached Matron's flat. The door was open.

'Come in, Mrs Dwek!'

I walked into an extremely untidy sitting room. Matron

29

shook hands with me, then threw newspapers off one of the armchairs and asked me to sit down. She was over-weight and dressed in a cotton house-coat, bedroom slip-pers and a multi-coloured towel, twisted into a turban. She had a lovely smile and spoke in an upper-class voice. She offered me coffee and while she shuffled into the kitchen to prepare it, I looked around me. Her various nursing awards and certificates hung on the walls and nursing magazines, books and papers were stacked in piles on the floor and table. The room was hot and smoky, despite an open window.

'Clear a space on the coffee table, will you, Mrs Dwek?'

I deposited a groaning ashtray and a couple of used glasses on the large table, then wiped the surface surrep-titiously with a paper hanky. She came in with the tray, plonked it down, turned off the telly and sat down opposite me.

'I'm sorry about the mess. I had a late night and since I'm not on duty until eleven, a late morning. I thought I'd make a start on the packing by sorting my books and papers; a mistake,' she said gloomily. 'Anyway, that's not your problem. Now I'll tell you about the home and how it's organized and then introduce you to the staff and residents. Have you had any previous experience?'

'No.'

'Any nursing experience?'

'I'm afraid not.'

'Never mind. Don't look so worried.'

Surely she knew that I'd never done this kind of work before.

'I've never done anything like this, Matron. I'm sorry that Professor Gottleib didn't think to tell you. When Frank and I married, he was a student with a small grant. I worked as a mini-cab driver during the day, and he did a few hours at night. Then our daughter, Gloria, was born, and I worked as a cook in a private school in Hampstead. My husband was very ill for months and until he got better and was able to continue his studies, I just did what I could to keep afloat. Later, I got a job as a clerk at the Court of Appeal and a year ago, enrolled as a mature student and started my teacher training course, but I gave it up in October. I'm sorry, but I don't know the first thing about this work.'

'You can drive and you can cook! I call that very useful experience! I got your papers from Doctor Thingummy two or three weeks ago, but what with all this, I've temporarily mislaid them. I recollect, though, that you seem to have done such a good job helping out in the wards while you were in hospital, that you were highly recommended.

'This house was donated by a Jewish philanthropist, an immigrant from Eastern Europe, who spent his childhood and youth in the East End of London. He made certain conditions as to its use. The people admitted must be Jewish, aged and in need of care, and not less than half the number must have lived in a particular area of the East End. A happy result of these conditions means that several of the residents either know each other or have mutual acquaintances and similar backgrounds. I don't have to tell you that the house wasn't purpose-built for old people. Plans *have* been submitted for a complete facelift, but work isn't due to start for at least another year. Once it's completed, we'll be able to accommodate as many as twenty-five residents very comfortably. At present, we're limited to not more than twelve at any one time and the facilities provide for a room each and two flats for couples on the first floor. We've two more good-sized rooms and facilities on this landing, on the other side of the fire door, but unfortunately we haven't a lift, which is a great drawback. Still the rooms are very pleasant and I like to ensure that people are able to have as many personal possessions with them as space will allow.

'It must be a terrible wrench to have to leave one's own home and move into another with a capital H. They've led full, independent lives; brought up families; worked hard, and just as you or I don't expect to end up in a Home, neither did they. You don't have to have nursing experience to imbue our residents with a sense of their own worth, and to make that H feel small. No one can learn how to do that. It's more important to make *their* lives brighter than pots, pans, kettles or floors.'

She grinned suddenly. 'They'll always give you a hand with the chores, anyway, and that's perfectly all right as long as they don't overdo things. Cook comes in four mornings a week for three hours and we have a part-time gardener, Tom, who also does the heavy cleaning. Voluntary workers – mostly ladies who live in the area – have formed a group called Help The Haven, and arrange outings and entertainment and so on for the residents, and we have Janet, an occupational therapist, twice a week. There always has to be a qualified nurse on duty, so when either Nurse Goss or myself is off, we use the agency, and Doctor Taylor pays a routine visit every Tuesday afternoon.

'Two part-time helpers left us at the same time three weeks ago, so we're very short-handed. What I really need from you is to organize breakfast, wash the dishes, set up for lunch and supper, help Cook with the vegetables, prepare and serve morning coffee and afternoon tea and help generally in keeping the kitchen clean and lending a hand where necessary. If possible, I'd appreciate it if you could make your hours fairly flexible until Matron Dixon takes over. She may want to organize things differently, though. By the way, the residents all call me Tinker. What should they call you?'

'Beattie. Beattie's fine. Will the new matron be taking over from you?'

'Yes. The end of this month.'

'And you'll be leaving?' She nodded. 'I'm sorry. I'm really sorry.'

'Why?' she asked, smiling.

I didn't know her from Adam, and was at a loss what to answer.

'I'm sorry,' I said truthfully, 'because you're friendly and easygoing and seem to care about people more than things.'

'Thank you, Beattie. It was true of me once, but not

any more. I care more about *that* than anything else.' She waved her hand at the empty glasses on the table. 'I got careless and was reported, quite properly, when I was somewhat the worse for wear one evening. Mind you, I've always been able to cope adequately in an emergency. Anyway, my health has been damaged, and before it gets worse, I'm going into a private nursing home to dry out. I'm quite nervous about the prospect, but I can't do it without help. I need help badly.'

'Someone told me that once you admit that, you're halfway home – and dry! I hope it's true – for both of us! I'm here only on a month's trial; it's quite likely we'll be leaving at the same time.'

'I'm sure that won't be the case! Will you excuse me for a few minutes while I get dressed? Then I'll show you round and introduce you to our residents. Here's a list of their names with some potted information for you to look at while you're waiting.'

'I promised Sarah I'd take her to Woolworth's this afternoon. Is that all right?'

'If it's all right with you and Sarah, it's fine with me.'

I read the names that hadn't been crossed out with the word 'Deceased' written over them, wondering how I was ever going to remember them all: Boris Berkovitch; Olga Berkovitch; Dora Cohen; Alter Freid; Golda Freid; Kitty Horovitz; Yetta Juggler; Rene Landis; Sadie Lypsic; Queenie Marks; Sarah Yanofsky. At least I knew one of them already . . .

Yanofsky, Sarah – Admitted 5 July 1982, after the death of her daughter, with whom she lived. Born 1882 in Rudenka, Poland. Right arm amputated in early childhood. Husband and three children killed in Zeppelin raid, 1917. Employment: machinist; market trader. Removal of kidney, 1951. Cataract removed, 1980. Needs a wheelchair for outside use and probably for use within the home eventually. Mentally alert. Relative to contact: Dr Jonathan Daniels (grandson), 21 Devonshire St, W1.

'I won't be long!' called Tinker. 'Could you pass me the hair dryer – on the bookcase.'

I jumped up and took it through to the chaotic bedroom, where she was rubbing her hair with a towel.

'I've just been reading about Sarah,' I said shakily. 'I wonder what else lies between these few lines!'

'Maybe you'll be lucky enough to discover a tiny fraction of what's missing. But Sarah isn't one to reveal too much. She has her own way of coping. They all have.'

I glanced through the short case histories, concentrating only on the sound of the hair dryer blowing in the bedroom. What the hell was I doing in a place like this! Tinker didn't know how lucky she was, getting away from it all to be tucked up in a nice safe nursing home along with all the upper-crust alcoholics. I sneaked over to the table and freshened my coffee cup with a drop of whisky from the half empty plastic bottle and swallowed it quickly as I heard the dryer switch off.

'I'm ready, Beattie,' she said. 'Are you?' She looked fresh and spruce in a pale green, short-sleeved, stylish overall.

'I haven't finished reading this,' I said.

'Why don't you keep it until you're familiar with everyone? It'll make a lot more sense in a week or two. The rest of the file mostly consists of the medical histories in detail and instructions for nursing and treatment.'

'I notice there are only two men to nine women. Isn't that a low ratio?'

'I received application papers for a male resident this morning. I haven't had the opportunity of checking his details yet, but in all probability the ratio next month will be three to nine. It's fairly representative in the over-eighties age group. In general, women endure and overcome calamity with more success and resilience.' She looked over my shoulder at the papers in my hand, then went over to the whisky bottle and poured out two tots.

'Here's to us. Don't let it become a habit, though!'

'I'll try,' I smiled.

'And I'll try – next month. Tinker, Daphne,' she said, as if reading aloud; 'Tinker, Daphne – Admitted 27 June 1982 after ten years' experience in the Royal Northern

Hospital, Manchester, on the geriatric ward. Born with a silver spoon in her mouth, April Fool's Day, 1935, Dorking, Surrey. Self-destructive; alcoholic; almost fifty, unlucky in love, confused but hopeful of full recovery. Unmarried. Numerous relatives, but none close enough to contact. Now it's your turn.'

'Dwek, Beatrice – Admitted, 1 March 1985 . . .' I looked at her and she winked and made a face at me. I drained my glass and took a deep breath. '. . . after discharge from the James Barrie Hospital. Born 10 December 1943, London. Frozen shoulder; occasional nervous spasms; obsessional and compulsive; depressed; mentally confused. Married. One daughter, murdered on 4 October 1984. Relative to contact: Frank Dwek, husband, 17 Friars Avenue, Cricklewood.'

'Let's go, Beattie,' smiled Tinker.

We walked down to the first landing lined with cupboards and she told me that Mr and Mrs Freid and Mr and Mrs Berkovitch occupied the two converted flats on this floor. Since there seemed to be a lot of yelling and shouting going on and I could hear Nurse Goss's voice, we didn't pay a visit and continued down to the ground floor.

Two enormous rooms off the hall had been subdivided very skilfully into pleasant little rooms off an open corridor, where the usual paraphernalia of invalids stood against the wall – commodes, walking frames and a wheelchair.

The kitchen led off a short corridor to the left of the hall bench and had been extended to accommodate a spacious dining area with Formica-topped tables and a sideboard. Two large stainless steel sinks, a fridge and a cooker lined the walls with working surfaces in between, and a pine table loaded with vegetables and cooking utensils stood in the middle with a couple of stools pushed underneath. A radio, a small television and a beautiful tabby cat sat on a shelf under some tall cupboards. There was an urn, a big wooden trolley and a pan stand in the corner. There was an old-fashioned hatch in the wall which apparently opened into the residents' sitting room. The kitchen floor was green and white and the curtainless window looked out on to the side of the garden. It was a light, homely room.

Tinker showed me the store room and the freezer and the week's menu pinned to a cork frame on the wall, together with an explanation and rules of the Jewish Dietary Laws, assuring me that I'd soon find my way around.

I wandered about, opening cupboards and drawers, while Tinker chatted to an invisible woman in the adjacent store room who was complaining about the amount of work she had to do, single-handed.

'I thought she was supposed to start work today.'

'I'll introduce you. Beattie!' she called. 'This is Mrs Jones, our cook.'

I shook hands with a skinny, disagreeable woman of about my own age, enveloped in a huge striped pinafore, who looked at me with distaste.

'I've no time to talk. There's too much to do.'

'Perhaps you'd better give Cook a hand, just for twenty minutes or so, before you meet the residents,' said Tinker. 'This overall should fit you. Take your jumper off, otherwise you'll roast along with the beef. We'll take the coffee round together, at eleven o'clock although usually it's served earlier. See you later.'

Mrs Jones told me what was for lunch and supper, and what needed doing, then went off for her coffee break. I peeled the potatoes, set the tables with glasses, paper napkins, condiments and cutlery, then set the trolley with cups, saucers and biscuits. Since I wasn't sure what else to do, I went over to the hatch, and peeped through.

Eight old ladies were sitting in a semi-circle knitting or winding balls of wool with the occupational therapist, and a little old man was standing at a bench making a lampshade. The room was full of sunshine and the huge windows opened out on to a verandah.

Mrs Jones came in and tut-tutted irritably because I hadn't made the coffee. Since it was instant, and I could see no necessity for making it in a jug when one could

36

just pop a teaspoonful into each cup, I felt like saying something back to her with a little more flavour. Compared to her, I was Sweetness and Light. Matron followed her within a minute or two, and we rattled through to the sitting room with the laden trolley.

'This is Beattie,' shouted Tinker, once we'd reached the middle of the room.

Everyone stopped what they were doing, and stared at me. Janet, the young occupational therapist, shook my hand and went over to clear spaces on the tables.

'What's she so scared of?' said one of the women.

'Of you lot,' said Tinker. 'I can't say I blame her. Maybe you could introduce yourselves when Beattie gives you your coffee.'

'How long is she going to stand there for? I'm dying of thirst.'

'Beattie, Shmeatie!' yowled Sarah. 'She's supposed to take me to Woolworth's.'

I poured the coffee but my hands were shaking so badly that Matron took over. I handed a rattling cup to an old, stout lady with blue eyes and beautiful white hair.

'I'm sorry. It's spilt in the saucer.'

'I like it in the saucer. I also like two biscuits and a sweetener.' I fetched them for her. 'My name's Yetta.'

'How do you do, Yetta.' I foolishly held out my hand and she fumbled with her cup and plate, and after an eternity, set them on the table and held out her knobbly hand. The others were all shouting at me to hurry up.

'I'm pleased to meet you.' She smiled. 'Take no notice of them. By tomorrow they'll all want to be your friend.'

'I hope that includes you!'

'Why wait till tomorrow? What's wrong with today?' Her voice was brisk and strong and demanded an answer.

'Nothing.' The blue eyes were sharper than her knitting needles. 'Everything.'

No one was helping me. Tinker was standing on the verandah, deep in conversation and cigarette smoke with Janet. All *she'd* done was pour coffee for the two of them. She didn't care about the old ladies calling out rudely and impatiently or that I was incapable of attending to their needs all at once. I handed Sarah her coffee and two biscuits. Something was wrong because she started shouting at me in Yiddish.

'You know what she said?' asked a little owl with untidy, feathery hair, big spectacles and red bootees. 'She's cursing you. She wants for all your teeth to fall out, but one, and that one should ache. You know why? Because you didn't give her a chocolate biscuit, that's why. And I have to live with a person like her!'

'There aren't any chocolate biscuits, Sarah. I'm sorry.'

'Sorry! Sorry!' she mocked. 'Give this ginger biscuit to the Old Maid. It'll help her to get a man!'

The red slippered lady gave Sarah a withering look and came up to the trolley to help herself, and told me her name was Rene Landis.

One of them called out that she was diabetic, and why didn't I know that I had to serve diabetics first.

'Be quiet, Kitty! How should she know? This is her first day,' said Yetta. 'Give her time.'

Give her time. Give me time. Give me time. The sentence caught up in the dented cogwheels of my brain, repeating itself with slight variations – the beginning of an obsessive merry-go-round. It usually happened in bed at night; not when I was busy. How much time? How much time, Sarah? Seventeen from eighty-five. How much time?

'Hello, Miss Cohen. I'm pleased to meet you. A little more milk? Of course, Miss Cohen.' Gaunt-faced; hollow-eyed; as frail as a late autumn leaf; iron-grey hair tied back in a bun, odd and old-fashioned; horn-rimmed spectacles, the lenses distorting her eyes, dominating her tiny face; high-necked white blouse and a dark shawl fastened with an oval brooch. A caricature of a retired schoolmarm – which, in fact, was what she was.

'Thank you, no biscuits. What did you say? You really must learn to speak up and speak clearly. It's extremely difficult for people of our age to understand you if you mumble.'

'I was really talking to myself, Miss Cohen. It's become

38

a habit of mine. I was trying to take seventeen from eighty-five. My mind's not very clear these days!'

'If you mean, as I suspect you do, that mental arithmetic is not a strong point, then always use the nearest round number. Subtract twenty from eighty-five, then add three to your answer. Well?'

'Sixty-eight.'

'Good. That method always works.'

I wanted to thank her for breaking the horrid circuit in my head, but didn't dare, in case she thought I was being impudent. Sixty-eight years. Sixty-eight years since the Zeppelin raid killed Sarah's husband and three children. Was there just the one left, who died a few years ago? Had she outlived all her children? She was over a hundred years old. Professor Gottleib said that bereavement is a part of the fabric of life; all of us endure it – unless we die young. The older we grow, the more frequent the experience. Did it follow that the adjustment was easier? What did he know about that? These people knew better than he did. Sarah was still complaining about her biscuits.

A diminutive lady, looking not a day over seventy-five and certainly not an inch over four foot eight, walked in briskly, came over to the trolley and began helping herself.

'Alter will be down soon. He takes black coffee and his wife, Golda, likes a milky one. They have their own sweeteners and biscuits upstairs. Are you from the agency?'

'No.'

'You're permanent then?'

'I don't know.'

'Well, you'll know soon enough whether you want to stay or not. My name's Olga. What's yours?'

'Beattie.'

'Are you married?'

'Yes.'

'Children?'

'No.'

'I don't know why women bother to get married unless

39

they want a family. If you had a husband like mine, you'd understand. There he is! There's my beauty!' she sneered, as the little man with the lampshade came over, looking like an elderly butcher in his red and white striped apron. His expression, so cheerful and benign, had altered the moment she stepped into the room.

'Get out of my sight, you old witch; the curse of my last years! Go from here!'

No one else in the room seemed to be perturbed by the behaviour of the couple. They continued to insult each other, while I served a very stout, deaf old lady who asked my name in a voice that shattered glass. I shouted as loudly as I could, everyone else complaining and telling me to be quiet.

Still she screeched, 'What! What did you say?'

The lady sitting next to her said quietly, 'Her name's Beattie. She's the new matron. You're shouting, Queenie. Stop it.'

'You don't have to shout to make her hear, Beattie,' said Yetta. 'It's because your voice is pitched too high. Try to speak low, like a man. She hears everything Sadie says. Her voice is just right. If you want to speak to Bubba, just tell Sadie.'

'Isn't the lady's name Queenie?'

'Everyone calls her "Bubba" except Sadie. It's a Jewish name for Grandma. Bubba has a grandson, Clive. He calls her Bubba and that's why.'

I didn't see why. I didn't care why. I didn't care that Bubba thought I was the new matron. Sadie was unable to manage her cup very well, so I held it for her while she took her teeth out and dipped a biscuit into the coffee, sucking noisily. She seemed a little confused, dipping her teeth in, as a pleasant change from the biscuit. Sarah was calling for a second cup and Olga looked after her.

An old man walked in from the hall. He was probably about eighty, smartly dressed in a spotless white shirt and a dark suit. He wore a black skull-cap and his thick white hair framed his exceptionally handsome face. He smiled at everyone and then at me and walked over to make my acquaintance.

'This is a pleasant surprise!' he said. 'I hope you'll be very happy with us. Perhaps later, when you've time, you'll come up to visit Golda, my wife. She isn't very well today, I'm afraid. My name is Alter – Alter Freid, but most of us like to be called by our first names. Have you ever come across the name Alter before?' I shook my head. 'It was a very common name where I came from. People were poor; hungry; sick. Parents lost their infant children, and after that happened in my family, and I was the only one left, my father re-named me Alter. It means "The Old One". It was the way of our people to remind the Almighty that he should spare a child of that name until such a time as it became appropriate. Well, at last my name suits me! And you are . . . ?'

'Beatrice Dwek, but everyone calls me Beattie.'

'Welcome to The Haven, Beattie. Perhaps we'll see you later, upstairs?'

'Yes. Thank you.'

He took a small tray from the sideboard and placed two cups on it. Two or three people asked after Golda, and he sighed and said she wasn't very well. We heard him going upstairs with the tray.

Matron and Janet came in and chatted to everyone while I collected the cups and wheeled the trolley through to the kitchen where the sour-faced cook was waiting for me to wash up and prepare the greens.

'I won't be in tomorrow, nor Sunday, you know. Did she tell you that you'll have to see to everything?'

'Yes, Matron told me,' I lied idiotically.

'Has she discussed the menu with you, then?'

'After lunch. We'll discuss it after lunch.' She knew I was saying the first thing that came into my head. I really disliked her.

'I leave at twelve sharp. If there's anything you want to ask me, now's your chance.'

'No, thank you, Mrs Jones. Matron will show me the ropes.'

'Well, I hope she doesn't hang herself while she's doing it. Those poor old people! Those poor, poor old people!'

'They seemed perfectly okay to me,' I snapped. This woman was making me really angry.

'With a matron like *her*! She's a walking disaster! I heard she's leaving. A good thing, too. Everyone thinks so.'

'Oh no they don't! The residents like her and I think she's an excellent matron.'

'The residents like her!' she sneered. 'They don't know how a place like this is supposed to be run. It should be run on oiled wheels. And what do you know? I'm talking about people who work here permanently, like myself and Nurse Goss. You'll be gone by the end of next week. I've been here over a year and I'm always right about staff!'

'This time you're wrong, you old cat!' I yelled, totally in control. 'I'm staying, so mind what you say! Now let me get on with the lunch.'

'You get on with it on your own then! I'm going! I'm not staying here to be insulted!'

She banged a huge, cast-iron pot on the stove, picked up her bag and marched out. Before I heard the front door slam, Yetta came hobbling through to the kitchen.

'I heard you through the hatch, Beattie. I'm glad you're staying. It isn't often I take to someone. At my age you don't make friends so easy. We knew about Tinker having to leave, but she'll be back, once she's recovered her health. Now, you leave the washing-up to me. Rene and Kitty are having their hair done, but they'll be in later, to help. We usually have lunch at one. Are the potatoes in the oven? Come on! Get a move on!'

'What if Mrs Jones doesn't come back, Yetta?'

'Course she'll be back! Monday first thing!'

'How can you be so sure? Did you hear . . .'

'I heard! And I heard it all before! That one's always threatening to leave. Tinker takes no notice. Don't chop all the cabbage stalks off. Shred the leaves. Like this. I've been here a long time and I know the routine. You come

42

to me if you want to talk about anything, and Tinker isn't on duty. You hear me, Beattie?'

'I hear you,' I said.

Frank was home before me. He was waiting at the front door, strained and anxious as I pulled in at the kerb, and he came out to the car to greet me.

'How was it, Beattie? Surely not as awful as you predicted?'

'More awful. I'm practically dead from exhaustion. I had a terrible morning and an even worse afternoon, but in spite of everything, I've decided to stay for a while. Anyway, I want to pay someone out, and as it happens, I made a few friends.'

I tried to tell him a little bit about the place and the people, but I couldn't remember the residents' names. My mind didn't work properly any more. I had Tinker's list in my bag, though.

'Frank, where did I put Gloria's notebook?'

'Upstairs on your bedside table. Why?'

'Why do you think? To squeeze oranges all over it, of course!'

'Excuse me for asking,' said Frank, grinning, 'but I seem to remember you being less than keen to write in it.'

'I need to make a few notes. My memory's terrible these days, and I want to jot down names and distinguishing characteristics so that by tomorrow, I'll be able to start.'

'Start what?'

'To become acquainted with the residents of The Haven. Tinker gave me some background information, but I need to enlarge on it. It's going to take time to get to know everyone properly, but you've got to start somewhere.'

'What made you decide to stay, Beattie? Is it preferable to the hospital?'

'No, it certainly is not!'

The furrows across his forehead had deepened and his hair was thinning into two Vs at the temples. I hadn't

43

noticed before. I hadn't noticed that the set of his face in repose was so melancholy.

'But I'd put up with anything to be at home – with you. Anything! I bet that crook Professor Gottleib knew the odds all along. I'll stay the course, Frank.'

Tinker and I stayed the course together for the next few weeks until the weekend of her fiftieth birthday, when she left to a sad farewell from all the residents. I promised to write the news to her, and hoped against hope that she'd be fit enough to return one day. Matron Dixon arrived, as smart and efficient as a new broom, and swept away all the mess. Not quite all. She didn't sweep me away, because by then I'd made a start.

4

The Therapist

My friend, Sarah Yanofsky, was born in Rudenka – a village in Eastern Poland. She began work as a sewing hand when she was seven, and recalls with ease and delight, twenty verses of a vulgar song she learnt at the time, from the older girls. The following year, the Cossacks galloped into Rudenka and lopped off her right arm. She sneers at Death's looming shadow and challenges it with a contemptuous cackle. She is afraid of no one and nothing – with the exception of one gruesome horror which lurks perpetually in the forefront of her mind. Sarah Yanofsky is terrified of tasting butter.

A hundred years ago, when Sarah was three, her mother left some butter in a bowl on the kitchen window sill. It was a hot, sunny day and the butter melted into liquid. Sarah toddled in, drank it up and was sick. I asked her if the sound of horses' hooves distressed her; the memory of the cavalry; the wild evil men waving their sabres in the wake of fleeing, innocent people. After all, the incident in which she lost her arm was a mere ninety-five years back, and was surely more dramatic, horrific and damaging than a temporary stomach upset.

'Horses! Who's frightened from horses? May they stamp your face into the earth! I can smell butter on this biscuit! You think because I can't see so well, that I don't know what you're trying to do to me, you sly, wicked poisoner!'

You can't reason with the old bat. Once in a blue moon it's possible to have a civil conversation with her, but it's difficult not to respond to her snappishly sometimes. She knows quite well that I'll never let her down, and her repeated bombardment of questions and suspicions is

45

offensive and gets on my nerves: 'Who mashed the potato? What's in this sandwich? You have hidden butter in the filling! May you catch the plague and be buried alive!'

'Shut up, you odious hell-hag! What possible reason could I have to waste good butter on you? All you can taste are a few mouldy toadstools marinated in arsenic. Open your mouth while I shovel some down your throat!' A slight show of temper tends to calm Sarah, and relieve her awful anxiety.

I was nice to her once, while helping her with her food, and she spat it all over me. I had failed to forewarn her that the custard was runnier than usual, and she thought I was giving her apple pie drowned in melted butter. I was furious and refused to go to Woolworth's with her and she screamed curses at me for a solid hour. The harmless, if hideous pimple which adorned my chin turned into a fearsome boil. After we returned from the shops she told me how to treat it by covering it with a hot tomato poultice. You've got to take the old witch seriously. She swore she'd cover me from head to foot with running sores if I ever gave her butter again.

The reason why I have infinite patience with Sarah is that I understand her anguish perfectly. I have suffered my particular phobia for a fleeting thirty-seven years, but what would it be like to be frail and slow-moving, my eyes too dim to search thoroughly; my reflexes a second too late! The idea was unendurable. My head swam. I thought of Alf Levene, due to be admitted to The Haven shortly.

Tinker told me about him two or three days before she left, after visiting him in hospital. It was her first and only meeting with him, since it was arranged that Dixon, the new matron, would make the final decision about accepting him. He was terminally ill and totally blind and Tinker went to see him to gauge the amount of skilled nursing he would need. She looked pale and tired when she returned. It was a difficult and distressing time for her – her last week at The Haven. I sat her down on the kitchen stool with a fresh pot of tea and an array of perfect biscuits, fresh from the cooling tray.

'These are heavenly, Beattie. What are they?'

'Sarah's recipe. She's been supervising me, making sure I don't use butter. She says they're called Hermit's Kisses. Indulge yourself.'

Tinker shuddered. 'Alf Levene, the man I went to visit this afternoon; *he's* a hermit.'

'How can a hermit come to live here?'

'I don't know. I can't think about it. His notes weren't available and whether he comes here or not will depend on whether he survives the next few weeks and on Matron Dixon. Not me, thank goodness. I've come across dozens of people with phobias – haven't we all? But this!'

'You mean he can't stand the sight or sound of people?'

'He's claustrophobic. He has to have doors and windows open all the time, whatever the weather. He's constantly listening; constantly suspicious; always anxious and fearful that a nurse or a cleaner will close the door. They've put him in a side ward, and wedged his door and window, but he must have asked me about them half a dozen times.'

'And to be blind as well,' I said. 'How sad!'

'Beattie,' said Tinker shakily, 'his head and face and neck are covered in spiders!'

An image of ghastly horror appeared before me and I had to grab the edge of the table to prevent myself from sinking to the floor. Of course, if I hadn't had Sarah pestering me all the afternoon, driving me mad, I would have understood that Tinker was suffering from DTs. If I'd had a few seconds to calm myself, I would have realized that perhaps she was referring to thread-like veins covering the surface of the old man's skin.

Tinker hovered over me. She knew exactly what was wrong.

'Beattie, listen to me! His face is tattooed all over, that's all! I'm sorry if I gave you the shivers. I didn't realize you'd react like this. Arachnophobia is a very common problem.' She spoke in her top-drawer voice as if she used

47

words like that all the time. 'There's a really excellent course of treatment available for sufferers. Why don't you ask about it when next you attend your group therapy? Promise me you'll mention it!'

'All I'm promising is that if Alf Levene is coming here, Beatrice Dwek is on her way out. I can't look at . . .'

'Beattie,' said Tinker, 'if I can tackle the booze, you can tackle this.'

I paid scant attention to the idea. I'd lived with my phobia for as long as I could remember. Still, after Sarah's most recent abusive assault, I *did* mention *her* problem during group discussion and practically the entire session was devoted to everyone's particular horror. I heard myself saying that I'd like to meet the person who claimed he could cure phobias, and would be fully prepared to undergo treatment.

Before I had a chance to reconsider, Velvet, Professor Gottleib's student who took our group and who'd been snoozing in the armchair, came to life and said he'd fix an appointment, and I told him to go back to sleep. Of course, these people only hear what suits them. Within a few days, arrangements were made for me to attend a unit for patients suffering from compulsive rituals, phobias and obsessive behaviour.

I rang Tinker at the nursing home and told her that if I could tackle this, she could tackle the booze – and informed the new matron that I would be having treatment for my frozen shoulder every Wednesday afternoon for the next six weeks, and she would have to manage without me for a couple of hours.

My therapist, Idris, greeted me with a much too cheerful smile and I followed him into a poky office. He left me there while he went to fetch coffee for us both, and I took the opportunity to glance at the papers on the desk. A letter from Velvet was there, explaining the nature of the phobia, the manner in which it affected my life – Velvet hadn't been asleep, after all – and a brief account of recent events. He also pointed out that he felt it was particularly important for this patient to surmount the difficulties she recognized and accepted as realistic, in order that eventually she might recognize and accept – and ultimately come to terms with – her present dilemma. I didn't follow the logic of the letter and found it of little interest, but the pages of scrawl written by another patient made fascinating reading, dwarfing my problems into insignificance. I was cut off in mid-stream by the sound of Idris's footsteps down the corridor, and was back in my chair, wringing my hands, when he entered. I told him at once, not to dare to try any shock tactics with me; I would have a heart attack and die – or worse.

'What's worse?' he asked.

'To lose control over my bodily functions.'

'That's worse than dying? You *have* got problems! Don't worry, though; it only happens occasionally. Remember, we're all experienced nurses here, used to handling embarrassing and distressing situations. I promise I won't do anything without your prior knowledge or agreement, if you promise that no matter how frightened you feel, you won't leave this room until the end of our session.'

'Show me the Ladies' this minute!'

Within a little while I had made my pact with Idris and was drinking coffee and smoking feverishly, telling him how it all began. In 1948, my mother was standing on the kitchen table, fixing up a new curtain rod over the window, and I was shouting to her that my friend, Liddell, was trying to look up her skirt. Instead of giving him a good kick over the head, she screamed, shuddered and whirled round. Her face was a mask of horror; her complexion as white and as waxy as a candle. She leapt to the floor, knocking Liddell down as she did so.

'Mum!' I shrieked. 'What's the matter?'

'Ugh! God!' she gasped. 'There's the biggest spider I've ever seen eating her husband up there, under the pelmet!'

She paid a heavy price for her reckless, uncontrolled behaviour and thoughtless remarks. I screeched my way through the following fifty nights, fleeing spiders in my nightmares. During my conscious moments, I searched for them diligently in cupboards, where great nests of them lurked just out of sight; in the bath; on the floor and ceiling; under my pillow. They took on a new life; a new appearance in my imagination – twenty swastikas superimposed, the compound eyes glaring at me malevolently through the horrid massy tangle of hair and legs; the females crunching up husbands by the dozen. What exactly was it that horrified me? The eighty legs? The manner in which they ran or crouched? The hellish thought that one might drop in my hair; scurry under the folds of my clothes, and while I stood, insane and paralytic, explore the entire surface of my skin unmolested? I wiped my slippery hands against my jumper. Poor old Sarah! I'd try to be nice to her on her birthday.

'Liddell . . .' said Idris thoughtfully. 'It's rather an unusual name.'

'I can't recall being acquainted with more than five or six Idrises among my vast circle,' I responded sourly. I felt aggrieved and not a little disappointed by his trivial remark after seemingly listening to me with such flattering attention. 'I really don't see what . . .'

'I'm sorry,' said Idris. He picked up the letter I'd been cunningly reading when he came in with coffee, and scanned the part I hadn't managed to get up to. 'This is the most amazing coincidence!'

'What is?' I snapped irritably.

'Nothing, nothing.' He scribbled something down on the top of Velvet's letter, then helped me to fill out a long questionnaire. No, I wasn't scared of eating in front of people. I didn't wash my hands five hundred times a day in boiling water. I was not unbearably distressed at the thought of hospitals or of going into Sainsbury's. Yes, I could look at the person I was speaking to, and travel on a bus by myself. My fantasies were my own business and I failed to see what my intensely personal life had to do with the problem. It seethed with the usual difficulties. I did not find half the population of the human species, male or otherwise, frightening or repulsive. I answered numerous such questions, suddenly more aware of the horrible sufferings of others, than hitherto.

'Now,' said Idris, 'do you understand what behavioural therapy means?' I didn't, but nodded. 'I want to assure you absolutely, that you cannot die of panic. It's actually impossible,' he lied outrageously. 'Panic can't last longer than fifteen seconds. Down the corridor we have a little zoo. We've got all sorts there – snakes, birds, mice, kittens, a couple of dogs, moths, wasps, spiders and so on. Charles is a new recruit – a friendly little soul and a favourite with us all. I'll bring him in to meet you – *breathe . . . breathe . . . slowly* – and again! Relax! That's a clever girl! He'll be in a jar with the lid on. There'll be just a few holes drilled in for air. No, we haven't got a dead spider. I'll be back in a minute. I'll put the jar on the desk. Now, please, remember our promise! You won't have to touch it or look at it until you're ready.'

When he returned, I tried to concentrate on keeping myself from fainting. I sat on Idris's knee and he held my hand and cunningly adjusted his position so that he could check my pulse. After twenty minutes I was able to touch the jar with a ruler and by the end of the session I could actually hold the jar on my lap with my eyes closed.

My homework for the week was to hold the jar for five minutes, twice a day, and write out a report about my feelings at the time. Idris carried it to my car and jammed it in the boot.

I felt enormously proud of myself; strangely elated by my miraculous progress. I drove with extreme care. It wouldn't do to have an accident today. What if some reckless fool bumped into me, though? What if the jar broke, and while I was lying injured . . . ?

I arrived at work with a splitting headache and all the symptoms of an impending attack of malaria.

Yetta, the most agreeable of the residents, was covering for me in the kitchen, preparing the vegetables. She, along with everyone else at The Haven, understood the nature of my malady and took the jar out of the boot for me, but

I insisted on bearing Charles myself. We ran along the pavement to the gate.

'Stop screaming, Beattie!' gasped Yetta. 'Everyone's staring!'

I didn't care. I had no shame. The sight of a middle-aged woman holding a jar in one outstretched hand, rushing along madly, dragging an arthritic, seventy-six-year-old with the other, must have given the neighbours and gaping passers-by something to wonder about.

I thrust the jar on the window sill and saw Charles for the first time. He was enormous and horribly active. Yetta suppressed a squeamish shudder and smiled.

'Who's Yetta's brave girl, then?' she said, as if I was a baby of two, getting ready to yell after falling over.

We sat on the same armchair in the residents' lounge while I held the glass cage on my knee for five interminable minutes, my eyes glued to *Play School* on the telly, waiting for the timer to ring the end of Round One. The bell went and I had won. I exchanged Charles for a tot of brandy, kept in Matron's cupboard for medicinal purposes. My life entered a new phase.

I did my homework diligently with Frank's help. I wondered, as I looked at his tense face and clutched his clammy hand, whether he'd counted on 'In sickness and in health' as this being part of the deal. Once I heard him murmur plaintively that anyone would think *he* liked spiders, but of course I took no notice. Charles dwelt in his jar in a dark corner, hidden by a dusty plant, and I kept daily records of my progress. After a few days, Idris rang and suggested I give Charles something to eat.

'Idris, I've just arrived home from work, which is to prepare food and clean up for eleven people. If you think for one moment I'm going to start cooking for Charles . . .'

'Shut up and listen.'

I had to reprove him and ask him to mind his manners. I was, after all, nearly twice his age.

'He can't get out,' he said, as if I hadn't spoken. 'Remove the lid. You can do it. Remember how I told you to breathe? One, two, in, out! That's better. *He can't get out*. Drop in a piece of wet, screwed-up newspaper and a few tiny pieces of meat. I'll phone again in fifteen minutes.'

'There's no one here to help me. I'm all by myself.'

'Fifteen minutes, Beattie.'

I prepared the banquet, put on my sun glasses and did as I was bid. I had a frightful dream that night, but awoke unafraid.

The following week I bore Charles to the Unit to see Idris. I had to park a good two hundred yards away and carried the jar hidden in a shopping bag. I shared the waiting room with a man of about my own age and smiled at him, asking if we'd met before, for there was something oddly familiar about him. He shuddered violently and averted his eyes, then ducked his head as if expecting a clout, and fiddled compulsively with his zipper. I had rarely seen anyone quite so wretched and distraught. What trauma had *he* suffered during his childhood, which had left him in so pitiable a state? He jumped up suddenly and paced the room in dreadful agitation, keeping his face turned against the wall away from me, as if I was a Black Widow with whom he was imprisoned. Then Idris opened the door and the poor man shot out of the room and followed him into the office.

'Well done, Liddell!' said Idris. 'Exactly seven minutes!'

The door closed and I heard no more. I looked at my watch, then stretched out my trembling legs. I still had only two. I came to my senses when I saw the jar rolling across the floor. I had kicked the bag without thinking. Indeed, I hadn't given Charles a thought for a full seven minutes.

I asked Idris about my strange companion in the waiting room. It was difficult to draw him out, as he maintained that information regarding individual patients was strictly confidential, but after some considerable probing, I elicited that Liddell had a phobia about women, thinking they were going to gobble him up.

53

'Oh, God, Idris,' I gasped, 'is he frightened of spiders, too?'

'No. He's very fond of spiders. Now then, today you're going to hold the jar without the lid on and do everything I tell you.'

I forgot about everything but the present horror of counting Charles's legs, examining the way his head joined his body and describing his markings. I actually met his eyes. Few can possibly comprehend the courage which this demanded. I screamed quite loudly but prevented myself from shaking as I didn't want Charles to stir unduly. Under battlefield conditions, I would have been presented with a richly deserved medal for valour.

Idris praised me to the skies and gave me coffee and my project, which was to draw the monster.

I performed this operation on Sunday afternoon, ashen-faced Frank in constant attendance, using a thick, black, felt-tipped pen. It took me an hour – a black, fearsome hour. Long after I had replaced Charles in his corner, his dreadful form was fastened in front of my eyes. Idris had warned me about the dangers of exchanging a phobia for an addiction to drugs or alcohol. I eschewed Valium and whisky for several glasses of weak lemon tea and *The News of the World*.

During the following few weeks, I felt that I broke all hitherto unknown records for Panic Time. We had Charles scampering in a plastic bowl and I touched one of his legs ten times – with a pencil – and held on tenaciously to my life, if not my dignity.

I continued to feed and water him at intervals, but one day I turned up for my therapy session with a web in the jar, some bits of food and a strangely withered Charles. He was dead. I'm sure he wouldn't have wanted me to grieve, so I didn't.

While Idris was emptying the jar somewhere, I riffled expertly through his papers, and turned swiftly to the signature at the end of the pages of spidery writing I had previously scanned. Poor Liddell! I felt sick with shock and misery and had to pretend I was desolated about the untimely passing of Charles, when Idris returned.

He endeavoured to comfort me by introducing me to Freda Girlie, and it was at this point that I felt the great wall of horror heave and crumble. She was quite charming – dainty, compared with the late Charles, with an inquiring mind and a lively little body. I was able to study her activities without a trace of dread – until Idris let her run playfully across his fingers and asked if I'd like to join in the fun. I told him he needed to be locked in a padded cell. He recounted a fairy story to me about a lady who had attended the unit, as phobic as I had been, who was now the proud owner of a pet tarantula. I wondered what that was supposed to signify, but was nevertheless impressed.

By the end of the session, Freda Girlie was permitted to run across my finger. It was a noisy performance, but did not prove to be fatal. I rushed into work and told Sarah.

She had been following every horrid inch of my progress with impatience and contempt. Today, she sneered in disbelief at my news.

'You can't abide the fact that you're a worse coward than I am. Your defence is to belittle my victory. You know perfectly well that for me to endure a spider running over my finger is just as terrible as for you to bite into a slice of bread and butter and feel it slide down your evil throat.' I was gratified to note that her false teeth rattled uncontrollably.

'Get out of my sight, you scavenging crow! May your fingers wither and drop off! I don't believe anything you say; I only believe what I see, Street Woman!'

'For a hundred years you've been scared out of your wits,' I taunted her. 'I'll show you how Freda Girlie runs over my hands. I can tolerate it for five minutes at a stretch,' I lied. 'I challenge you to a duel of courage!'

I didn't wait for an answer. I ran to the car and brought Freda Girlie into the sitting room. Usually, the hours between two and four are for nodding off, but there was no slouching about this afternoon. The atmosphere was electric when I placed the jar on Sarah's table, then took a slice of bread and butter from the trolley and put the plate next to the jar. With a vicious swipe of her hand, she knocked both to the floor. I rushed to Freda Girlie's rescue. She frisked about on my hands, from one to the other. For a horrid moment I thought one of her legs was trapped under my wedding ring and even Bubba Marks, who's as deaf as a door-post, jumped to attention on hearing my foul-mouthed shrieks; but Freda Girlie was just curious, and continued on her adventuresome way.

'Look, Sarah! Look! This is you, eating butter! You, too, can be freed from fear! Anything's possible if I can do this! Let me help you!'

She pretended to be asleep, which meant that she was suitably impressed. I edged Freda Girlie back into her jar, euphoric with success. Idris would be so pleased with me. Perhaps he'd forget to nag me about visiting the Insect House at the zoo. But he didn't.

'I want you to look at the tarantulas and the crab spiders and all the other whoppers. Surely your husband would go with you, or your mother or a friend.'

'My nearest and dearest seem to have gone off spiders in a big way,' I snapped. 'And my friends are reminded of urgent business whenever I attempt to mention the subject of an outing there.'

'Well, you'd better find *someone* to accompany you,' said Idris briskly. 'This is an extremely important part of your treatment. It isn't a good idea to procrastinate at this stage.'

I asked Sarah if she would tell Matron that she had a fancy to visit the crocodiles before she got too old to enjoy their pleasant habits. She should refuse absolutely to go with a voluntary worker and it was her last wish; a strange but particular caprice that I should escort her. In this way I could make the trip during working hours, with a companion, and get paid. Sarah understands about killing three birds with one stone. I promised that if she looked after me in the Insect House and gave me kindly encouragement for once in her life, I'd pack up some dry bread and cheese for a picnic, pinch the medicinal brandy and we'd spend an hour at the band stand.

The following Tuesday, I shovelled her into the car and stowed the wheelchair in the boot. She behaved badly all the way to Regent's Park, making out that she was doing me an enormous favour, and if she hadn't been such a sloppy-hearted fool, she could be lolling at home in her armchair. I was already extremely nervous at the thought of my impending ordeal and was uncharacteristically rather tetchy and short-tempered.

I couldn't find the Insect House. It was badly sign-posted, and I was continually misdirected, although Sarah was pleased to ask everyone where it was. While I was pushing her past it for the tenth time, she yowled out that she knew all along what I was up to and she'd blow the whistle to Matron about me if we didn't enter the building immediately.

It was dark and oppressively hot inside. Sarah said that she wanted to stay there for at least an hour as her blood was frozen and the Insect House was the warmest place in the zoo. I stuck my sun glasses on my nose and stumbled along, but the venomous old devil produced a powerful torch from her rag-bag and flashed it around, claiming that she couldn't see a thing without it. It was she who peered into all the glass cages, ramming on the brakes with her one mighty hand. I could hear her wheezing excitedly, leaving hardly any oxygen for me.

'Take your glasses off, or I'll give you cholera,' she ordered.

Two interfering busybodies heard me threaten to thump her, and stuck to us, asking her if she was all right and where did she live. She told them she was on a visit from Rudenka in Eastern Poland, then cursed them horribly in Yiddish, telling them to mind their own business.

The tarantula had red knees and piercing eyes. I looked at a huge knot of wood, and when Sarah flashed her torch, it detached itself from the small branch. A praying mantis performed appalling antics. Hideous creatures crouched or scuttled in each cage. Sarah crouched in her chair, watching; waiting for me to break. I didn't. It was she who said that the heat was killing her, but I strolled around, pouring with sweat, for an extra two minutes, just to spite her. She got me out by yelling that she wanted to go to the toilet. We got there just in time. I'm still never quite sure when she's trying to manipulate me.

We told the band leader that it was Sarah's hundredth birthday, and although she looks much older, he was gallant and congratulated her most kindly. He announced the event to the smiling, lunch-time crowds, and at her special request, played a medley of Polish and Russian folk songs, while she sang her twenty obscene verses along with the music. A man sitting on the seat next to us organized a collection for her present. She persuaded me to be her guest and we hurried off to the Rose Garden Tea House where we ordered lavish refreshment with a fraction of the proceeds.

'Well?' she said. 'You think you're cured, eh? What's that big black thing dangling next to your ear?'

She cackled maliciously and I regarded her scornfully and continued to sip my tea, then gave my thickly buttered scone a sudden push towards her. For a dreadful few seconds I thought I'd killed her. She stopped breathing and stared in ghastly horror at my right hand. I followed her gaze.

My hand, which was resting on the table between us, was covered by a monstrous spider, striped ginger and black. Charles was a microscopic dot of delight in comparison. I was entirely unprepared. Panic paralysed me, yet terror and frenzy threatened to cause a jerking spasm in my stricken muscles. If I moved, the Thing would meander up my arm. My heart pumped a farewell drumbeat in my throat.

'Sarah,' I quavered. 'Help me! Help me!'

Very slowly she moved her shaking hand across the table, but instead of swiping the spider away, she took my left hand in hers, willing me to look at her. Her expression was soft and tender; her smile, brave and bright.

'Remember that panic can't last for more than fifteen seconds and you can't die of it.'

I thought she was talking to me, but she wasn't; she was talking to herself. She loosened her grip and raised her voice.

'Beattie, I challenge you to a duel of courage!' she said. Then my friend, Sarah Yanofsky, picked up the buttered scone and popped it into her mouth.

5

The Teacher

Miss Cohen didn't mix much with the other residents. She preferred to spend her time in her room, sitting on the chair near her bed listening to the radio or her talking book. She was in constant pain and Nurse Goss gave her two injections every day, which I think contained morphine. At night, she swallowed a 'black bomber' with a cup of hot milk, and this gave her seven hours of blissful sleep. She needed several pillows to support her back, but with the help of two sticks she always managed to struggle in for her meals. Sometimes, if she was enjoying a programme, I would sneak in her coffee and biscuits or her afternoon tea, so she wouldn't be disturbed by having to join the others in the sitting room. For some evil reason, Matron insisted that the residents took their tea and coffee together, and that no special arrangements could be made, unless the circumstances were exceptional. Personal, private pleasure did not come under that heading. You had to be dead or dying.

'We like everyone to be sociable here – one big happy family! Come on, Miss Cohen! You're no different from the rest of us; no better and no worse! You'll get very stiff sitting for so long in one place, and it's not good for you to be alone all day!'

I saw Matron with my own eyes turn off the *Afternoon Play* while Miss Cohen was totally engrossed in it. I had just crept in with tea and cake for Miss Cohen, and Matron didn't know I was watching until she turned to fetch the walking frame and our eyes met – acknowledging our undisguised, mutual contempt and dislike. The incident occupied my mind for some hours and that evening I looked up Tinker's notes in Gloria's notebook:

'Cohen, Dora. Admitted 1 October 1984, from the Royal Free Hospital. Date of Birth, 1892, London. Retired school teacher. Hysterectomy; mastectomy; cancer of the spine; glaucoma. Support collar, arm crutches or walking frame essential. Mentally alert. No known living relative.'

No known living relative. No known living relative. No known . . .

'Frank, do you believe in hatred at first sight?'

'Are we talking about the matron and how much you detest her?'

'She's been at The Haven now for nearly three months and it's getting worse. I mean she can't stand the sight of me, either. All the folks notice how she . . .'

'Has it occurred to you that she might be jealous?'

'Jealous!' I shouted, pleased that Frank might think so. 'You're mad! She's thirty-four, tall, blonde, blue-eyed, gorgeous and irresistible to men. Can you imagine her being jealous of a dark, small, skinny, forty-one-year-old skivvy?' Is there anyone in the whole world who could possibly be jealous of me! Sometimes Frank's insensitivity shocks and upsets me.

'I was thinking of the residents,' said Frank. 'She might be resentful of the special relationship you seem to have developed with them.' I had expected a different response from him and felt angry and hurt. 'But if hatred at first sight lasts as long as love at first sight, you might as well prepare for a long, long war.' He smiled. My Frank! There were probably dozens of women who were jealous of me!

Apropos of absolutely nothing, I asked him how his new colleague was shaping up, and almost immediately afterwards, regretted doing so. His enthusiasm depressed me; the passionate interest he felt for his work would always be a source of solace and joy.

'I wish I was like you, Frank. I wish I was involved in – in things outside myself. I can't concentrate. I can't take a sustained interest in anything. While I was talking to Miss Cohen today, I was reminded of that time when you had to give a paper to some people from Nebraska and you had a raging toothache. I kept wondering how you managed to answer questions so patiently and good-humouredly when you were in such agonizing pain.'

'What a nightmare that was! I pretended that I was in the French Resistance and all our information was hidden in my tooth. The Gestapo was watching; waiting. If I flinched or showed any sign of discomfort, I'd reveal the secret place and betray my comrades. I think most of us possess far more strength and courage than we give ourselves credit for. How's *your* toothache today, Beattie?'

I wished I was like Frank.

'I've got enough with this frozen shoulder.'

He got up and stood behind me, massaging it. Some days were worse than others. I looked down at Gloria's notebook.

Miss Cohen never grumbled or lost her temper. Whenever I took her tea in, she would smile and say, 'I hope you won't get into trouble on my account, Beattie. You shouldn't really be doing this. I'm enjoying the concert so much, but . . .'

'The Queen is in the parlour, eating bread and honey. Have a good time!' I'd ease her up into a more comfortable position, and hurry out to see to the loud-mouths in the sitting room.

On sunny afternoons the folks sat on the verandah, dozing or quarrelling, and on these occasions Her Royal Highness allowed me to take the trolley out to them. Miss Cohen sat on the garden seat near the bird table, wearing her green eye-shade, and I knew she wasn't listening to anyone but the birds and the sounds of early summer. She could no longer read print, but she could see the lawn and the flower borders and shrubs.

All the residents called each other by their first names, or, when they were ill tempered, by rude ones, but no one called Miss Cohen anything but Miss Cohen, and neither did I. Perhaps it was because she had been a teacher all her working life and the aura of respect still remained, as if we were her pupils and were touched by her authority. It was as if she sat at a separate desk on a slightly elevated plane, while we jostled noisily on a lower level, yet oddly constrained by her presence.

Miss Cohen's favourite programmes were *Poetry Please* and *With Great Pleasure*. If the folks were at the Friendship Club or one of them had insulted me and I didn't feel like mixing with them, I would tiptoe into the Green Room – so named because of her choice of wallpaper and coverlet – and drink my coffee with her. She knew every poem read out by the actors; every one. Her lips moved along with Dame Peggy Ashcroft or Sir John Gielgud, and at these times I basked in her great happiness and felt cheated and disappointed when Cook called me or Matron burst in.

I knew Miss Cohen didn't mind me being there, for she'd say, 'Beattie, Lord Byron is on the menu next week', or 'Dame Peggy is reading her favourites on Thursday afternoon.'

One day, she asked me when I had begun to enjoy poetry and whether I had developed my love for it at school.

'I never learnt anything at school. I passed my scholarship by a pure fluke and got stuck at the bottom of my class. I've always been a dunce and didn't get on with the teachers.'

'Didn't your parents encourage you?'

'They tried, but they eventually had to accept that they were on to a loser. Dad used to go on and on, saying that if only he'd had the opportunities offered to me, and my mother would tell me how she wept because she had to leave school at fourteen. *She* taught me all the poetry I know. She loved school, especially English lessons. Her English teacher was the first love of her life. I suppose you can learn from someone you love very much. My parents always maintained that I was too wild and arrogant to accept authority, but you don't take notice of anyone when you're fifteen. I'll be forty-two next birthday, and to tell you the truth, Miss Cohen, I don't think I've changed that much in certain respects.'

63

'As at seven, so at seventy,' said Miss Cohen.

'I wish I'd had a teacher like you when I was a kid.' I felt foolish and embarrassed after I'd said that.

'You would probably have spent much of your time standing in a corner or outside the classroom door,' she said briskly. 'I was an extremely strict disciplinarian. I never slackened – not until the day I retired. Perhaps I was wrong to be so unbending. I was never popular with the pupils or the younger, more easygoing teachers.'

'What do you think of Matron as a disciplinarian, then?' I asked.

'She has her job to do. She runs this establishment in the way she thinks best.'

I daren't argue with Miss Cohen, but I couldn't resist mentioning Matron Tinker.

'If you're trying to engage me in a discussion about her and Matron Dixon, you'll be disappointed. It isn't necessarily the more affable people who are best at their work.'

'I agree with you, Miss Cohen. A wardress at a top security prison doesn't have to be an imaginative, easygoing . . .'

'You know, Beattie, when you make these unsuccessful attempts to provoke me, you remind me of . . .'

'Matron Dixon?' I shot in cunningly. 'That hateful, sadistic, bossy . . .'

'That will do!'

'Of who, then?'

'I do wish you'd allow me to finish what I was about to say! Now it's slipped my mind. It happens when you're ninety-three years old. Don't you think you should assist Cook with the lunch? It's always pleasant to have your company, but your duties come first. There's a veritable feast of literary delights on the World Service at eleven o'clock tomorrow. If your coffee break coincides, perhaps you'd like to join me then?'

I got up at once. I felt about ten years old, but I could accept that sort of reprimand from her. I wondered why

I had never been able to tolerate similar rebukes from my own teachers; from anyone else but Miss Cohen.

The next day I hustled everyone into the voluntary workers' cars. They were going off to a coffee morning at Lady Muck's fancy house, but Miss Cohen was too unwell to accompany them. I was glad to be shot of them for a couple of hours and slipped into the Green Room. I saw at once that she was in great pain, and that for anyone less controlled it would have been unbearable. There were tiny beads of perspiration on her forehead, and her skin was grey and blotched.

'Hello, Miss Cohen,' I said softly. 'I've brought your coffee – and mine. Is there anything I can do? Would you like to be left alone? Shall I call Matron?'

'You ask far too many questions, Beattie. Turn the wireless up a little.'

I did as I was told, then adjusted her swivel table and put the coffee down so that she could manage it without too much movement. ' "The Listeners" is first,' she said. 'Walter de la Mare; an underrated poet, I think. Stop fidgeting and sit down.'

'Is there anybody there?' said the Traveller,
Knocking at the moon-lit door;
And his horse in the silence champed the grasses
Of the forest's ferny floor . . .

We listened, and I waited for that delicious prickling at the back of my neck.

. . . But only a host of phantom listeners
That dwelt in that lone house then
Stood listening in the quiet of the moonlight
To that voice from the world of men . . .

Then came 'Spellbound' by Emily Brontë; 'I Remember' and 'The Song of the Shirt' by Thomas Hood. We sat in silence for a few moments after it was all over.

'You know "The Listeners" by heart, Beattie. Would you give me the pleasure of hearing it again?'

'Never the least stir made the listeners,
Though every word he spake
Fell echoing through the shadowiness of the still house
From the one man left awake . . .'

I came to the end. No one had ever listened to me more attentively.

'You recited that beautifully. Thank you. What do you think it means?'

'The Traveller was a man with a great and important message,' I said softly. 'A prophet; perhaps the Messiah, who tried in vain to impart it; to open our eyes and ears to what we should know; what we should see and hear. Perhaps it was the Truth, but we weren't ready. We didn't respond. We didn't want to know. He tried, but he failed to resurrect us.'

Miss Cohen sat very still, looking at me as if I was someone else. I felt quite sure that she was deeply impressed. 'That is an interesting interpretation,' she said at last, 'but not original, I think. I recall a young pupil of mine whose version was very similar to yours. Oh dear me! She was such a romantic! I remember . . . I remember . . .'

I continued for her:

'The house where I was born,
The little window where the sun
Came peeping in at morn;
He never came a wink too soon,
Nor brought too long a day,
But now, I often wish the night
Had borne my breath away!'

I sat back, waiting for Miss Cohen to praise me.

'I do wish you would allow me to finish what I was

going to say,' she sighed. 'I was trying to recollect her name, but it's gone now. Do you know "Spellbound"?'

I shook my head sheepishly. 'I haven't heard Emily Brontë's poems before, but I think *Wuthering Heights* is my favourite book. I know great chunks of it by heart, I've read it so often. I love all the Brontë novels. My husband and I went to the Yorkshire moors last year, in the spring, and I re-read them all – and Mrs Gaskell's *Life of Charlotte Brontë*. My mother knew someone who knew someone who knew the Brontës!' I boasted.

I could hear Cook blasting off in the kitchen, but we took no notice. Miss Cohen wanted me to stay. I felt heady; uplifted; elevated to the same level.

'When I was a young girl, I went to stay with my friend in Keighley. Her great-grandmother lived in a cottage in Haworth and we went to visit her. She knew the Brontë girls. She told us how shy they were and rarely spoke more than a greeting to their neighbours. She said that the three of them used to walk up the hill together; tiny little figures, very much wrapped up in one another. They considered themselves very plain, especially Charlotte, and she had a habit of covering her mouth with her hand when she was confronted. Her teeth stuck out, apparently. Ann was the most forthcoming. This old lady remembered Elizabeth and Maria, too. They died in childhood, and Emily always maintained that they were unusually gifted. She remembered Branwell very well. Everyone knew he was a genius, but a wild, sad, self-destructive young man. Do you know, Beattie, listening to that old lady all those years ago was the most unforgettable, and perhaps the most thrilling, day of my life.'

I felt the hair on the back of my neck prickle again, and tears of excitement and tension stood in my eyes. 'Miss Cohen,' I whispered shakily, 'listening to you is . . .'

'Call Matron will you, Beattie!' she gasped. Even Miss Cohen couldn't keep this blast of agony under control.

I leapt to my feet and flew to Matron's office.

'Quick, Matron! Please be quick! Miss Cohen's in terrible pain!'

'Don't be hysterical, Beatrice. Find Nurse Goss, then return to your duties in the kitchen. Cook has been looking for you.'

She didn't dawdle, but grabbed the tray of instruments and hurried across the sitting room to the Green Room. I found Goss, told Cook to shut up and ran back to Miss Cohen. The door was closed, but I didn't care. I wrenched it open and saw Goss and Matron hovering over her.

'Phone Doctor Taylor, Beatrice. His number is Sellotaped to my desk. Tell him that Miss Cohen is very poorly.'

I obeyed her orders slavishly.

'I'm on my way, Beattie,' he said.

I sat in the office, waiting for my legs to stop shaking, then picked up the phone again and dialled my parents' number.

'Mum, can you come over to The Haven? It's urgent.'

'What is it, Beattie? Beattie! You're crying! Is it Frank? Have you two had another row?'

'No,' I said. 'No.'

'Is he ill? Is he . . . ? Are you . . . ? What's the *matter*?'

'It's Miss Cohen.'

'Miss who?'

'*Cohen!*' I shrieked. 'Miss *Cohen!* I think she's dying.'

'What can *I* do? I'm just cooking Dad his dinner. You get too attached to the old people. Are you there by yourself?'

'The doctor's coming, and Nurse Goss and Matron are with her.'

'How old is she?'

'Ninety-three. What's that got to do with anything?'

'We should all live so long,' she said. 'Beattie, if you can't take the heat, get out of the kitchen. Ninety-three isn't a bad innings. One can't go on for ever.'

I wiped my face with a handful of Matron's tissues. 'Globe Road Girls' School,' I said. 'What was the name of that English teacher you worshipped when you were thirteen?'

There was a long pause.

'Oh, Beattie!' she gasped. 'Not *my* Miss Cohen! Did she say . . . ? Does she remember? There were three Miss Cohens – sisters – all teachers in Stepney. They taught thousands of kids. There were dozens of Miss Cohens apart from . . .'

'I know,' I interrupted irritably. 'You've told me thousands of times. This one's yours. Remember when she told you about the old lady who knew the Brontës and Charlotte thought her teeth were ugly and kept her hand . . .'

'God!' she screamed.

'Remember "The Listeners" and your idea about what it might mean? Miss Cohen remembers. I never made the connection until today.'

'Dad will see to his own dinner. I'll ring for a cab. To hell with the expense. Tell her I've never forgotten her. After all these years, I've . . .'

'Tell her yourself. Hurry up!' I slammed down the receiver and rushed to open the door for Doctor Taylor. I could see the voluntary workers arriving in their cars, hauling out the folks, calling for me to come and lend a hand, but I was in no mood for their carryings-on.

'Please, Doctor Taylor,' I cried. 'Help her!'

'Help her to what?'

'To live! To live!' 'But now I often wish the night had borne my breath away.' 'Help her! Take the pain away!'

They were too busy to bother about me standing in the doorway. I heard Miss Cohen cry out, and then Doctor Taylor's voice, deep, soft and comforting.

'After this, you're going to feel much better. When you wake up, the pain will have gone, I promise.'

I had to serve up lunch to the folks. I told them that Miss Cohen was very ill and that Doctor was with her.

'She's the last of the sisters,' said Kitty. 'They lived in Rothschild Buildings. Even when they were young, they never mixed with the other girls and boys. All old maids.

Not a husband among the lot of them. Not a son or a daughter; not a nephew or a niece. No one to hold her hand during her last hours. Terrible! Terrible!'

'Have you quite finished?' I snapped, slopping cabbage on to her plate so that the water splashed her pinafore. I didn't apologize. Kitty was forever boasting about her three horrid sons, and how rich and successful they were. They took it in turns to visit her every other Sunday, most dutifully, but never took her out or to visit their homes, to spend a few days with the family.

'What's the matter, Beattie? What have I said that's so terrible? Look what a mess you've made!'

'Terrible, terrible,' I sneered. I banged the colander on the table, making a worse mess. Even Sarah stopped chewing. I wondered if Kitty's sons would arrange a rota for holding *her* hand. 'I'm sorry, Kitty. Take no notice of me. I'm upset, but I didn't mean to snap. As a matter of fact, Miss Cohen *has* got someone.' The front doorbell rang. 'That's her, now. Serve yourselves while I let her in.'

I took my mother through to the Green Room. She waited outside while I tapped on the door and tiptoed in. Nurse Goss was sitting by the bed, reading *The Daily Mirror*. Doctor Taylor and Matron were probably up in her flat, having a quickie under the eiderdown. Miss Cohen seemed to be sleeping peacefully.

'Miss Cohen has a visitor, Nurse Goss,' I whispered.

She looked at me suspiciously. 'What a turn-up for the book! I thought all her relatives and friends were dead.'

'You thought wrong, then, didn't you? Miss Cohen happens to be much more than a friend to the lady waiting outside. They lost touch for a few years, that's all. Perhaps you would allow them to enjoy their reunion privately. Kitty has spilt hot cabbage water over herself, and needs immediate attention.'

She actually pushed against me as she marched out, causing me to knock against the bedside locker. Miss Cohen opened her eyes.

'You have a visitor, Miss Cohen,' I said, smiling down at her.

'Who is it, Beattie?'

'A girl called Flora Fielding.' I led Mum over to her.

'Flora! This is a most unexpected pleasure. I was thinking about you today. Do stop hovering and fidgeting. Sit down.'

I pushed Mum into Nurse Goss's chair and she took Miss Cohen's old, feeble hand in her old, strong one.

'I've never forgotten you, Miss Cohen. You have been precious to me all these years. I was so fortunate to have you as my teacher. Everything you taught me – the thrill and romance of words, poetry and literature have been a source of joy and solace to me. I loved you so much! If only my Beattie had had the benefit of your influence; but there isn't another teacher in the world like you!'

'Nonsense, Flora!' I could see, even from where I stood, that she was smiling. 'I'm afraid you have not learnt to think before you speak, otherwise you would not exaggerate so foolishly.'

I could hear a commotion from the dining nook; Kitty calling my name.

'Are you there, Beattie? Is that someone calling you?'

'Yes, Miss Cohen. I'm just going.'

'No. Not yet. Come here, sit down beside your mother and pay attention. I want to tell you something.'

I did as I was told. She released her hand and placed it on Mum's cheek.

'Beattie, sitting next to you is the best teacher in the world,' she said.

6

The Inventory

'The state of the silver is an absolute disgrace, Beatrice,' said Matron. 'I felt thoroughly ashamed when Doctor Taylor took coffee with me yesterday. See that the cutlery, the two tea services and the coffee set are cleaned this morning. After lunch, I would like to have a private talk with you in my office.'

You have to hand it to the deceitful cow. She can look at you without batting her silver-blue eyelids when she mentions Doctor Taylor. They get under her eiderdown every Tuesday afternoon to discuss the health of the residents and she serves up a few extras with the coffee. Bubba Marks is the only one who doesn't know. I asked Yetta to help me with the polishing, and we got to wondering what Dixon wanted to talk to me about. Had she noticed that one of the catering cans of pink salmon had disappeared from the stores? My brother Teddy's three teenage kids had phoned me at work on Friday evening announcing their arrival on my doorstep, I didn't have any emergency provisions in the house so I'd snaffled this and that from the store room and made them a pile of salmon rissoles and chips. I'd also run out of clean bed linen, so I'd borrowed a few sheets and pillowcases and hadn't had the opportunity to launder and return them. Yetta said she'd swear blind that they'd had salmon for supper on Matron's weekend off, and she'd make sure all the residents remembered the occasion. The linen cupboard key wasn't hanging in its usual place, so I guessed she might have cottoned on to something. We discussed whether or not I should tell Matron the truth if the subject came up, but neither of us thought that a very sensible solution.

Hawk-Eye Goss was hanging about all morning, watching me gleefully. She saw Yetta helping me in the pantry, and hauled her back to the sitting room, making out that she was abusing her arthritic hands. Yetta isn't one to be pushed around, and she managed to jab Goss in the bum with a handful of forks. Sarah fell out of her chair laughing and had to lie down, after swallowing a paper cup of brandy to help her over the trauma. Goss prowled around her in case she died, and there was no chance of borrowing a few sheets from the cupboard downstairs, for an emergency replacement.

I served lunch, then cleared away and washed up. Matron buzzed for me three times before I had the opportunity of answering her summons.

'Sit down, Beatrice,' she said. 'You've been working at The Haven now for how long?' She knew perfectly well, but she was always repulsively twee, before she came to the point.

'A month longer than you.'

'That makes five and a half months, yet you still don't seem to understand exactly what your duties are. Perhaps Miss Tinker never made them clear to you. She wasn't in a very balanced state of mind, poor thing, and I'm afraid you learnt some rather unfortunate habits from her.'

'Matron Tinker explained my duties to me very clearly. We were in full agreement regarding the priorities here.'

'In that case, my priorities are not hers. When I accepted this appointment I was quite frankly horrified by the lack of organization and hygiene. Our collective duty is to make the last days of our residents as pain-free and as serenely happy as possible. We have a team of voluntary workers to come in at intervals to have a sing-song or a chat, and lend a sympathetic ear when needed. They take our people for short walks and drives, and for their weekly outing to the Friendship Club. We have an occupational therapist and our social worker. Daily restoratives, sedatives, injections and dressings are handled by Nurse Goss and she or the agency nurse helps them to bathe and undress for bed, and wash and dress

73

in the mornings. Cook sees to the main meal and the special diets, and last, but not least, Rabbi Ezra attends to the spiritual needs of our residents, and sustains them when their lives draw to a close. You see, we're one big family, each with a well-defined responsibility. What do you consider yours to be, Beatrice?'

I was so relieved that she hadn't cottoned on to a few missing tea bags that I let her babble on, ad nauseam, and didn't bother to remind her that she and Doctor Taylor had not had *their* duties well defined.

'I prepare and serve breakfast, serve lunch and lay out the supper trays. On late shift, I do exactly the same, except that I help the folks to get into their dressing gowns instead of doing the breakfasts. In between times, I set up the trays for Mr and Mrs Freid, the trolleys for morning coffee and afternoon tea, wash the dishes, the tables and the kitchen floor, scrub the pans, vacuum the sitting room, your office and flat; keep the mice at bay in the store room and check on the stuff in the fridge and pantry. I'm expected to polish the silver, clean the cooker and assist Cook with the vegetables. I'm on the go from the moment I arrive until the moment I leave.'

I knew damn well what she was getting at. I thought of Tinker. She was the sloppiest, merriest old drunk you could ever wish to work with. It was Goss who'd spilled the beans about her habit, probably hoping she'd be upgraded. We all missed Tinker.

'In short, your work is in the kitchen and keeping The Haven fresh and neat. There is no necessity for your presence in the residents' sitting room, except for taking in the trolley and bringing in the supper trays. There is absolutely no need for you to sit there, gossiping. Their outings do not concern you. Your job is not taking them for walks or to shops and cafés. Their shopping, as well you know, is done for them by the voluntary workers and their meals are more than adequate. One of the ladies on the House Committee saw you coming out of the Eagle and Child at two-thirty with Mrs Marks, and Nurse Goss tells me that Mrs Juggler was setting up the tea trolley in the kitchen, unattended. I, together with the House Committee, make the rules for The Haven. No resident is allowed in the kitchen alone, but if the occupational therapist thinks that it would be a good idea for them to feel usefully employed, now and then, she suggests a little job for them to do, with Cook's cooperation, but on the whole, they are very happy with their hand-work and knitting.'

The sly, patronizing bitch! I'd seen her and that OT woman pulling out the knitting when the drawer got crammed to capacity with dishcloths, then serve the folks up with the string again.

'We have more than enough voluntary workers, and I will not have you wasting paid time on noisy and wearying activities during our old people's rest time, or on irresponsible expeditions. If you feel that your work here is too arduous, it might be wise for you to look for a job elsewhere. The committee has already discussed looking for a live-in help – someone considerably younger, who would be glad of a home.'

She sat opposite me, at her desk in her neat little cap and cuffs, telling me with a movement of her hand that I was dismissed from her royal presence.

I felt myself going hot and cold. Tinker had been pushed out by the committee, and since this matron was appointed, Tom, the old gardener and odd-job man, had been given his marching orders. Now, she was trying to get rid of me! Since the death of Miss Cohen two weeks ago, she'd allowed her violent dislike of me to free-wheel. It seemed that Miss Cohen had held her back somehow and compelled her to apply the brakes. I tried to figure out the reason for this. There was something . . . some moment . . . but I couldn't pin it down. It had been such a sad time recently. A few months ago I hadn't thought it possible that I could miss someone; someone else, so much. I actually told Professor Gottleib when I attended his monthly clinic the day before yesterday. I regretted doing so, since he quite openly and disgracefully seemed to relish my distress.

'I would be grateful for another chance, Matron. I like my work here,' I said, pretending to be crushed and mortified. I'd get my own back on her; discuss the position with the residents at the earliest possible opportunity, and we'd organize a plan of action.

'Then go and get on with it!' she bellowed. 'The inventory of bed linen, pillows, blankets and tablecloths should have been completed last week. There seems to be a discrepancy in the number of new sheets we bought. See that the list is on my desk before you leave today. Here's the key.'

Goss must have told her that I'd planned a rather busy time. The big race at Doncaster was due to start at three o'clock, and we'd arranged the chairs around the telly, so that we could all watch and hear. Kitty had collected the pocket money, and we were going to blow the lot on Amazing Grace, an outsider, at 20 to 1. If we won, we were all going for a trip to Southend. Yetta's grandson-in-law was a taxi driver and he and two of his friends had volunteered to take us and bring us home. Bubba's grandson, Clive, worked as a croupier at a small casino. He told me that he'd seat us all round one of the roulette tables and he and another croupier would make themselves available to us and serve us with free coffee and sandwiches, with the compliments of the manager. All he required was forty-eight hours' notice. We needed a good win in order to buy enough chips for everyone to play at the tables and also to pay something towards the petrol money for the journey.

There was no way I could get to the betting shop now. Only four of the residents were mobile enough to walk up to the main road – Rene, Alter, Olga and Boris. I asked Rene if she would do the errand, but of course she wouldn't dream of entering a betting shop. She hadn't been brought up to frequent such places, and I should really know better than to ask her to start now. Rene is sometimes quite intolerable. Olga and Boris had already gone out. They were *always* out somewhere – leaving separately and returning separately – painfully demonstrating their dislike of each other, yet unable to forego the activities they had once enjoyed together; feeding the ducks; playing bowls; walking round the flower beds in the park; going for a bus ride. Well, that left Alter, my only hope!

Alter was the most active and physically fit of all the residents, but he had less fun than anyone else. From my very first day at The Haven, I'd noticed how everyone seemed to know and like him, yet he and his wife had moved in just a few weeks before.

'. . . Freid, Alter – admitted 4 February 1985. Date of birth, 1905, Trzcianne, Poland. Retired beadle. Nervous exhaustion and depression; physically active and vigorous. Mentally alert. Closest relative, Golda Freid (wife) – The Haven.'

'. . . Freid, Golda – admitted 4 February 1985. Date of birth, 1905, Bialystock, Poland. Retired milliner. Diabetic; doubly incontinent; extremely confused. Closest relative, Alter Freid (husband) – The Haven.'

They occupied the flat across the landing from Boris and Olga, on the first floor, right next to the huge linen cupboard. I could keep an eye on Golda while he went on the errand.

Alter rarely went out, and then only if his wife was asleep or being bathed. His utter devotion to Golda was touching, and made me terribly sad. Sometimes, when he came down to the kitchen for the tray, he'd say, 'Oh, Beattie, why doesn't the Almighty have mercy, and take me and my Golda to our everlasting peace?'

Golda was senile, and could no longer offer or accept the love and companionship they had both enjoyed during their fifty-five years of marriage. They had given up their home when he could no longer cope with the situation, refusing to allow her to go into residential care without him.

Most of the residents remembered Alter and Golda Freid from years back. Yetta and Kitty had been neighbours in the East End and Alter was the beadle of their synagogue. They often spoke about what a handsome couple they were, not blessed with children or material wealth, but always ready to help out in a crisis in the neighbourhood. Their tenement flat was crowded with refugees, during the bitter, pre-war days, and they'd worked night and day at the Jews' Shelter; but now, if one of the residents struggled up the stairs to see them, Golda would shriek dreadfully and become insanely agitated, jealous of her husband's attention; and Alter had asked that they should be left alone.

Goss was rubbing alcohol into Golda's heels and back when I went upstairs. Golda was shouting and screaming, and poor Alter was standing in the middle of the room, looking wretched and lost. I beckoned to him and he followed me on to the landing.

'Alter, please run to Ladbroke's with the purse. All the instructions are inside, and there's a man there called Salim who'll help you to fill in the betting slip. The Queen of Darkness has loaded me with work and I daren't leave the premises, but I promise I'll stay with Golda until you get back. I won't leave her for a minute. The race starts at three and we've got to place the bets before then. Afterwards, just pop into the Bird and Baby for a can of Watney's Red Label for Bubba – and buy one for yourself. A treat from me. No! I insist! You look as though you could do with a drop.'

I think Alter was glad of the break. He said he wasn't born yesterday and knew how to fill out a betting slip, and it didn't take me long to persuade him. He reckoned he'd go out by the garden door so that none of the voluntary workers would stop him, to talk. All they did was ask him about Golda, and what could he say? Tears were never far from his eyes and voice. I handed him the cloth purse, together with the name of the horse, and helped him on with his coat and scarf. He picked up his hat and stick and hurried off.

I told Nurse Goss that Alter had gone out for tobacco and that as I had work to do up here, I'd keep an eye on Golda until he returned. She said that *she* hadn't time to hang about; she had three diabetics waiting for injections downstairs, meaning that some people, excluding me, had important matters to attend to.

I pulled out armfuls of sheets and pillowcases from the cupboard and heaped them on to Alter's bed, so that I could talk to Golda while I sorted and counted. She shouted for Alter repeatedly, and banged her frail old fist against the arm of her chair. Nothing I could do or say seemed to quieten her. Her milky-blue eyes were wild and she pulled aimlessly at her dishevelled, sparse white hair.

'Where's Alter? Alter! Alter! Alter!' She tottered over to his bed, feebly trying to dislodge the linen, as if she thought he was lying beneath it. 'Wake up, Alter! Alter! Alter!' No doubt she did this during the night, and I wondered if he ever got any undisturbed rest.

'He'll be back soon, Golda. He isn't in bed.' I threw everything on the floor to show her he wasn't there, but she tore at his coverlet and pillow in ghastly agitation, calling his name over and over again.

'He's with a prostitute!' she howled.

I speculated as to what frenzied delusions tormented her. I guided her back to the chair, and pushed her into it gently, then knelt in front of her so she couldn't get up. I reached over to the window sill and grabbed one of the framed photographs.

'Look, Golda! There's Alter! Isn't he handsome? And who's that beautiful girl next to him?'

She looked briefly at the picture and then thrust it away fretfully, beginning to cry for Alter again. It must drive him quite mad; the constant, inane, repetitious shriek.

'What a lovely hat you're wearing in the photograph! What colour were the flowers on it?'

'Red. Red roses.'

I held my breath while her mind erased fifty intervening years, competently; scrupulously.

'I made the hat myself – yellow straw with red roses. I painted the roses, but when it rained, the paint stained the hat and ran down my face. We sat in the shelter, and Monty wiped the paint away and kissed me. Every Sunday afternoon, while his ugly wife and her brother were at their mother's, Monty and I sat in the shelter in Shadwell Park. He can't get enough kisses from his Golda. Where's Monty? Where's my straw hat? It's raining! The rose paint is running down my face! Monty! Monty!'

Tears poured down her withered cheeks. I wiped them away with a pillowcase, and tried to take the photograph away from her, but she held on to it, as if, at last, she had found temporary peace.

'Monty! Monty!' she crooned.

'Alter kissed you, Golda,' I said shakily. 'Alter! Alter! Alter!'

She looked at me blankly, then turned again to the picture of her and Alter, and sat quietly, rocking backwards and forwards. I adjusted the shawl around her tiny, bird-like bones, and went back to my inventory. I remade Alter's bed, and tucked his prayer shawl back into its velvet bag from where Golda had grasped it from under his pillow. The bag was beautifully embroidered. She was shouting for Monty again.

'Did you make this bag for Alter, darling?'

'Monty darling! Monty darling!'

'Shut up!' I said sharply. 'Shout for Alter!' He would be back soon.

A tortoiseshell snuff box fell out of his velvet bag. If I gave her a pinch of this, she might sneeze, instead. I opened it. There wasn't a whiff of snuff inside – it was crammed with black and yellow capsules. It was a sacred rule at The Haven that no one was allowed to keep his or her own medication. Pills were doled out with scrupulous efficiency, as individually prescribed. Even Tinker had been exacting on this point.

I grabbed Alter's clip-board, which was attached to the end of his bed. One, every night, before retiring. The black bombers which Miss Cohen had swallowed, to help her through the long nights. I remembered how quickly she had sunk into a deep and peaceful sleep; her respite from the unremitting pain caused by the tumour on her spine. So Alter was given a nightly dose, too, of the black and yellow capsules – perhaps for similar reasons, but for him, it was respite from mental torture. Why was he hoarding them? You didn't have to be a genius in order to guess. He wasn't going to hang around, waiting for the Almighty's mercy.

I stuffed the snuff box into the bag along with his prayer shawl, and placed it under his pillow where it belonged, then started throwing the sheets on top, trying to get Golda to count along with me, but I couldn't change her tune.

'Monty darling! Monty darling!'

I thought I heard a soft step on the landing and began singing loudly, but when I paused for breath, all I could hear was the telly in the sitting room. The race was about to begin. I hoped Alter had managed to place the bet in good time. He came in.

'Alter! Hello! You managed to place the bet? Marvellous! Why don't you join the girls downstairs and enjoy your beer – and watch the race for me? Golda's fine!'

'Thank you, Beattie. I'll stay here with her. Here I am, darling! Who's Golda's sweetheart?'

'Monty! Monty! Monty!' she cried, looking up at him vacantly.

'I've been telling her a story about a man I used to know called Monty,' I gabbled wildly. 'Give me a drop of that ale.'

He poured out a brimming glassful, but I took the can and drained it, so that he had to take the glass. The froth clung to his moustache. He took out a snow-white handkerchief and wiped his mouth and then his eyes.

'I put all the money on Rose of Tralee, five to one,' he said. 'Amazing Grace has three legs, and two of them are wooden.'

'You did *what?* My life won't be worth a penny! You go down this minute and tell them what you've done, before the race is over.'

I gave him a little shove and he went out without a backward glance. I could hear his deep voice clearly, amongst all the female ones. Talking. Laughing. Rose of

Tralee must have come in. He came bounding up the stairs.

'Well, Beattie, I told you I wasn't born yesterday. They're working out their winnings down there. I think the trip to Southend is on!'

'You're a brave man, Alter,' I smiled, 'or, rather, a reckless one! Well done! I wish you could come with us.'

'Maybe I will. I'll help you to count the pillow cases.'

'Monty!' shouted Golda. 'Look at my hat! It got spoilt in the rain! Kiss me, darling!'

I wrote down fifty pillowcases; thirty-eight sheets; fifteen blankets; seventeen pillows; ten coverlets; ninety-nine towels. A few less – a few more. What difference did it make? Fifteen black bombers. Alter was as balanced, as good and as kindly a man as you could ever wish to meet. A private man, deprived of his privacy and independence. He seemed more cheerful after his outing. Perhaps the pills were a safety valve, just in case his life became too intolerable. His safety valve; his life. Both belonged to him.

I rushed downstairs to make the tea. The sitting room buzzed with excitement and everyone was saying how they knew Rose of Tralee would win, but Beattie, of course, was that pushy and bossy about Amazing Grace that no one had a chance of voicing their preference. Good old Alter! He'd saved the day! It took a man to put Beattie in her place!

I didn't bother to straighten them out. I yelled for Yetta and Kitty to come into the kitchen to help me, and sat on the stool having a quick smoke, while they set the cups and put out the biscuits and cake.

'Listen, girls, I need to draw on your wisdom, knowledge and advice but before I do, just rack your brains and try to remember a man by the name of Monty, who was close to Alter and Golda about fifty years ago.'

'That must be Monty Katz. He was married to Alter's sister, Julie. They lived in the same building. They were always in and out of each other's places, but one day there was a terrible row. I think Julie insulted Golda, and Alter never forgave her. Isn't that right, Kitty?'

She nodded. 'Julie and Monty moved away after the war. When Sam, my husband, asked after them, Alter said he never wanted to hear their names mentioned again. God only knows what the row was about. They used to play cards together nearly every night. Maybe somebody cheated. Sam said that's what comes of living in each other's pockets. Something's bound to flare up and cause bad blood instead of a few minutes' bad feeling. I'd forgotten all about them until just now.'

'I've often thought about them,' said Yetta. 'About that row. If Sadie's mind was clear, she could tell you everything that led up to it, but all she remembers now is the carryings-on and the terrible things Julie was screaming all through the Buildings. Reach the tea down, Beattie.' I threw in a handful of tea bags. 'How did Monty Katz's name come up?'

'Golda remembers bits and pieces from the past, and I noticed Alter looked a bit put out when she mentioned his name, so don't say anything. Forget about that; I've got far more pressing problems.' I gave them a full report of my interview with Matron and how uneasy I felt. 'Try to think of something that'll stop her giving me the elbow. Talk to the others over tea. I've got to see her with the inventory in a minute, but I want to get my position clear before I go home tonight. I'll meet you in the cloakroom before supper. Come up with something, for God's sake.'

I needn't have worried. The residents have never let me down in a crisis. Yetta reminded me about the afternoon I'd seen Matron turn off the radio while Miss Cohen was listening to it – and how Matron hadn't realized I was there until the moment our eyes met and I'd seen the guilt; the fear. Yes! That was it! I've got into the habit of telling Yetta everything. She's so wise and clever and understanding.

I was knocking at Matron's door again after I'd served the supper.

'Matron,' I said. 'Since you prefer me not to mix with

the residents any more, I'll probably have more time for cleaning your flat. I've noticed that the bed needs remaking on Tuesday afternoons, so a second tidying up won't come amiss. I hope Doctor Taylor will notice how beautifully the silver is polished, but I suppose he has other things to think about?'

Of course it worked! That look, that same guilty, fearful, sideways slide of the big blue eyes. The smile; the white teeth touching; grinding.

'Perhaps you'll help me to work out my timetable of duties tomorrow morning?' I asked sweetly.

'I don't think that will be necessary, Beatrice. You've worked extremely hard and well this afternoon, and so long as all your jobs are carried out as thoroughly, and not neglected in the future, I think we may turn a blind eye on your occasional chats with the residents. I'll put in a good word to the committee on your behalf.'

'Thank you, Matron. That saves me the task of speaking to the committee myself.' I smiled brightly and hurried off to say good night to the residents, and give them the thumbs-up.

I knew something dreadful had happened when I turned up for work the next day. The radio wasn't blaring, and no one was in the hall waiting for me. Goss, Matron and the agency nurse were nowhere to be seen. Death is a not infrequent visitor to The Haven and it brings more of a chill than a feeling of grief, as if all the folks are saying to themselves, 'Not me, this time, but who will be next?'

Don't let it be Yetta! Please, God, don't let it be her, or Alter or Sarah or Kitty or Boris or . . .

I shouted 'Hello' and peered fearfully into the cloakroom. Yetta was there, drying her face. I gasped with relief.

'It's Golda, Beattie,' said Yetta. 'She passed away in her sleep during the night. Alter raised the alarm not half an hour ago. Don't be upset. It's a happy release for her. For him.' She wiped her eyes. 'They had a long and happy life together. I lost my husband, may his dear soul rest in peace, when I was thirty-three.'

I sat down on the stool. My legs were trembling, and I needed a little time before I started work in the kitchen. Kitty came in, wearing a black headscarf.

'Alter's joining us for breakfast. Come and help me look after him, Yetta.'

No more trays, I thought. No more isolation.

I followed them after a minute or two, into the kitchen. His face was red with weeping and he sat in the dining nook, between Yetta and Kitty, for he had known them both when young. I went over to him, kissed the top of his skull-cap and massaged his shoulders for a few moments.

'I'm so sorry, Alter,' I said. 'Take comfort from your friends. May I go up to see her later?'

He nodded and squeezed my hand.

I heated up the milk, put the eggs on to boil, and started the toast and coffee. Matron and Goss came in and I slipped up the stairs to Alter's flat and asked the agency nurse there if she would mind if I said goodbye to Golda in private. She looked at me curiously then shrugged and walked out.

I kissed Golda's forehead and her hand, then searched briefly for Alter's velvet bag. I found it in his drawer, wrapped in his prayer shawl. Then I took out his snuff box and made a careful inventory.

7

Kissy-Kissy

'Something odd is going on, Yetta. But of course you haven't noticed.'

'Pass me two more Spanish onions.'

I watched her, the knife blade missing her fingers by a whisker, slicing paper-thin rings faster than I could count. 'Between Olga and Boris,' I said, observing the next few slices carefully. They were thick and clumsy in comparison. More my style. 'Why are they always quarrelling in public; hurling insults at one another? You know how upset the children are? Pat was crying last Sunday. She said . . .'

'And what about Paula? Was she crying last Sunday?'

'At this moment we are talking about Pat!'

'No,' said Yetta. 'You are. I'm talking about Paula who was three years old on Sunday and didn't have a birthday visit from her grandma and grandpa, even though they promised . . .'

'You're unbelievable! I really think you should speak to Doctor Taylor about the way you've been deliberately forgetting what I say! I *told* you that with Matron and Cook away at the same time, it was impossible for me to take the time off.'

'And did you tell me that Miss Shapiro and her two friends offered to help out so you could stick to your arrangements? I remember what you didn't tell me! Where are the tomatoes?'

We didn't speak for five minutes. Yetta picked out the squashy tomatoes from the box, then started cutting them up as if her life depended on it. I lit a cigarette and made sure the smoke blew in her direction.

'As I was saying,' I said deliberately, '*Pat* was crying

on Sunday. She said her parents had a wonderful marriage and seemed so happy until a few months ago, just after Boris had his heart attack. Pat said her mother was distraught while he was in hospital, and promised God over and over that if he spared him, she'd do what was right. She just kept on hollering that she'd do what was right. Pat says that since her dad recovered, they've turned against one another in the most dreadful manner. What do you make of it all, Yetta?'

'Pat, Pat, Pat!' scoffed Yetta. 'Everything must be done right for little Pat! She talks too much. The paper towels, Beattie.' I ripped off a couple of sheets. She wiped her eyes and glasses. 'Why isn't the oil hot? Are we having goulash or raw onions and squashed tomatoes for lunch?'

Mrs Jones was away with a trapped nerve in her wrist, and Matron was on a week's holiday. Yetta acted as if she was both of them rolled into one.

'Will you stop that!' I banged the pan down on to the stove, poured the oil and lit the gas. 'Are you going to tell me why Olga and Boris act as if they hate each other and as soon as they're on their own, they're kissy-kissy, lovey-dovey?'

'Don't you ever quarrel with Frank?'

That was really hitting below the belt. Since I told Yetta every time Frank started a row, I didn't bother to answer, but she ignored my silence.

'And before you can have another quarrel, you have to make up, don't you? Have you and Frank made up after the row you had on Sunday?'

'Frank is acting unreasonably and childishly. Sometimes plans have to be postponed.'

'Paula's birthday? Was that postponed?'

When Yetta's got a bee in her bonnet, she's more tiresome than all the residents put together. I'd been foolish enough to mention to her that our son-in-law, Dave, had invited us down to help Paula celebrate her birthday, but it was out of the question to take up Miss Shapiro's offer of help. I didn't want to be unkind about her to Yetta, but she was really quite incapable of managing the meals and helping Goss if there was an emergency. On top of everything, Frank had been in a mood all week.

'So, Boris and Olga quarrel sometimes, and make up sometimes – like you and Frank.'

I took a deep breath and tried to keep calm. 'Remember last week when Boris yelled at Olga that he wanted a divorce, and she said that's all she wanted from him and walked out of the house? Remember?' Yetta nodded, and concentrated on scraping the carrots. 'Well, not ten minutes later, *he* left the house – and I went out to post a parcel for Matron. I popped into the play-park for five minutes' peace and quiet, and who should I find on the seat there, but Boris and Olga – smiling, talking, holding hands. I pulled back before they saw me. Do you know why? I'll tell you. I pulled back because I knew that this was real between them, and the other things – the shouts and curses – were not! Yet since then, Olga's slept downstairs, and they haven't spoken one word to each other. What do you think all that's about?'

'A lot of divorced people don't speak to each other, or share the same bedroom.'

'They're not divorced. You can't get divorced in five minutes.'

'How do you know? Are you a solicitor? Are you a rabbi?'

'The most ignorant, stupid person knows people can't get divorced without a whole lot of palaver,' I said spitefully, 'unless you're an Arab with four wives and no sons. Is Boris disguised as one, then? It's possible, since he seems to be giving a stage performance every time I see him and Olga in the sitting room.'

I threw the cubed meat into the spitting oil.

'Boris and Olga are *Jewish*,' said Yetta coldly. 'You might know about Arab divorces but you don't know anything about Jewish ones. Rabbi Ezra gave them a special quick divorce because they're old and don't have all the time in the world.'

'Does Pat know anything about this?'

'She's in Majorca. How *could* she know? They waited

88

until she left for her holiday, so dear little Pat wouldn't be upset by it.'

'What have you got against Pat, Yetta? I thought you liked her, and under the circumstances I think she deserves your sympathy.'

'And what about Paula and Dave? And Janice?'

I scooped the tomatoes from the board and threw them into a bowl. A few pieces dropped off the table on to Yetta's slipper. I walked over to the trolley, popped a spoonful of coffee into a cup and filled it at the urn. My hands were shaking and I barely avoided scalding myself.

'Your remarks are offensive,' I said stiffly. 'I have endured a week of keeping this place going, single-handed, together with Frank's moods – and the knowledge that Gloria's husband has, with unseemly haste, found himself a girlfriend. But that's not enough for him!'

I could hear my voice getting louder and louder. Yetta seemed unperturbed. She got up from the stool, shook the pan and tossed in the onions.

'Oh, no! He wants us to meet her! Smile our approval! He wants us to see how much our Paula likes this Janice and she's being encouraged to . . .' My voice melted into self-pity. 'And now you . . . my friend . . . ! It's a miracle you've actually heard a word *I've* said to you since Golda died. You should watch it, Yetta. From where I stand you're paying far too much attention to Alter. He's just got to get used to being without Golda and he needs time to grieve. You shouldn't be at his beck and call all the time. You're spoiling him.' I was sickened and ashamed to hear what I was saying, but worse was to follow. 'Don't you think *I* deserve a little sympathy?'

'At this moment we are talking about Pat,' said Yetta calmly. She wiped her hands and leaned back for a few moments. 'I remember when Pat was born, like it was the other day, but it must be sixty years. Olga and Boris docked in the Pool of London on a ship from Hamburg. They were sixteen, maybe, but looked a lot younger. Only because they were both very small,' she added quickly. 'Alter helped them to find a room, and work, then Olga had to leave because Pat was on the way. My mother used to go every day, and not empty-handed, either. They were so poor and couldn't speak a word of English between them. But look at them now!'

'Olga and Boris aren't from Germany. Their notes say that she was born in a town called Nikolayev in the Ukraine, but Boris was from Riga – about a thousand miles apart.'

'So what?' shouted Yetta angrily. 'People travelled around in those days as well. Trains didn't just run in England, you know. There were railway lines in other places in the world. Just because you and Frank lived near each other when you were kids, and went to the same school, doesn't mean to say that Olga and Boris had to live on top of each other. And so what if they were poor and didn't have train fare! People weren't lazy in those days. If your parents decided they wanted you to meet a nice, respectable boy or girl from a good family a few miles away, they didn't waste time looking for train fares. They went over in a horse and cart or they walked. An unmade road or a bit of bad weather didn't worry them!'

She chopped at the carrots so viciously that a few slices jumped across the table, and practically landed in my open mouth. I chewed slowly, completely taken aback by her peculiar outburst. I decided to ignore it completely.

'Look at them now, indeed!' I said. 'Maybe they were happier then, in spite of the poverty. I wonder why their lives have become so bitter.' For a few moments I forgot about being upset, exasperated and puzzled. 'Frank and I were married when I was eighteen and he was nineteen, and everyone told us we were too young. But sixteen! And arriving in a strange country with a baby on the way!'

'Plenty people got married at sixteen, especially from where they came from. Fifteen even! In those days you grew up fast. You had to.'

'Maybe they didn't have a long enough time to be single and they've started to resent each other. Maybe they should see a marriage guidance councillor or a psycho-therapist.'

'Don't be foolish, Beattie,' said Yetta sharply. 'Rabbi Ezra knows better than those people.'

'But he doesn't know that they meet up in the bus shelter or the park! He hasn't watched them sitting in the Bird and Baby, laughing and talking, or having coffee together in Owen's after shouting horrible names at each other through the hatch, right here, in front of me and everybody! I'm going to tell him!'

'I wouldn't do that. Rabbi Ezra knows everything about what's going on with Boris and Olga, and you telling him what he knows already would only make him embarrassed. People go to their rabbi with private problems, and don't expect they should go tittle-tattling to nosy parkers. Rabbi Ezra is a gentleman, but he might have to tell *you* to mind your own business! Maybe Alf Levene wasn't far off the mark when he accused you of being a spy!'

She had offended me deeply. I turned my back on her and concentrated on measuring out the rice. Kitty and Olga came bustling in to set the trolley and tables, as giggly as naughty schoolgirls when the headmistress is off the premises. I could see Yetta through the reflection in the window, making gestures at me, and saying something in Yiddish. Olga came straight over.

'Sit down and drink your coffee, Beattie. We'll see to the rest of the lunch. Has something upset you?'

'I'm feeling very distressed about you and Boris, Olga, that's all, but it seems as if I'm the only one here who is,' I said maliciously. 'I hope poor Pat will react as calmly as your friends, when she discovers you and her father are going your separate ways.'

'We're not going to Separate Ways,' said Olga, as if it was the name of a residential hotel. 'We're moving into our new flat as soon as it's ready. We only stayed here while Boris was sick and until the flat is finished. But it's not good here for a couple. Rabbi Ezra did our divorce, but straight away we decided to get married.'

'Again,' said Kitty loudly. 'You shouldn't forget to say "married *again*".'

'Our flat is nearly ready,' said Olga quickly. 'Sheltered housing. Very nice. You bring everyone to visit us, Beattie. If you walk across the golf course it'll take you twenty minutes. We're having the carpets down on Friday. Pat's been on and on to us about moving there. It was Boris's idea to pretend we weren't interested, then arranging it all behind her back. She's always wanted us to live nearby. She'll have a *good* surprise when she comes home. And Beattie, my Boris and I want to make a little wedding party for all our friends here. We've been so well looked after and happy. Sunday, eighth September. Rabbi Ezra will be coming too. Will you help us with the arrangements?' She looked excited; radiant.

'Of course! But shouldn't we speak to Pat about it first? I know she'll want to help.'

'She's not invited,' said Olga. 'You don't invite your children to your wedding, and Boris and I would rather she didn't know about it anyway.'

The three of them looked at one another, and spoke in Yiddish again, then Yetta nodded slightly. I went into the store room and stayed there until they went out with the trolley, leaving Yetta alone at the table. She called out to me. I went over to the table and started clearing up the mess, not looking at her.

'Beattie,' said Yetta softly, 'I've known Olga and Boris on and off for sixty years, and for sixty years, on and off, they've had something on their minds which has made them ashamed. No one else thinks badly about them. The children, if they knew, would only feel sorry that their mother and father carried this burden and hid it from them. On September eighth that burden will be lifted and when their time comes, they will be able to meet the Almighty without shame. He wouldn't blame them anyway. But you can't tell folks they're not guilty, when they've convinced themselves they are. Can you? Don't *you* take sixty years, Beattie.' She took my hand and I turned my face away until I'd managed to pull it into place.

'Would you answer me one question, Yetta? After all,

you've known me nearly six months and I won't breathe a word to Pat.'

'Or go tittle-tattling to Rabbi Ezra?' I smiled. She shook her head.

'I can't answer any questions about Boris and Olga. They don't know you like I know you, and would never give me leave to tell.'

'Did immigrants from places like Latvia and the Ukraine usually travel across land, then go by cargo boat from Hamburg?'

Yetta nodded.

'I suppose they had to sleep on deck. It must have been so cold.'

'My Debbie still has the feather eiderdown Father brought over. He used to tell us how he and my mother rolled themselves up in it and stayed snug in the worst weather. Some of the immigrants were very poor and didn't have an eiderdown; but children, couples, clung together and shared body heat.'

'It must have been so cold,' I repeated. 'If you were very poor *and* on your own, with no one to share body heat with.'

'Throw in the carrots and the tomatoes,' said Yetta, giving the saucepan a shake and a stir with the slotted spoon. 'Now give me the paprika, salt and pepper. A garlic clove as well. It's got a good taste, Beattie. Two pairs of hands are always better than one.' She added a little water, brought the mixture to the boil, then lowered the gas flame and watched it simmering gently. 'No one froze to death, as far as I know. Kissy-kissy, lovey-dovey.'

8

Touch of Evil

The voluntary workers were a group of ladies who gave their spare time to the residents at The Haven, organizing bingo games, sing-songs and outings to the Friendship Club and, now and then, a trip into the country or to one of their homes, where a special tea would be prepared. Miss Shapiro, one of the most active members of the group, was sharing the celebration of her sixtieth birthday with the residents, and had organized a wonderful day for them – a ride to the canal in Kennet where a barge had been hired, with coffee and lunch on board.

The weather couldn't have been more perfect – unusually hot for mid-September. Nurse Goss and umpteen ladies from the Help The Haven team went along too. Matron and I waved them off, then I went into the kitchen to make her coffee. I decided to tackle the somewhat overdue chore of spring cleaning the sitting room while it was empty. The Haven Garden Party was to be held next week, to coincide with the Jewish Harvest Festival. It was also Open House and I wanted the sitting room looking its best. The House Committee had decided to buy a dishwasher with some of the funds we hoped to raise, but I doubted if it would make me redundant. I seemed to be the only one who did any real work these days. Refreshments were by courtesy of Beatrice Dwek, since Mrs Jones's trapped nerve seemed to be enjoying a long stay in ambush. Our huge freezer was crammed with my goodies. I told Matron what I intended to do, when I took her tray in.

'Bring another cup, Beatrice. There's more than enough for two.'

This was the first time I'd ever been invited into her

royal presence for a break. I managed to contain my surprise and suspicion. She seemed genuinely friendly. Maybe Doctor Taylor had told her he couldn't live without her; or perhaps her week's holiday had sweetened her up. I responded politely.

'Okay, Matron. Thanks.' I sat down while she poured.

'It's much too hot for heavy housework.'

I've never fainted in my life, but I was near to it when she said that. Something odd was going on. 'Why don't you take Mr Levene out?' she suggested. 'You could keep all the windows of the car open, and take him to that pub with a garden, off the A404. He'd enjoy that.'

'Oh, I don't think so, Matron. I don't mind the idea of cleaning. The heat doesn't bother me. And you know him. He hates going out except on his own.' Had she twigged that I was frightened of him? Was she being malicious or merely ingenuous?

'He can't go out on his own any longer and he actually asked if you could take him for a drive when I could spare you. I can spare you today. Go up and tell him to get ready.'

'Matron, I'm sorry. I don't want to. I appreciate your thoughtfulness, but to tell you the truth, we don't get on well and I'm a bit afraid of him.' I shouldn't have said that. One should never reveal one's vulnerability to an enemy. But the trouble was she was being so uncharacteristically nice, that I forgot myself.

'Why, Beatrice? He's an old, blind man. He can't hurt you.'

'It's nothing to do with physical fear. He gives me the shivers. I can't explain my feelings towards him. They're irrational.'

'Wouldn't this be a good opportunity to try and conquer your fears? It's such a beautiful day and he spends so much time alone. He's not been out for his usual walks for three days and he won't be in this world much longer. Doctor Taylor seems to think that it's the strength of his will that keeps him going. I suppose you must have noticed that the knitting machine hasn't been so active this week.'

Perhaps she wanted me out of the way today. Maybe she and Doctor Taylor were planning a wild orgy. I'd been thinking about their affair quite a lot lately; ever since Frank had told me his new colleague's name was Fenella Taylor.

'I'll take the old devil out, but he'd better behave himself. A couple of weeks ago, I saw him sitting on the seat at the top of the road, and said Hello and who I was. He swore at me and accused me of spying on him. But certainly I'm not afraid of him! That was a stupid thing to say. I dislike him, that's all.'

'I would have thought that one could only feel compassion for him.'

By the way, Matron, my husband is a bio-chemist. He works at the Institute of Tropical Diseases and guess who's on his team? Your lover's wife! Frank says she's very clever and original and he admires her ability; but I would have thought one could only feel compassion for her.

'His personality doesn't invite compassion,' I snapped. 'He's the nastiest man I've ever come across, blind or not. It can't be just crude vanity that impelled him to have himself stamped all over with those disgusting patterns; it's a gesture of contempt to his fellow men.'

'I suggest you reassess your views, Beatrice. From the brief report I received from the hospital, it seems that Mr Levene didn't have himself tattooed voluntarily. His psychological problems, handicap and disfigurement are all due to events beyond his control. Have you ever considered that it might be *your* attitude that should come under scrutiny? No, of course you haven't!' she chuckled, wagging her finger playfully. 'If you treat Mr Levene courteously, he responds well. He's always polite to me. Simply because he prefers working alone in his room to gossiping to you, doesn't necessarily mean that he's an unpleasant character. Aren't you being rather immature?'

'I don't think so,' I answered coldly. 'Are you telling me that someone forced him to cover himself with tattoos?'

'I'm afraid I'm not at liberty to discuss the details of a confidential report with anyone other than his social worker and the nursing and medical staff,' she said mendaciously.

Would you be so high-minded, so scrupulous, if I mentioned to you that I had a notion to spill the beans to poor old unsuspecting Fenny? Perhaps a note addressed to her, tucked into Frank's lunch box.

'But since you'll be taking him out today, I feel I should try to soften your heart a little for Mr Levene's sake. If he decides to confide in you, that's up to him, but I don't want him pressured in any way. He's a very private man, as well as a sick one.'

Alf Levene came to The Haven from hospital, in August, shortly after Golda died. He, himself, had been at Death's door two or three times since Tinker saw him, but had rallied sufficiently to be admitted. To give Matron her due, she had agreed to take over the responsibility of caring for him, and it was obvious to all of us that he was a dying man.

Before his illness he had lived alone in a council house in Stoke Newington, where he apparently augmented his pension by knitting sweaters on his knitting machine. She had installed him in the large room on the second floor, which had a small balcony overlooking the garden. Although he was so ill and emaciated, he was still capable of doing the stairs quite easily. He had a morbid dislike of company and would have starved rather than eat or mix with the residents, and since he suffered appallingly from claustrophobia, he had to keep his windows open all the time. Matron had, for once, been understanding, and allowed him to take his meals in his room.

He worked at his knitting machine incessantly and compulsively and repelled all friendly approaches. He knitted the most exquisite sweaters, and his room and the cupboard in the hall were full of different wools and yarns of all colours and textures. His patterns were in Braille, and all you had to do was tell him your size and what pattern and colour you wanted, and within a few days the garment

97

was ready. He charged high prices for his work. Matron probably got hers at a hefty discount in exchange for her uncharacteristic tolerance. Kitty's daughters-in-law, their families and friends, were all good customers of his.

He had been blind for many years, and was capable of getting around by himself with the help of his white stick. Everyone in the neighbourhood knew him. Once seen, never forgotten. He was the most terrible sight. He was primitively tatooed, not here and there, but all over. His bald head was covered in blue and red spiders, webs, abstract shapes and animals; there wasn't a square centimetre of his face, head and neck which was free of the ghastly artistry. The backs of his hands; the bony wrists which protruded from his jacket sleeves were patterned and inscribed with vulgar words and obscene pictures. He wore black, opaque glasses with shields on the sides, so you couldn't see his eyes at all.

I wondered sometimes why he didn't grow a beard and moustache; perhaps hair didn't grow properly over tattooed skin. Short of wearing a bag over his head, and gloves, there was no other way he could hide his ugliness. The horrid sudden knowledge that these tattoos had been forced on him made me shudder.

'You're shivering Beatrice, yet it's so hot today. Are you unwell?' Was it my imagination, or did I detect a flicker of pleasure at my discomfort in those cold blue eyes?

'It's the atmosphere in this place today. There's a touch of evil in the air. I'll be okay once I'm out of here. I'll take Alf his coffee now and see if he's in the mood for an excursion.'

I went upstairs with his coffee. He was sitting at the open window, working the machine.

'Alf!' I yelled, over the din, 'it's me – Beattie!'

'What is it? What do you want now?'

'I've brought you your coffee.'

'Where is it?' His fingers travelled over the table and I placed the tray within his reach. 'Mind you leave that door open as you go out.' Since he'd wedged it open with an iron door-stop, his comment was quite unnecessary.

'It's a lovely morning and everyone is away. Would you fancy coming for a drive and a drink at the Cherry Tree? There's a garden and a duck pond there, and the House Fund will pay.'

'So the old hags have been dragged off, eh? I hope it's for ever. Get away from the window.'

'I'm nowhere near the window,' I lied, moving silently to the other side of the table.

'You're all liars, the lot of you. I know where your voice is coming from, you silly bitch.'

'Do you want to come, or don't you? I'll be ready to leave in twenty minutes.'

He felt his watch. 'You got your car?'

'Yes.'

'I'll meet you at the front door, then.'

'He's coming, Matron,' I said. 'He accepted the invitation with his usual charm.'

She gave me seven pounds and I signed the chit.

'Have a ploughman's lunch as well. You don't have to hurry back. If it comes to a bit more, let me know, but remember, you're driving, so don't drink anything alcoholic. Have a pleasant time. If you don't rub Mr Levene up the wrong way, he behaves quite well.'

'Why is he always polite and respectful to you, yet vile to everyone else?'

'He only needs a little patience and understanding.'

'Doesn't he ever call *you* names?'

'No. Never.'

'I wish I knew your secret.' I looked straight at her and for a fleeting moment I saw that my flippant remark was not received as such. 'I'll be off, then.'

I exchanged my overall for my blouse, and fetched my bag. I could hear Alf locking his room and then walking downstairs. I opened all four windows of the car while he climbed in carefully, declining the front passenger seat, then placed his stick across his knees. He was wearing a cream straw trilby, an open-necked shirt, a light jacket

99

and grey flannels. He carried a capacious, zipped bag on a strap across his chest which he kept in position, even after he was seated. I watched him as I pretended to adjust my mirror. He took off his glasses and polished them with his handkerchief, although they were already gleaming. Whatever he did to them, he couldn't see a thing, anyway. I got the impression that in spite of his dreadful appearance, he was a vain man. A disagreeable notion jostled my mind that perhaps he didn't know what he looked like. Maybe he went blind before the tattoos, and no one had ever dared to tell him what a sight he was.

'How long does it take you to start the car up?'

I drove towards Hertfordshire, planning to make a detour to the pub, so we'd arrive there about midday. At least I didn't have to make polite conversation.

'Have you got a map?'

'Yes.'

'I don't want to go to gardens and duck ponds. I want to go to Lancing Green. You know where that is?'

'No, but I could look it up.'

'Stop the car and look it up, then.'

I turned left down a tree-lined residential road, pulled up and opened my AA book.

'It's quite an easy run. About half an hour, I suppose.' I started the engine.

'Wait. I want to speak to you. You're employed as a cleaning woman, aren't you?'

'Yes.'

'A cleaning woman doesn't earn much money. Do you like money?'

'Certainly I like money.'

'I want you to write something down for me. I would also like you to write a letter, and deliver it to Lancing Green. I'll give you twenty pounds.'

'Alf,' I said, 'if you could see, you would be able to write your letters yourself. I certainly won't do it for twenty pounds.'

'For how much?'

'For nothing, for God's sake! I don't want your damn money!'

'Don't worry. I'll pay you.' I ignored him. 'When one of the old hags dies at the home, what happens?'

'Rabbi Ezra and the family are informed. The funeral takes place the following day at the Jewish Cemetery.'

'And who pays for all the palaver?'

'I'm not quite sure. I believe there's some arrangement with the synagogue. Most of the residents are members. Otherwise, I think the family make a financial commitment.'

He took an envelope out of his bag, opened the flap and unfolded a piece of paper, then handed it to me. It was a receipt for five hundred pounds, dated a month previously, to cover funeral expenses, and signed, Dorothy Dixon, Matron. I read it out to him.

'I told her I wanted to be cremated. The bitch hasn't written that down.'

'It must have been an oversight, Alf. Speak to Matron about it, if you're worried – or to Rabbi Ezra.'

'Are you a Jewish woman?'

'No.'

'Jews don't go in for burning. They go in for burials. She says that if I'm living in a Jewish Home, I've got to abide by the rules. I don't want a burial! Nobody's going to stuff me six feet in the ground, and shovel dirt on top of me! You understand? I want to be cremated! I told her. I told the bitch fifty times. She's got to send away for some paper or other to get special permission. I told her to get a move on, so I can sign the paper. "All in good time, Mr Levene! You concentrate on getting well and if you behave yourself, I'll see what I can do. But *only* if you behave yourself! Remember I'm in charge here, and what I say, goes!" ' He mimicked her voice. Beads of perspiration drowned the blue and red patterns on his brow.

'Do you want me to write down your instructions and see that they're carried out? I'll get her to sign them for you and witness them.'

101

'When? When will you do it?'

'Today. If she's gone off duty by the time we get home, I'll see that she signs your paper first thing tomorrow.'

'And what if I die today?'

'I swear to you that I'll see you're cremated,' I said, banking on the improbability that he'd die in the car. He wiped his forehead, then felt around in his bag again, produced a pen and a notebook and handed them to me.

'I'll pay you for your trouble. I've got money. Are you ready?'

'Yes.'

'Write the address and the date.' I did as I was told. 'I, Alfred Levene, wish to be cremated on my death. I understand that this is not the usual practice among Jews, but special arrangements must be made. The Matron, Miss Dixon, of the above address, has received five hundred pounds to pay for my cremation. The receipt will be found in the lining of my overcoat pocket. Signed . . .' I placed the pen in his right hand, and guided it to the appropriate place, then added my own name as a witness.

'Read it over to me.' I did so.

'Here. Here's twenty pounds. Now I want you to write a letter for me.'

'If you wish to pay, you'd better see a lawyer.'

'I don't want any business with lawyers.'

'And I don't want any of your money! Is that quite clear?'

'And how can I be sure you'll keep your mouth shut? This is a private letter.'

'You'll just have to trust me then, won't you?'

'Who's there?' he shouted.

'A woman walking two dogs.'

'Move off. Move off to some place where there's no nosy bitches walking around.'

'*I do not like the human race; I do not like it's ugly face,*' I shouted at him.

'That's right.' I drove on in silence.

'We've just passed a signpost for Lancing Green – five miles. There are fields on either side of us. Do you want to write your letter here? All I can see are a few cows. Shall I pull up in the next lane or lay-by?'

'Yes.'

I turned on to a bumpy track and switched off the engine. A soft breeze blew pleasantly through the open windows.

'Is there anyone about?' he demanded.

'No.'

He handed me the notebook and pen again.

'You keep your mouth shut, do you hear? Or I'll shut it for you!'

I felt ridiculously uneasy. Afraid. What was the matter with me? The old, blind man at the back of my car was more helpless, physically, than a small child, wasn't he? But what if he had something in his bag to hit me with? What if he leaned forward and grabbed me by the throat? I was ten times stronger than him, but maybe he knew certain tricks. Why had someone gone to such meticulous lengths to make him so repulsive? Was it vengeance for some unspeakably evil deed? Violence and hatred seemed to emanate from him. I twisted round in my seat and watched him.

'I told you. You'll have to trust me. Don't you ever try to threaten me. Do you understand, you uncouth old devil?' I gripped his shoulder and pressed my fingers into it. 'You mind your manners and speak to me with respect!'

'I want a letter written to my son and delivered into his hands. *Please!*' he sneered. 'After I'm dead, you can blab for all you're worth, but I'm telling you for your own good, it would be better for you if you didn't. Don't write an address. Print in capital letters. That's how I want it, because that's the way I used to write. He isn't to know I'm blind or that someone has to write this for me.'

It was the second time today that I'd almost passed out. Alf Levene being the father of someone was so absurd, so startling and oddly moving, that it took me several moments to pull myself together.

'Whatever you wish me to write will remain absolutely

103

confidential. Please try to believe me. Money or threats don't influence me. I'm ready.'

'My beloved son,' he said, while I wrote, 'I last saw you when you were a boy of eight, and now that I have reached the end of my life, I want you to have what is in this envelope. It belongs to you. I worked hard for it, and while I worked, I thought of you. I do not ask to see you. After so much time it would be pointless to meet. Give the woman who is delivering this, some token of receipt. I send you my blessings for a happy and successful life, and hope that your son will be as proud of you, as you were of me. Your father . . . That's all. Read it back to me.'

I did as he asked, then handed the letter to him.

'Leave me alone for five minutes, please.'

It was peculiar to hear him say 'please' as if he was a normal person. I got out of the car, then leaned through the open window, told him to reach over the back of the driving seat, then placed his hand on the horn.

'I'm going to walk up the lane towards a field gate about twenty yards away and wait until I hear the horn. There's no one about. Take your time.'

'Thank you. I won't be long.'

I sat on the gate, thinking of the old man sticking the fruits of his wretched life into an envelope for a son who, for probably about forty years, had never seen his father, and was never likely to, ever again . . . My beloved son . . . please . . . thank you. After a few minutes I heard the horn and returned to the car. He had his arms folded on the back of the driving seat, his head resting on them. How could I possibly have ever felt afraid of him!

'Alf,' I called. 'It's me – Beattie.'

He raised his head and moved his arms away. He looked ill; ghastly.

I got into the car. 'Shall we go now?'

'In a minute. Turn round. What do you see?'

'I see you.'

'Am I a pretty sight?'

'You're okay.'

'I was once a very handsome man. Black hair; brown eyes; clear skin. Would my son recognize me, do you think?'

'The passage of time and dark glasses are fairly good disguises. Did he ever see you wearing them?'

'Did he ever see me with a mask over my face and neck, you mean? No.'

'Did you ever see yourself with the mask, Alf?'

'I lost my sight at the same time as the paintwork. Maybe it was good timing, eh?'

'You mean – while you were being tattooed, something happened to your eyes?'

'That's what I mean.'

'How dreadful!'

'Not so dreadful. At least I never went inside. They never locked *me* up! You ready to take this letter?'

'Yes. Have you the address?'

'No address. It's the house next to a pub called the Goat and Compass.'

'I'll find it.' I reversed out of the lane. 'What if your son isn't at home?'

'He's at home. His business is there.'

'What's his first name?'

'Michael. You don't tell him anything about me or where I live.'

'Why, for God's sake!' I shouted. 'What if he wants to see you? What if your grandchildren . . . ?'

'Would you like to see your father blind and covered in *this*? Why do you think I left my son and never returned? Should I let my son be sorry for me; ashamed of me?' He made a sweeping gesture over his face. 'But it could have been worse. I never went inside! My son doesn't have a penniless jailbird for a father!'

'Who did that to you and why?' I yelled. 'I'll take you only if you tell me what this is all about!' I turned the engine off. His anxiety clogged the air.

'Who did this to me? Friends!' he hissed. 'Why? You want to know why? I gave names to the Belgian police,

105

that's why! I walked straight into a trap in Antwerp, and I had no option. I couldn't take the rap for them; I'd rather be hung, drawn and quartered than go inside! So I traded their names for a suspended sentence. I knew what they'd do once they came out, if they caught up with me. The knock on my head damaged the optic nerves. That wasn't part of the deal.'

'Your friends were criminals, then?'

'My friends were criminals.' He mimicked me unpleasantly. 'And *my* name wasn't Honest Joe either.'

'That picture – there – is that why they tattooed that picture?' I pointed at his forehead, forgetting myself; forgetting that he couldn't see where I pointed; might not know. His two fingers touched it; covering the crude red bird, its beak open, a bubble issuing from it with the words, 'squawk, squawk' printed therein, a blue cage surrounding it. 'I'm sorry, Alf. It's hardly noticeable,' I gabbled.

'I might be blind but I'm not an idiot! When are you going to deliver my parcel? Now or next week?'

'Now.' I started the engine. 'Did your friends know you suffered from claustrophobia?'

'No. You think they'd have let me off more lightly?'

I drove into the village and saw the pub immediately. There were a couple of cars in the small gravelled car park and I pulled up next to them and told Alf where we were.

'Would you like me to fetch you a drink and a sandwich before I go to Michael?'

'Go now. Can you see the house?'

'Not from here. Do you want to wait in the car?'

'Where else? Go!' He thrust the bulging package into my hands. He'd tied it neatly and very firmly with string. He crumpled his long, skinny body so he was barely visible to anyone passing by, and bent his head down, almost to his knees.

Half the tables in the garden of the pub were already filled and a couple of youngsters were playing on the swing. Houses lay only to the right of the building and I looked over the low hedge which bordered that side of the car park. The land sloped at quite a steep gradient, and I could see the house – a cottage really – in its own small plot of land. I crossed over to the car park entrance and turned left on to the downhill path. The sun shone; the kids on the swing shouted; a dozen people not twenty-five yards away were enjoying a lunch-time break; yet I felt cold, frightened and alone, as if there was a touch of evil in the air.

The front door was open and I could hear a radio playing. I rehearsed what I had to say. 'Are you Michael, the son of Alf Levene? He sent you this.' The whole exercise seemed unreal, nightmarish.

There was a sign to the right of the door, advertising the name and business of the occupants – J. Frostig and Son: Tattoo Artists. A dog barked from somewhere behind the house. I turned and fled like a bat out of hell back up the slope and into the car park. Alf Levene would be listening for my footsteps. I skirted the hedge, went into the pub and asked if I could have a word with the landlord. The barmaid called him over and he greeted me cordially.

'I've got a letter to deliver for a Mr Levene. I know he lives in the village but I've stupidly forgotten the address. I wonder if you could help me?'

'I know all our regulars; but I don't know anyone called Levene. Sorry. I'll check in the local phone book, if you like. No, it's no trouble – nothing's too much trouble for a lady in distress.' He reached under the bar and leafed through the directory. 'Levene . . . No. Nothing. I've only been here for two years, though; ask the customers in the garden, or you could try the post office, when it opens again at two.'

'I'm sure I was told he lived next to the pub, but I've already tried the house there – ' I made a vague gesture.

'Frosty and his son live there and have done for years. The old chap may be able to help you. He'll be here for his beer in about ten minutes. Sit down and wait for him.'

'Thanks. Thanks very much. I'll pop back in a few minutes.'

I bought two cheese rolls and left, as if to go out into the garden, but made straight for the car. Alf Levene was sitting bolt upright; every muscle painfully tensed. I thrust the envelope and the sandwiches at him and jumped into the driving seat.

'We've got to leave here. I'll explain as soon as I can.'

I didn't wait for an answer, but jammed in the key and careered over the gravel and out into the village street. He didn't speak; didn't question me. I didn't know where I was heading; nor did I know how long I kept going, away from that place. The tap on my shoulder frightened the life out of me. I pulled into a lay-by without signalling, causing the driver behind me to hoot and swear.

'You said you would hand this to my son. Why didn't you?'

'Your son isn't there. Your damned friends are, though – one of them, anyway! Does the name Frosty or Frostig mean anything to you?'

'My wife's maiden name. Her brother was one of the men I betrayed. Did *he* say my son wasn't there?'

'What!' I shrieked. 'Are you telling me that your bro-ther-in-law blinded and tattooed you?'

'I gave his name to the police. He spent five years in prison because of that. The loss of my sight was an acci-dent. I resisted the punishment that we'd all agreed on. He promised to take care of my wife and son and never to tell them how I'd betrayed him and the others. He adopted Michael; taught him our trade. He kept his word. I had to keep mine – to stay away. Go back and deliver this envelope to my son. I'll pay you. I'll pay you well.'

'You let one of the bastards who did that to you bring up your son?' I gasped. 'You're mad! And you're even more mad if you think for one moment that I'm going back there! Send your blinking package with the postman!'

'I want a personal delivery. This is for my son and for no one else. How will I know my brother-in-law won't get his hands on it first if I send it by post?'

'Don't you trust him? He kept his word in every other way.' My voice sounded like a death rattle.

'I trust no one where money is involved,' he said, ignoring my cynicism. 'I trust him in every way, except with money. He brought up my son, taught him our trade and kept silent about the betrayal. That doesn't mean that he won't steal my son's money. People do anything for money. I've known him since we were boys. We're two of a kind. I made a mistake. I shouldn't have resisted. Don't you make the mistake of going back on your word, Beatrice Dwek,' he said softly. 'People do anything for money.' I hadn't known until that moment that the helpless old man knew my name. 'Now, go back to Lancing Green and make the delivery. You've wasted enough time already. I want you to get back home in time to see that Matron signs my cremation papers, as you promised. Don't worry. I'll pay you for your trouble.'

The sun blazed down but a cool breeze blew through the open windows. I shivered, as if there was a touch of evil in the air. I turned the car round, feeling his hand resting gently on my shoulder, and drove towards Lancing Green.

'People do anything for money,' he chuckled.

9

Gloria's Birthday

I arrived at work two hours late on the morning of Gloria's birthday. Yetta was the only person at The Haven who knew, because her granddaughter, Debbie, is exactly the same age. She was waiting for me on the pavement and hurried over to the car as I pulled up.

'You'd think the world was coming to an end in there. The three monkeys have been huddled together discussing your faults. Come to the cloakroom and wash your face. Don't give them the satisfaction of letting them see you're upset.'

I always try to take Yetta's advice. She's the wisest old witch in the business of muddling through. I know about incidents in her life which would have driven a lesser person into the safety of madness, or at any rate bitterness and self-pity – and she knows more about me than anyone, and is probably my best friend. She took my hand and stayed with me while I splashed my face and held the towel to my eyes. I put on my overall and she helped me to button it up, put her arms round me for a minute, then pushed me towards the kitchen.

'Good morning, Cook,' I said briskly.

'Good afternoon.' She dropped the potato peeler on to the table and marched out. I felt like sticking it between her shoulder blades, but Yetta was hovering in the doorway, making faces, both crooked thumbs held up as straight as possible. Matron came in and slammed the door shut in her face, but I knew that she was still loitering nearby.

'So you've condescended to turn up,' she sneered. 'Of course, it's too much to expect of you to phone and explain that you're going to be two hours late.'

'I'm sorry, Matron.' I busied myself with the potatoes. 'I did try, but there was something up with the line.'

'Really? I received several calls this morning. I hope you appreciate that it's my "menu" morning and that Cook is supposed to be here for two hours only today. We and Nurse Goss are not employed to do your chores as well as our own. What's your excuse this time?'

'I reckon you've cracked open the mystery of relativity, Matron,' I babbled, playing for time. 'Two hours is a short time for Cook to work, but a long time for me to be late. I'm afraid the car wouldn't start.'

'So you came by bus? Or did you walk?'

'No. I got it going after I'd given the battery a long rest. I was messing about for ages outside my house. It felt like a week, I was so anxious.'

'Well, well! We did try to telephone you, but there was no response, so I rang Mrs Colley who said she'd seen you leaving at the usual time.'

My next-door neighbour is a good sort, but not too quick off the mark. I couldn't think of anything to say, except that she must have been mistaken. Matron knew I was lying, of course, but I didn't care. My mind felt dull and heavy. All I could think of was Gloria's birthday and the long weekend ahead of us; Frank and I going to Brighton, to stay with Dave and Paula – and to meet Janice. The visit filled me with dread, and I wished, now, that I hadn't let Frank prevail on me to go.

'How much longer can we put it off? Just pull yourself together and try to imagine how they feel about it.'

'Do you think I give a damn? Do you really think I care twopence . . . ?'

'What about me, then? Do you ever consider how I feel?' he shouted. 'And Paula! Remember her?'

'It's Gloria's birthday. Perhaps next weekend; or the one after that.'

'No. *This* weekend! It's been one excuse after another! Last time it was Gloria's . . .'

'Shut up!' I screamed. 'Just *shut up!*'

He turned away from me and walked to the door like

111

an old, broken man. 'I've had enough. I've just about had enough.'

I heard the gate scrape closed, and when he returned, hours later, he went straight into the bedroom. By the time I joined him there, he was already asleep. This morning I'd found his note telling me he was going to Brighton that evening, and to be ready by five thirty if I was going too. I was okay when I left for work, but all of a sudden, at the traffic lights in Ballards Lane, the wretched thoughts swelled up in my chest, black and suffocating, and I'd had to pull up in Waitrose's car park, unable to see where I was going.

I felt much better after I'd cleared up the after-lunch mess. Yetta gave me a hand with the washing-up.

'Debbie will be here soon,' she said. 'Will you wrap her birthday present for me? Clive's coming too. Maybe he'll play the piano and we'll have a bit of a sing-song.'

Clive was skinny and pushing forty, with a Woody Allen face and known to Matron as 'that pathetic little queer'. He not only visited Bubba every week, but also took her out and sent her letters, postcards, flowers and gifts. He was charming and witty and made each one of us feel special and interesting. We all doted on him.

Bubba had difficulty in hearing but not in speaking. Clive might be telling her about his landlady's antics or about a customer who'd lost hundreds of pounds at the roulette table, and right in the middle, she'd say, 'When are you going to find a nice girl and get married? Why don't you make your old Bubba happy? Are you waiting for me to be dead and buried before you find yourself a wife?'

We always laughed at the way he answered her, and I'd never seen him irritable or short-tempered. He'd brought a present for Debbie, too: a necklace made out of carved peach-stones, painted and varnished. It was beautiful. He put it round her neck and she took his hands and smiled right into his eyes, then kissed him on both cheeks. For some reason, I felt a lump in my throat which had nothing to do with Gloria's birthday.

112

Yetta gave Debbie a leather-bound photograph album and the residents and I gave her a volume of Katherine Mansfield's short stories, which she said she was going to save for when she was in the maternity hospital. Clive played 'Mighty Like a Rose' and 'My Curly-Headed Baby' while Debbie sang with her hands spread dramatically over her tummy. Even Sarah was smiling and beating time and actually refrained from cursing while Rene sang 'My Yiddishe Mamma'. Alter and Boris left their card game on the verandah to join in a medley of Red Army songs. There was no end to Clive's repertoire!

I went into the kitchen to cut the birthday cake Debbie had baked, and prepare the tea. I could hear Clive thumping away at the piano and all the folks joining in, then Debbie walked in and plonked herself on the stool.

'Grandma won't be in for supper, Beattie. Joe's picking us up in his cab at six. He's cooking a celebration meal for us.'

'I wish everyone at The Haven had grandchildren like you and Joe and Clive,' I said, mopping my eyes cunningly while I stuck my head in the cupboard. Without a scrap of warning, I felt her arms around my neck.

'They've got *you*, Beattie,' she said in my ear. 'I want you to know that I remember it's Gloria's birthday too. Grandma told me that you're going to Brighton for the weekend. I'm so glad. I'll be thinking of you.'

Frank was closing our suitcase when I arrived home. We stowed it into the boot and put the presents on the back seat – a tent and sleeping bags for Dave and Janice, and a tiny doll's pram for Paula. Frank packed the wine and cakes, and the dolls' furniture he'd made for Gloria's birthday, nineteen years ago, in a cardboard box, while I went up to wash and change my blouse.

'You drink and I'll drive,' he said. He handed me a huge sherry, then fastened my brooch and kissed the top of my head.

'It'll be good to mix with young people for a change,'

I said to Frank as we crawled through the South London traffic.

'Does that include me?' he asked, smiling.

'Yes, sweetheart. Will you talk to me about Edna and what it felt like for you – for all of you – when your dad married her?'

'Poor Edna! She had a hard time! Especially from my mother's mother and father. Oh, Beattie, it isn't easy for anyone! Let's get the weekend over first.'

I put my hand on his knee, and as soon as we reached the open countryside he held it in his. He held my hand all the way to Brighton, right through the weekend and all the way home again.

We stopped at Box Hill and climbed to the top, remembering Gloria aged ten, racing down, away from us, flying the kite that we'd given her for her birthday.

'It's time to say "Goodbye" and let her go,' said Frank. 'Squeeze my hand when you're ready.'

'Goodbye, Gloria!' we shouted. 'Goodbye, darling!'

I arrived at work early on Monday morning, and hurried into The Haven to look for Yetta and to tell her about the weekend. Alter and Kitty were sitting on the bench in the hall. Alter got up and walked painfully towards me.

'Joe passed away, Beattie.'

'Joe? Joe?' I shook him by the shoulders. 'Who's Joe?'

'Debbie's husband; Yetta's grandson-in-law. Friday. He didn't turn up. Clive drove Debbie and Yetta home. They found him dead on the kitchen floor. Thirty-two years old and as strong as a lion.'

'What are you talking about?' I shouted harshly.

'Debbie gave birth to a daughter late on Friday night. The Lord giveth and the Lord taketh away.'

I could hear this horrible shriek in my head and sat on the bench with my hands over my ears. Matron came running up and slapped me over the face.

'Mr Freid, fetch the brandy, please. Pull yourself together, Beatrice. The residents are badly shocked as it is. Mrs Juggler has been asking for you, but I don't want her over-excited. She hasn't eaten a thing since that – since Clive Marks brought her back on Friday night. She's helping no one, least of all herself, by being foolish and stubborn. I hope you'll try to persuade her to be sensible.'

It was a toss-up as to whether I should drain the glass or throw the contents in her face. The brandy revived me, and after a couple of minutes I was able to go in and see Yetta. She was sitting on the chair near her bed, a black scarf covering her lovely white hair.

Fate doesn't deal out fair shares with justice and merit in mind. He doesn't care whether he aims a blow in the same place repeatedly. They all know that, here . . .

Juggler, Yetta – Admitted 4 June 1983 from the Middlesex Hospital after heart attack; born 1909, London. Retired milliner and dressmaker. Angina. Osteoarthritis. Mentally alert. Widow, two children. Whereabouts of son unknown; daughter, severely brain-damaged after overdose, died 1970 in Friern Barnet Hospital. Relative to contact: Deborah Schlesinger (granddaughter). Miss Schlesinger married 1984, now Mrs Joseph Gold, 24 Cecil Road, Palmers Green . . .

Yetta knows about Fate. I held her hand.

'Beattie! Take me to see my Debbie! Now! Now!'

'Miss Shapiro has kindly volunteered to take you, Mrs Juggler. She'll be here at two o'clock. Beatrice has her work to do. After you've eaten breakfast and a light lunch, Miss Shapiro . . .'

'Beattie! Take me now!'

'You are my responsibility,' said Matron, 'and you are not going anywhere until . . .'

'Get away from me, you!' She stood up, swaying slightly, glaring at Matron with hard blue eyes, her fingers gripping mine. 'Come on, Beattie.'

'I'm afraid I cannot allow it.'

'Let's have a cup of tea and a slice of toast first, Yetta. Matron, would you jot down the directions for me, and ask Nurse Goss to bring us a tray? I'll be fit to drive in fifteen minutes, and my friend will be fit to sit beside me.'

Under different circumstances, Yetta would have been

proud of me. I knew that Matron could stop her going and be entirely within her rights, yet for a few moments we had both been afraid of Yetta. Grief is a terrifying and awesome contender.

After breakfast, Matron called me into her office. 'Sign this,' she said sharply. 'You agree to take full responsibility for Mrs Juggler in so doing.'

Her idiotic jargon made me sick, making out that I was signing Yetta's death warrant.

'This is how you get to the Evergreen Maternity Hospital.' She handed me a torn paper from her pad with a few pencil lines scrawled on it. 'Take the first on the left after Luffley Post Office, then follow this route. Visiting hours are from two until four. You'll have a long wait.'

I could feel Yetta egging me on, although she was nowhere to be seen, and I stood my ground for a full half minute. 'Please phone the Evergreen and ask for a wheelchair to be put in the entrance hall, for our use. I hope the staff there are a little more flexible and compassionate.'

She snatched the signed paper away from me. But the wheelchair was there when we arrived.

Sister met us at the entrance to Azalea Ward and greeted us kindly.

'Hello, ladies. Mrs Juggler, I'm so glad you managed to make the journey here. The staff and I would like to offer you our sincere condolences. We thought that under the very sad circumstances, your granddaughter would be more comfortable in a room by herself for the first few days. She's awake, but sedated. Don't be too upset if she doesn't seem to want you. It's quite natural after such great shock and sorrow. Mr Marks told us that you're Mrs Gold's closest relative – in every sense of the word, he said. I gather you brought her up from a small child. Poor Mrs Gold! It will do her good to see you. The baby is absolutely beautiful! Would you like to see her?'

'Has my granddaughter seen her?'

There was a slight pause.

'Oh, yes!'

116

'Has she held her? Fed her?'

'Give her a day or two. She's still quite distraught and her grieving leaves her no room to take an interest in the baby. In a little time . . .'

'Give me the baby and take me to my granddaughter.'

Sister didn't flinch. She called for a nurse to bring Baby Gold and the tiny bundle was placed on Yetta's lap.

'Hello, darling!' said Yetta.

Tears poured down my face, but Yetta didn't cry.

'Let's go, Beattie.'

I looked at Sister, who smiled and nodded, and then walked ahead of us to a small, private room. She opened the door and I shoved Yetta and the baby through it.

Debbie was lolling against three huge pillows. Her eyes were open, but she didn't look at us.

'Take that thing away,' she growled.

I looked wildly about me. Did she mean the wheelchair?

'Take that thing away.'

My heart banged like a sledgehammer. Yetta was seventy-six years old and suffered from angina. This horrible dead voice flecked with madness, coming from this catatonic creature – her lovely granddaughter – would kill her.

'What thing?' Yetta's voice was clear and strong.

'That thing. *That thing*.'

'What thing?'

The frightful dialogue went on and on. I couldn't stand it. The baby started to cry. My courage failed me. I crept towards the door. Sister was standing against it, but moved aside. Yetta sat in the wheelchair, her back towards us.

'Where are you going, Beattie?' she called, without turning her head. 'You don't like this thing either? What is this thing?'

'Debbie's beautiful baby girl.'

'Debbie's and who else's?'

'Joe's,' I quavered.

'Joe's baby daughter is a thing – a hateful thing. Joe! Debbie is calling your daughter a thing!'

'Joe!' screamed Debbie. The baby yelled. Sister went over to take her from Yetta.

'She wants her bottle, Mrs Juggler. It's time for her eleven o'clock feed.'

'I'll feed her,' said Yetta, 'since her mother won't.'

The bottle was brought. Sister helped Yetta to place the baby comfortably while Debbie stared out of the window, twisting two plastic drinking straws together. The baby sucked noisily and eagerly.

'*You* had a daughter, didn't you, Beattie?' said Yetta pleasantly. 'An only child, wasn't she?'

'Yes.' I felt frightened; ill.

'It was her birthday on Friday, too. How old would she be?'

'Twenty-two.'

'The same age as her?'

'As Debbie; yes.'

'When did she die?'

'A year ago.'

'She went suddenly, like Joe?'

'I prefer not to talk about her just now.'

'You prefer to eat yourself up!' she said scornfully. The bottle slipped out of the baby's mouth. She spluttered and waved her tiny fist angrily. 'You prefer that your son-in-law should be lonely for the rest of his life. You prefer that little Paula should never have a mother to love and care for her.' Debbie glared at Yetta. 'Did it ever cross your mind whether Gloria would have preferred it that way? You are as cold and as heartless as that one there, hating Joe's only daughter.'

The baby finished her bottle and Yetta held her against her breast and stroked her back.

'Beattie!'

I quaked, then sat down on Debbie's foot and jumped up again.

'Beattie,' said Debbie, patting the bed. 'Sit down next to me. Don't listen to Grandma. Don't cry!'

'Why shouldn't she cry?' shouted Yetta. 'She lost her only child! She loved Gloria more than anyone in the

118

world!' Suddenly she thrust the baby into my arms. 'When I'm dead, this baby will have no one to love her. She has no father and no mother. Take her, Beattie! She's only a thing! I'm tired. I need to go to the bathroom and I want a cup of tea.'

'Would you take the baby for a moment, please, Sister?'

'You stay here with Mrs Gold and the baby for a while. I'll show Mrs Juggler our facilities; I know my way round,' she smiled. 'I think Mrs Juggler would enjoy a well-deserved rest and refreshment in the staff sitting room. I'll have coffee and sandwiches sent in to you and Mrs Gold.'

'Thank you, Sister,' said Yetta. 'I don't usually laze about in a wheelchair. I help my friend Beattie in the kitchen, every day.'

We could hear them talking as they moved away from us along the corridor, and I failed to suppress an idiotic urge to smile. The baby slept, and I looked at Debbie and thought I saw her mouth twitch. She punched one of the pillows and I leaned my shoulders against it.

'Put your feet up. They don't care in here. Grandma's probably boasting about how she's the assistant matron and has to dole out the medicine.'

'She's a dab hand with injections,' I said. 'I once saw her give Goss an accurate shot in the backside with a couple of forks.'

Debbie burst out laughing and crying at the same time. I rocked her in my free arm until I heard a nurse plonk a tray down somewhere. Before Debbie had time to think, I gave her the baby while I poured the coffee for us. She didn't want any, so I drank hers, too, while she kissed the baby's wet, salty forehead.

'Tell me about your weekend, Beattie,' she said. 'One day I'll tell you about mine.'

I talked and talked. I told her how Paula looked like Gloria when she was three years old and that she was coming to stay with us while Dave and Janice were in Greece. I rattled on and on about the fun we'd had swimming, boating, telling stories and playing with the dolls'

119

furniture. On Saturday night, Dave and Janice took us out to a restaurant and afterwards, Dave and I danced and talked about Gloria. On Sunday, he spoke to Frank and me about Janice. I lay on Debbie's bed, telling her about my weekend, as if I couldn't stop. I knew she wasn't listening but it didn't matter. Now and then I paused to wipe my eyes and recover myself, and Debbie would say, 'Go on, Beattie. Go on.' So I told her how Frank and I climbed Box Hill, remembering the day Gloria flew her kite there: laughing, shouting; running. Running away from us.

'I called to her to come back. I called and called, and then Frank and I held hands and we both said Goodbye.' I knew Debbie couldn't possibly be listening. She had so much to bear. But I was listening. Listening to myself for the first time.

'Gloria,' said Debbie, smiling at me and the baby. I knew she wasn't listening, but it didn't matter. She examined the baby's fingernails closely and tested each one against her lips. I felt so weary. As if I hadn't been to sleep for a year. I closed my eyes. Debbie sang a lullaby and I fell asleep.

It was past tea-time when Yetta and I returned to The Haven. Clive took her to visit again, in the evening, because he didn't start work until ten thirty that night.

When the time came for Debbie to take the baby home, Yetta went with her, for she had brought Debbie up, single-handed, from infancy. But now she was old and tired and ill. After three weeks she returned to The Haven and Debbie brought her daughter to see Yetta as often as possible.

We all watched her progress – gleeful when she smiled; concerned when she yelled; loving her and spoiling her outrageously.

As usual on Friday afternoon, Clive was playing with Debbie's baby and showing her off to Bubba.

'Why don't you make your old Bubba happy?' she shouted at him. 'What are you waiting for? Why don't

120

you find yourself a nice wife and raise a child like this little beauty?'

'I don't want to hear you say that again, Bubba! Stop pestering me! It gets on my nerves!'

I'd never heard him speak like that before, and looked at Yetta to see what she made of it, but all she did was slide her eyes in Debbie's direction. For some reason, a lump came into my throat and I slipped into the kitchen to make the tea.

Clive and Debbie followed and insisted on preparing the trolley, twirling it around the kitchen and shoving it into each other like a couple of wild kids. I held the baby in my arms and she smiled and touched my face.

'Hello, Gloria,' I said. 'Hello, darling!'

10

A Candid Chap

Doctor Taylor visited The Haven every Tuesday afternoon to check over the residents and to examine more fully, Matron and anyone who was feeling or looking under the weather. His attitude towards pain and suffering was to alleviate it as quickly and as effectively as possible. On one occasion, to my certain knowledge, he had administered an addictive, dangerous drug in order to enhance life at the expense of prolonging it. Matron always accompanied him on his first round, reminding him of who was taking what medication; then she would leave him to it, and shimmy up to her flat to prepare for his ministrations, and he would do his second round alone, talking and listening to each resident in turn with generous and courteous attention. Occasionally he would still be in the sitting room when I trundled in with the tea trolley, perched on the arm of a chair, deep in conversation. His affair with Matron in no way diminished my liking and respect for him as a genial and compassionate man and a gifted doctor.

On this particular Tuesday, Matron was in Nottingham for the opening of a swanky new home there, so Nurse Goss did the round with him. After he'd finished, he popped into the kitchen to say hello.

'What's that you're doing?'

'Ironing out soup for the folks. It's a job that demands skill and concentration. Sarah, Sadie and Kitty remove their dentures to savour the flavour, so it has to be smooth for them. Bubba and Rene enjoy the texture of the butter beans, but can't cope with the leeks and onions. The rest of them are tough guys and like more body.'

'Likewise,' said Doctor Taylor. 'I'm starving. I never have time for lunch on Tuesdays.'

'Sit down, tough guy. There's a baked potato going too. Would you like cheddar with it, or butter?'

'Cheddar, please. This soup is delicious! Why don't I get this every week?'

I didn't think it was my position to point out to him that Matron's menu plan made provision for another, more exotic kind of feast for his delectation; nor did I want to tell him that her menu for the residents provided for only one hot meal, served at midday, and that suppers were always cold. On the days when she was away or off duty I did as I damn well pleased, since she couldn't keep track of the vegetables we ordered; but I didn't want him blabbing to her. I decided to take the bull by the horns.

'Matron and Cook work out the menus. I shouldn't be doing this. I'm supposed to be laying out egg salads and cleaning the top cupboards. Don't tell.'

'While the cat's away, the mice play?' He smiled. 'Your secret is safe with me. A little more, Beattie, if you can spare it?' I ladled out another gallon. 'They'll enjoy this. Old people deserve all the pleasures of life we can offer. A wonderful taste along with nourishment, without the effort of chewing; relief from pain; the comfort of a warm bath and a warm bed; smooth, soft clothing; pleasant surroundings; the stimulation of change, friendship and love. Someone to cuddle – and someone to cuddle them; good company and conversation, and the absolute knowledge that they're needed; that they're important to another individual.'

'You're talking about the ideal human condition. This is The Haven, where sick, old, lonely people live. Not Utopia.'

'I'm talking about your soup and jacket potato – with a few additions. Egg salads and spotless cupboards are not among them.'

I detected a note of criticism, which, coming from him, sounded disloyal and rather pleasant. He probably knew that Matron and I detested each other. We talked about the residents for a few minutes, including our latest departures: Olga and Boris, who had moved into their new home – and Alf Levene. I told Doctor Taylor a little bit about my last outing with him, scrupulously avoiding placing Matron in a bad light.

'You have very strong likes and dislikes, don't you, Beattie?' he said, right out of the blue.

'Who . . . what do you mean?' I was taken by surprise and spoke rather sharply.

'. . . Regarding the residents,' he said, smiling.

'Alf Levene was certainly not one of my favourite people,' I said, relieved, 'but since he's been dead two months, he can't be counted amongst their number now. I'm very fond of all of them.'

'Really?'

'Yes. Really!' I felt quite angry. 'Alf Levene had a unique place in my disaffections.'

'You know, Beattie, that old man was a medical puzzle to me. I've never understood how he remained active – let alone alive – for as long as he did. I've never come across such defiance of death. The quality of life doesn't necessarily tally with our unwillingness to relinquish it. He was a tortured soul, poor devil. Not a very attractive character. You obviously eased his mental suffering that day you took him out. He didn't last a week after that.'

'You sound like a suspicious policeman with murder on his mind! And did Matron tell you that he left twenty pounds for me in his room?' He grinned and nodded. 'It would have to be at least twenty-five to motivate me. Not guilty!'

At that moment I suffered a sudden, most painful muscle spasm in my shoulder and I felt quite faint from it. I sat down on the stool for a moment.

'I've upset you, Beattie. I wonder if *you're* really such a tough guy.'

'More coffee?'

'Yes. Thanks. I'd like to make a phone-call.'

'Matron's office is open, I think.'

He took no notice and carried his cup over to the phone

on the kitchen wall and I rattled out with the tea trolley. Miss Shapiro and Mrs Temple, two of the voluntary workers, had started a game of bingo with the folks, and they said they'd serve tea, so I was back within a couple of minutes. Doctor Taylor was sitting at the table again, glancing at the crossword I filled in, in spare moments.

'While the cat's away, the mice play,' he said in a low voice.

'This mouse does crosswords when the cat's here!' I said sharply.

He looked across at me, genuinely puzzled. 'Oh, this! I don't mean *this*!'

I pulled out the step-ladder and started emptying the top cupboards. 'The mouse never realizes that the cat might be a mouse in disguise – or vice versa,' he said.

'Pushkin's a mousy old cat when it comes to dealing with the catty, spiteful mice in the cellar. But I'm not sure what you mean. I'm not good at riddles.'

'Nor at crosswords – or spelling. I'm surprised at you, Beattie. There's no F in morphine!'

'Really, Doctor Taylor! Please curb your language! Use curare instead, then!' He managed a feeble chuckle at my rather vulgar joke. 'Of course I know how to spell morphine! It's the wrong answer, though, because eleven down has got to begin with F. "Candid chap – five letters". Frank's always appearing in crosswords.'

'Yes . . . Yes, indeed! Crosswords and cross words, as in "irritable units of expression".' He seemed abstracted; sad. He must be missing the comfort of Matron's embrace. Perhaps he was deeply in love with her. There was no accounting for tastes. 'I hope I'm not in your way here.'

'Not at all.' I wondered why he was hanging around. Probably because his schedule was upset, and he had an hour to kill.

'Let me help you with those.'

He got up and I handed everything down to him from the shelves, and he put the storage jars on the table for me. He rested his foot on the bottom step of the ladder as I reached up for the last one.

'You've got very pretty legs, Beattie.'

'All the better to kick you with, my dear.'

'Can't you accept a compliment gracefully?'

'No. You're terrific with eighty-year-olds, but you haven't a clue when it comes to dealing with women of nearly forty-two.'

'My wife's age,' he sighed. 'You never spoke a truer word.'

'Pass me that wet dishcloth, please.' I hoped Mrs Taylor was having an affair, too – a thoroughly enjoyable one. I'm all for a bit of rough justice. 'I happened to notice that your wife has very pretty legs. I'm sure *she* could accept a compliment gracefully.'

'Perhaps,' he said. 'But not from me. I didn't know you knew Fenella. When did you meet her?'

'At The Haven Garden Party. I served her strawberries and cream and she introduced herself to me. Then my husband came into the summer house with a bottle of Asti and some more goodies just as the speeches started, and we hid there, guzzling, until the Mayor finished talking.'

'Well, you weren't there when I came by!' he said irritably.

'Why are you getting so ratty? I left in her very good company. Someone had to wash and wipe the mountain of mucky pots. My name's Drudge Dwek, not Lady Muck.'

'What did you say?' he barked.

He really was being unnecessarily edgy. If he had personal problems with his wife, I was certainly in no way accountable. He was probably scared I'd spilled the beans to her about him and Matron. Maybe Fenella was on to it. Well, that was his look-out. I'd been the soul of discretion.

'I didn't say anything to upset your wife, Doctor Taylor,' I said, slowly and carefully. 'She told me a bit about her job, and I told her about mine. I remember we discussed the number of microbes on a tea towel after drying a single plate. I said I had to go and wipe up a few more billion and came back here.'

'What's your husband's job, Beattie?'

He sounded so tense and agitated, that I turned and looked down at him.

'If it's okay with you,' I said sarcastically, 'he works in the Institute of Tropical Diseases. He's a biochemist, researching into antibody defence mechanisms. In fact Mrs Taylor is on his team.'

'Good God!' gasped Doctor Taylor. 'Good God!'

'What are you Good Godding about?'

He didn't answer. His face was the colour of dirty snow. I thought he was having a heart attack, and hoped he'd stay conscious long enough to tell me what first aid to administer. I scrambled down the wobbling ladder. He had slumped into the chair.

'Goss!' I screeched. 'Goss! Quick! Doctor Taylor's very ill!' That bloody woman was never around when she was wanted.

I tried to undo his tie. He shook his head, backed off and pushed me away.

'You're sloshing Fairy Liquid down my neck! What a mess here! Give me a towel!'

I chucked one at him. I was relieved he was obviously okay, but deeply offended by his churlish manners. I turned my back on him while he stuffed the towel down the front of his shirt. I banged three saucepans on to the stove, poured in my soup and lit the oven.

'Next time you imagine I'm knocking at Death's door, put down that soap thing before you half throttle me.'

'Physician heal *thyself!*' I said crossly.

'Don't be so touchy.'

'Me! *Me*, touchy? I tell you your wife's charming; I tell you we had a pleasant time in the summer house; I tell you that she and Frank work in the same lab, and you pounce on everything I say, grouching and Good Godding, then turn green at the gills, and *then* lose your temper when I try to give you first aid. And *you* tell *me* I'm touchy!' I adjusted the ladder, stomped up the steps and got busy rubbing at an inch of grease on the rim of the cupboard door.

'I didn't realize that Dwek was your husband. I'm sorry.'

It wasn't what he said, but the way he said it that infuriated me, as if he was talking about a dirty floorcloth.

'I'm not!' I shouted, purposely misinterpreting him. 'I'm proud and happy that he is! His name has a handle to it – the same one as yours, but of finer quality, *Doctor* Taylor! Doctor Dwek is a man of integrity who doesn't cheat or exploit vulnerable women, or hand out cheap and unwelcome flattery to married ones!'

'I wouldn't be too sure of that!' he roared back at me. 'You left my wife in *very* good company! I won't dispute with you about *that!* Too damn good for my liking! Maybe your Candid Chap isn't as candid as you think!'

I looked down at him. He was sitting at the table, glaring at the crossword, his face white with rage. My head swam, making a rushing sound in my ears, and my knees turned to jelly. I hung on to the cupboard door, but it swung fiendishly away from me as the ladder tipped sideways. I lost my balance and tried to grab at something; anything. Doctor Taylor gripped me round the knees as the step-ladder crashed against the table.

'I've got you, Beattie. Let go of the shelf. I've got your weight.'

I slithered through his arms, my overall and skirt over my ears, but I managed to save my neck, if not my dignity. The ladder had smashed the storage jars and a mixture of broken glass, butter beans and barley littered the floor and table. I adjusted my clothing then sat down on the chair for a moment while he brought me a cup of water. I was shaking so much that it rattled against my teeth. He held it for me; hovering; concerned; his arm around my shoulder. Nurse Goss came into the kitchen.

'And what's going on here?'

'What the hell do you think's going on!' he shouted. 'That step-ladder is a danger to life and limb and Beattie could have had a very serious accident. As it is she's banged herself about and has had a bad shock. Fetch the brandy from the surgery and bring it to the office, then clear up this mess and ask the voluntary workers to serve the supper. It's all ready. Beattie can't do anything else today.'

When he was satisfied that I hadn't broken or dislocated any bones, he helped me to my feet, put my arm round his shoulder and his round my waist, and walked me slowly to the office, without my feet touching the floor. He lowered me into the easy chair and knelt down in front of me, feeding me brandy.

'Have you suffered from vertigo before?'

'No. Give me some more.'

'I want to give you a thorough check-up. Blood pressure, heart . . .'

'Will you *shut up*! How dare you make insinuations about my husband!'

'I didn't know your surname until a few minutes ago. I didn't know Doctor Dwek was your husband. Fenella and I have been going through a rough time lately, and your prissy complacency wound me up. Now, Beattie, I must insist that you keep still and as calm as possible. Let's forget all this nonsense and be friends again. We both went too far and said things we didn't mean.'

'Speak for yourself! How dare you make insinuations about my Frank!' I screamed at him again. 'How dare you!'

'You made insinuations about *me*. I lost my temper, that's all. I apologize for upsetting you. Perhaps you should do the same.'

'Apologize! To you? What I said was the truth! What you said was a lie – a wicked, spiteful lie!'

'You're overwrought. Where's your bag? I'll drive you home.'

'Liar! Liar! You're a contemptible liar! Add that to your list of virtues!'

He turned on me with such fury that for a moment I thought he was going to strike me. If he'd had one of his lethal injections handy, he would have stuck it into me, without a doubt. Instead, he crashed his fist on Matron's desk with such insane force that the framed photograph of her late, lamented budgie bounced on to the floor.

'Haven't you done sufficient damage in the kitchen? Have you got to smash Frisky, too? Matron will be *very* pleased!'

'Damn Matron! Damn Frisky! And damn you!'

'Go to hell.' I started to cry. I felt ill and frightened. Frank, my Frank, busy with that horribly attractive, uppity Fenella. He'd spoken about her to me. What had he said? That she was a brilliant chemist; that she'd got an original and lively approach to . . . Oh, God! Doctor Taylor was half sitting on Matron's desk, his foot grinding into Frisky; not knowing or caring. There was only one thing to do. Grovel.

'Doctor Taylor,' I blubbed, 'I am deeply sorry for my insulting remarks. I can only explain and try to excuse my behaviour by telling you that I am acutely distressed. If I was suffering death pangs, you would kindly and generously relieve my pain. I beg of you to tell me what you know about my husband and your wife, because I cannot endure this anguish any longer. I must know the truth. Whatever you have to tell me can't possibly make me more wretched.'

'All right,' he said. 'Perhaps it's best all round that you should know.'

A cold shiver of ominous terror zig-zagged through me. I gripped the arms of the chair. This was a nightmare.

'I saw your husband and Fenella embracing in the summer house,' he said. 'They didn't see me and I didn't confront them. I hate public rows, and anyway, The Haven Garden Party wasn't the ideal circumstance for an encounter. When we got home, I told her I'd seen them together, and she didn't deny it or appear confused. She seemed pleased, for God's sake. "Good!" she said. "Now you know. Now you know what it's been like for me, having your sordid little affairs pushed in my face. Frank has given me back my self-respect. He makes me feel pretty and clever and worthwhile." I love my wife, Beattie. I told her she was making a fool of herself; that she'd destroy our marriage; that I was angry; jealous; bitterly ashamed and sorry for all the heartache I'd caused her. I swore I'd change if she would just give us both a chance. She said a leopard doesn't change its spots, but that she'd think about it. The trouble, she said, was that she was in love. I can't tell you what I've been suffering, Beattie. We've had the worst rows I can ever remember. She seems to thrive on them, but I'm devastated. I can't work. I can't think. These last seven weeks have been the worst in my life. I'm only thankful that our sons are away at college, so they don't know what's happening to us.' He covered his face with his hands.

'Take me home.'

He fetched my coat and bag, and I got into his car like an old, cold woman. We didn't speak on the journey. The people shopping and walking on the pavement seemed to come from another planet. This was the end of my life and they didn't know; didn't care. He stopped at the top of Friars Avenue, a few yards away from our house.

'Beattie,' he said, 'I'm so sorry to have caused you such pain. I understand how you feel.'

'No. You don't understand. There's never been anyone else for me. Frank is my life.'

He leaned across and held me in his arms, stroking my back, while I drenched his soapy shirt with my tears. He didn't seem to mind. I don't know how long we sat there, in the car, but it was only the sound of his bleeper in my ear, summoning him to an urgent call, that made me realize how late it was and that Frank would probably be home. Doctor Taylor waited until I turned in at my gate, and I watched him turn on his headlights, reverse the car and drive off. I fumbled for my key. Frank's briefcase was lying on its side in the passage as if he'd just thrown it down as he came in. I stepped over it. The house was dim and silent and he didn't call out to me. I crawled into the living room. He was sitting by the window, his shoulders slumped, white-faced and haggard.

'Frank! What's the matter?'

'I don't know what to do. I don't know what to say.

131

We've been married for twenty-three years. I . . . Oh, Beattie!'

I realized in that instant that he was trying to tell me he'd fallen in love with Fenella Taylor, and that our marriage was over. This horror, this anguish that I was feeling now, was only the beginning of imponderable misery. Desperation made me calm, strong.

'Don't say anything, Frank. You see, I know. I know about you and Fenella Taylor. I don't blame or condemn either of you,' I lied. 'No, let me finish. She's a beautiful, clever, charming woman and you're the handsomest, cleverest man in the world and I love you. I love you, and I can't face my life without you. I won't make a fuss. I won't stop you seeing her. I'll put up with anything; everything, except living without you. Please, Frank, please! Don't destroy me. I know how dreadful I've been since we lost Gloria. Mad; self-absorbed. I'll change.' I ran over to him, knelt down and put my head on his lap and my arms round him.

'Have you gone clean out of your mind?' He stood up, pulling me with him, grabbing me roughly by the shoulders. 'Is this your idea of trying to change the subject? Do you think I'm as stupid and shallow as that? I saw you! I saw you with my own eyes, kissing and canoodling in a car parked on the corner, practically on our doorstep! Just tell me how . . . who . . . why? *Why*? And don't lie to me! Don't give me some damn story! I've told myself too many this last wretched hour!' There were tears in his eyes. His fingers dug into me like iron rods.

I was so utterly astonished that for a few moments I could only stare at him, unable to speak.

'You're the one who's crazy,' I gasped. 'That was Doctor Taylor. He was at The Haven today, and told me about you and his wife. I was so numbed and shocked that he had to drive me home. I was crying; dying!' I screamed. 'He put his arms round me to comfort me. You beast! You twicer! Do you think everyone's like you?'

He heaved a great sigh, closed his eyes and enfolded

me, crushing me against his chest so that I could hardly breathe.

'Beattie! Sweetheart!'

'You're suffocating me! Let go!'

'Only if you promise to listen and not talk. I don't love Fenella Taylor, you lunatic! I love you, and she loves her awful husband. God knows why, but she does. Have I ever lied to you?'

'Dozens of times. Why were you cuddling in the summer house?'

He sat down and pulled me on to his knee.

'Shut up, and I'll explain everything. Fenella told me to tell you that afternoon. I didn't; I should have. All this trouble and grief for nothing. She started crying in the lab one afternoon. I'd been talking about you – boasting a bit, I suppose. She said, "I wish my husband was as proud of me as you are of Beattie. I'd give anything for him to talk about me like that." She wept so bitterly, it was heart-breaking. I asked her if there was anything I could do. She told me her husband was having an affair; that it wasn't the first time, but that now their boys had left home she felt unwanted and rejected. The main trouble was that she loved the bastard. Anyway, the subject never came up again, and in fact she did her best to avoid talking to me unless it was absolutely necessary. I thought that she might have regretted confiding in me, and was embarrassed about it.

'Then that afternoon in the summer house, she said, "Frank, you once asked me if you could do something for me. I want you to hold me in your arms, just for a minute. I'll explain later, to you *and* to Beattie. I promise you, she won't mind. She'll approve." She sat close up to me, then put her arms round my neck and buried her face in my shoulder. She was actually looking at her watch all the time, telling me when half a minute had gone by, then forty-five seconds, and so on. Then she stood up and told me, as cool as a cucumber, that her husband had just walked by with his girlfriend in tow, and she'd deliberately used me to provoke him. I was very annoyed, but she swore she'd see to it that I wasn't compromised and then she said, "I'm going to find Beattie and tell her what's happened. I don't want her to get the wrong idea." I told her that you wouldn't get the wrong idea, anyway, and if she didn't mind, I'd prefer to tell you myself. "Okay," she said. "Just as you like, but see that you do."

'If you don't believe me, Beattie, you can check up with her yourself, but it would make me look a terrible fool, because I *didn't* tell you – until now.'

He kissed my hair and stroked my bruised, swollen leg. I must have given it a crack against the step-ladder when I fell. The pain was awful. I hadn't felt so happy for months.

'Why didn't you tell me all this before? I wouldn't have minded. Fenella understood that. Oh, Frank, why didn't you? I would have believed you. Did you think I wouldn't?' There was a moment of stillness – so fleeting, that I thought I'd imagined it. I touched his face to bring him back to me, and saw his eyes, looking above my head, beyond me. 'Frank,' I said softly, 'are you sad?'

He smiled and shook his head.

'I knew you'd believe me. Perhaps that's why. You'll never understand, Beattie. Why should you? I wanted to pretend that another woman found me attractive and sexy; that I'd been embraced for that – not merely as a vehicle to rouse a wayward husband. I wanted to indulge a private fantasy; a stupid, vain illusion that I was young and lean and handsome – and irresistibly desirable.' I heard him swallow, as if there was a lump in his throat.

Frank underestimated me. I understood. I tried to control the bleak, lonely feeling that suddenly swamped me. My leg ached and throbbed almost as painfully as my heart.

'That's no vain illusion, darling,' I said bravely.

I told him about my accident. I took off my tights and Frank had a look at the damage. There was a great swollen bruise, stretching from my knee halfway up my thigh.

'What a hell of a knock you've had!' He brushed his hand and lips over the swelling. 'I'll fetch an ice-pack.

134

Put your leg up here on the cushion. Don't move. I want you to see the doctor first thing tomorrow. They'll have to manage without you at The Haven for a day or two. Now! Get ready to shiver! I'm going to press this here.'

'Doctor Taylor said he'll give me a thorough examination next Tuesday.'

'That quack! What does he know? I'm not letting *him* loose on my wife's bruises!' He moved the ice-pack to my thigh. 'Has anyone told you lately that you've got very pretty legs?' He looked at me so tenderly that my heart eased at once. For a fleeting moment I didn't answer him. 'Beattie?' he said softly.

I swallowed the lump that rose in my throat. It didn't do to be too frank.

'My Frank! My Candid Chap!' I said, smiling. 'Indulge your fantasy. It's okay with me. Unfortunately, no one tells women over forty they have pretty legs. Just you.'

11

The Wedding Guest

Kitty's three horrid sons were rich and successful and had married eminently suitable, odious women, more alike than a set of triplets, with solarium suntans, slim, girlish figures and carefully arranged, gold-tipped hair, well-lacquered to hide their face-lift scars. It took me forever to work out who was who. Each vile couple took it in turns to visit Kitty every Sunday from two until four. They sat on either side of her, bored and silent, waiting for the clock to strike, then exclaiming that they must be off, would give her a brittle peck on the cheek and leave with unseemly haste, no doubt sighing with relief at the three-week respite ahead, and sweep away in the sable and sand Bentley to the stockbroker belt. They never took her out; never invited her to their homes, yet she doted on them and boasted endlessly about their attainments. I felt both irritated and touched by her devotion and loyalty to these unlovely people who treated her with such contempt and neglect. I longed to give them a piece of my mind, but I knew that any intervention on my part would only cause Kitty distress.

Yetta and Alter told me that Kitty used to peddle needles and combs, door to door and in the street markets, while her husband Sam worked in a tailoring sweat shop, literally sleeping on the counter so that he could start again at the crack of dawn. The family lived in two rooms in a wretched tenement, but since nearly all the immigrants were poor, their situation was not remarkable. Few children brought up in these circumstances could hope to continue at school after the age of fourteen, but Kitty's sons did. She made their uniforms and did piece work, sewing linings for jackets, in order to buy the necessary

136

books and equipment. They took their entrance exams for university while their father worked himself to death.

'Even so, how did she manage to pay for it all?' I asked Yetta. 'You're always telling me how poor everyone was in the East End and how the factories and workshops were full of geniuses who could never hope for further education, so how did Kitty and Sam send all three boys to college? Did she spend her nights with Rumpelstiltskin weaving straw into gold?'

'Something like that,' said Yetta softly. 'Kitty was a very pretty young woman. Pride in herself was a sacrifice she made in order to achieve an education for them. Her husband slept three nights a week in the shop but they had no secrets from each other. Their ambition for their children consumed them.'

'What!' I gasped. 'Are you telling me that Kitty sold *herself*?'

'So what if I am? So what if she did? She and Sam knew what they wanted. Something from Dreamland for the boys. Neighbours shunned her and mocked her, but some of us understood. Those boys were as bright as buttons – Solly, Abey and Yankel – and as soon as they got their fancy education they changed to Selwyn, Arnold and John. Fine, nice Englishmen,' she sneered, 'ashamed of their roots; casting their mother aside! For this sin, this terrible sin, may God punish them. Are they the same people, the little boys I knew? Sometimes I wonder!'

'Is Kitty the same woman?' I looked across at her, snoring gently in her chair.

'The same,' said Yetta. 'Old and tired and sick, but still the same. Vain, stupid and stubborn, seeing just one thing at a time.'

'What was her husband like?'

'Who knows what a beast of burden is like? Who knows what goes on in its heart and soul? Alter and my Jack used to sit next to him in the synagogue, but he never had the time to cultivate friends or pass the time with a neighbour. On Saturdays he slept and on the other days he slaved. He never had time for his own children; all he seemed to want was a different life for them; something better than *his* life was. It was a madness with him and Kitty was infected by it. Poor Kitty! You think she doesn't get on my nerves as much as yours? You think I don't want to lose my temper with her when she's boastful and arrogant! But Yetta ain't Beattie! Yetta's got more sense; more patience; more tolerance. You only think from yesterday.'

John, Kitty's eldest son, had one daughter who was twenty-nine, although Yetta insisted that her real age was thirty-seven. Her name was Angela and she was about to be married. I listened with grinding but well-hidden impatience to the attributes of the wretched bride-to-be, about ten times a day. She was not only gloriously beautiful; she was also brilliant, charming, domesticated and modest and would make the perfect wife for the man who had been lucky enough to win her. She was an angel; an angel with one tiny flaw. She'd been a little too choosy. Men had flocked around Angela since she was sixteen: doctors, lawyers, top businessmen. The cream of the cream!

I exploded to Yetta that if I heard Kitty say 'the cream of the cream' just once more, I would go stark staring mad, because there was only so much that a human being could stand. I couldn't help noticing after my outburst that Yetta took malicious pleasure in encouraging Kitty to yatter on even more, whenever I was around, and I was driven to walloping Yetta with a wet dishcloth when there was still six weeks to go to the wedding.

Cynthia, John's wife, was going to take Kitty shopping for an outfit to wear for the wedding which was to be held in a marquee in the grounds of a stately home. Kitty's excitement knew no bounds and she sent me to the post office to withdraw all her savings, for she wanted to buy Angela a present, too. It drove me to distraction that she might spend the little money she had on her pig of a granddaughter who never came to visit her, but there was nothing to be done.

Eventually, the shopping day arrived and Kitty was up,

bathed and dressed in her best frock and hat by eight
o'clock, although Cynthia wasn't due until eleven. She
arrived, late and irritable, in a two-hundred-pound pink
track-suit, complaining about the traffic and embittered
by the chore of having to take her mother-in-law out.
Cheerfulness was a virtue she saved only for her equals,
and it was in short supply when it came to the staff and
residents of The Haven.

I had persuaded Kitty to wear her flat, comfortable
shoes for the outing, knowing how her ankles swelled with
walking and standing.

'Mother, you can't go out in those shoes. They may be
acceptable here, but I'm afraid you're not wearing them
when you're with me. Haven't you any others?'

'Yes, darling, yes. Beattie, run to my room and bring
me my black suede ones.'

'No. You know what the chiropodist said. You're going
to be on your feet a lot and you need to be comfy.'

Cynthia lifted her eyes to heaven in exasperation. I
imagined raking her hair with the yard broom.

'I think that Mother knows her own mind. She can't
try on an outfit wearing those things! They look like old
potatoes and the hat will be just a nuisance. If you'll
excuse me saying so, I suggest you let Mother make up
her own mind. I strongly disapprove of the way you people
try to institutionalize your patients. Some of them do
have family, you know, who care. Is she wearing decent
underwear?'

I controlled myself for the sole reason that Kitty was
already upset and only wanted to ingratiate herself with
her daughter-in-law. But as soon as she went to the bathroom, I gave Cynthia a long overdue piece of my mind.

'This is *not* an institution! The residents are *not* patients
and I didn't realize Kitty had a family who cared! Our
matron is absolutely scrupulous about standards of cleanli-
ness and tidiness and she would have something to say
about your impertinent remarks. The suede shoes are at
the back of the top shelf of her closet, in a green box. Get
them yourself!'

139

She crammed Kitty's feet into them, then she stalked off to the car while I followed, more slowly, with Kitty. I managed to shove a plastic bag, containing her soft shoes, on to her lap, while I fastened the seat belt and kissed her.

'You look so pretty! Don't overtire yourself, and have a lovely time.'

I slammed the car door and waved as she was swept away, and wondered if Cynthia had any notion of what it might be like to be very old and vulnerable and too eager to please. I'd rather have gone swimming with a shark than on a shopping expedition with that cold, proud, cruel woman, and felt tense and anxious all day.

Avril, the young agency night nurse, was late as usual, but I always covered for her without letting on. Matron was on holiday and Nurse Goss had gone off duty. Yetta, Rene and I were on the last knockings of clearing up from supper when the pink track-suit barged in, golden curls still perfectly lacquered; but ill temper had found a crack in the make-up and exuded with ugly malevolence.

'I need help in getting her out of the car. She seems to be stuck. Hurry up, please.'

'Who seems to be stuck? The cat's mother-in-law?' Rene and Yetta laughed.

'Are you trying to annoy me?'

'I don't *need* to try,' I said. 'Drive up to the window. Kitty won't have to walk more than ten steps – and neither will I. It's rather a tight squeeze for cars the size of yours, so please try not to scratch the gateposts. I hope you don't mind me telling you, but your lipstick is very badly smudged.' I turned my back on her and lit another cigarette.

All the pleasure of aggravating Cynthia was forgotten when I hauled Kitty out of the passenger seat. Her eyes stared ahead; dark, glittering holes in her dead-white face. She was wearing her soft shoes, and I could see the swollen ankles and puffy feet, and the sore places on her heels as she hobbled into the bathroom with me. She had wet

140

herself, and I thought that because of this, she was deeply distressed.

'It doesn't matter, sweetheart! Not with friends, and who gives a damn about enemies? You're overtired, that's all. Why didn't you tell Cynthia you wanted to go to the Ladies'?' She didn't answer. 'Anyway, it didn't go through to the seat – more's the pity.'

I helped her to undress and wash, while Yetta fetched a clean nightie and dressing gown. Cynthia came in to adjust her mask.

'I've put all your paraphernalia on your bed,' she said coldly, to the mirror. 'My woman will shorten the dress and I suppose I'll have to make some time on Sunday to come here again so you can try it on. And it's just as well I put old loose covers on the car seat. Really, Mother!' She pressed her jammy lips together. 'Really! I didn't realize you were . . .'

'Were what?' I shrieked. 'Your mother-in-law is fine as long as she's able to spend a penny every two hours. You leave her alone! She's had enough of you for one day! Come on, Kitty. The girls have got a bowl of hot water and soda ready for your feet and a cup of Ovaltine. Cynthia will come to say bye-bye before she leaves.'

'I'm going now. I've people coming and I'm very late. I won't kiss you; my lipstick hasn't set.' She marched out to the car. I was pleased to note that she knocked her wing mirror as she drove through the gates.

I took Kitty through to the kitchen where Yetta and Rene were waiting. She sat between them, her feet in the bowl of water, her head bent, her crooked old fingers stroking her wedding ring. Yetta signalled to me to be quiet and get Kitty something to eat. She was so much wiser, so much more knowing than I, and I always obeyed her in times of crisis.

'Thank you, Beattie. I'm sorry you've been troubled. I thought I would be invited into my son's home for a rest and a snack, but I wasn't. We stopped by the house. She said she'd only be a moment; she had to leave a message for her cleaning woman and it would take too long to help

141

me out of the car. She didn't come back for twenty minutes. I saw Angela at the window. She didn't bother to pop out and say hello to me. I would like to eat my supper now, but I can't until you promise to do me a favour.'

'I promise,' I said. 'What is it, sweetheart?'

'Take the yellow notebook out of my bag and on the first page you'll find my children's telephone numbers. Ring up and say that I never want to see them or their families again.'

'What!' I gasped. 'What about Angela's wedding? You're tired and disappointed and depressed. See how you feel tomorrow.'

She put down the spoon. I sat opposite her and took her hand, but she pulled it away and glared at me.

'Should I listen to *you* or should I listen to Sam?' she asked, in a voice so full of contempt that I shuddered. 'Take yourself, your supper and your promises out of my sight!'

I looked at Yetta and Rene but they turned away from me, muttering to each other in Yiddish.

'Eat your supper,' I quavered. 'I'm sorry. I'll do it. Will one of you come with me?'

Yetta got up while Rene handed Kitty the spoon. She started to eat and Yetta and I went into her room.

'Why are you letting her do this, Yetta? You know you could talk her out of it. I can't ring them up! I can't and I won't! She's been looking forward to this damned wedding as if it was her own. She'll be okay tomorrow, and very upset if we pander to this mood. She lives for those horrible sons; she'll die if she cuts herself off from them. I can't understand how you can be so blind and unsympathetic to the hysterical state she's in. You know as well as I do that it's temporary.'

'You fool, Beattie. You think you know everything, and that's why you know nothing.'

She pushed aside the department store bags containing Kitty's new accessories, found the handbag, opened it and took out the notebook. She held it out to me.

142

'Do it yourself,' I said, knowing that she was unable to use the telephone without help. 'You're not going to pull me into this madness.' I stood watching her.

'Call Alter in here, please. He's smoking his pipe in the summer house.'

'Certainly I'll call him, since he's the only person with any sense in this place.'

'Fetch him now,' said Yetta, 'and when Avril arrives, go home. No one needs you here. Meanwhile, be careful of what you say. Sam is watching over Kitty and can hear everything. During his lifetime he always suppressed his anger; a dumb, patient, wretched man, who was never able to express what he felt. Now he has spoken. At last he has unburdened himself.'

I sat on the bed, trembling with rage. 'How *dare* you threaten me, you silly, superstitious woman! I'll tell Alter about these crazy goings-on and maybe he can sort you out. Sam's been dead for over forty years and if he's haunting this place, he'll know who Kitty's true friend really is; that is, if *he's* got any sense!'

I stood up and pushed past Yetta and ran out through the verandah and across the lawn. It was an unusually hot, sultry evening for mid-May, and I had a ramming headache. Alter was sitting in the summer house playing solitaire. He rose gallantly and waited until I was seated.

'What's wrong, Beattie?' He spoke so kindly. I wiped the sweat from my face.

'It's those three in the kitchen – Yetta, Kitty and Rene – they've ganged up on me! They've wounded me more than they can possibly realize!'

'Why is that? Tell your old Alter.'

'Kitty came back from shopping with her daughter-in-law and it suddenly dawned on her that her family isn't as perfect as she thought. Now she says she doesn't want anything more to do with them and wanted me to phone and tell them. I tried to dissuade her – Angela's wedding's in three weeks – because I know she'll get over this and think differently tomorrow; but she was so rude and dismissive and Yetta and Rene backed her up and are being horrible to me as well. Yetta said I wasn't needed and didn't understand anything. When I refused to telephone she threatened me with the wrath of a paranoid ghost and told me to come here and fetch you. I thought they were my friends,' I whined. 'I thought they were Kitty's friends, but they're not; they're humouring a whim which could destroy her. Thank God you're around. They'll pay attention to you.'

Alter had been patting my knee, listening to me sympathetically. When I'd finished he clasped his hands, rested his chin on them and closed his eyes. For a few moments I thought he was praying, for his lips moved and his attitude was one of reverence. He always spoke in Hebrew when he addressed God, and in English when he addressed me. Now he spoke in Yiddish, and didn't seem to notice that I was beside him, even when I tentatively tried to interrupt. A singular sense of isolation oppressed my spirits and I watched his handsome old face, trying to catch what he was saying. Then so suddenly, that I jumped, he stood up and raised his head and his arms, as if bestowing a blessing.

'Sam,' said Alter, as if I wasn't there, 'rest in peace, my old friend!' For perhaps half a minute he stood quite still with his head bowed, then without a glance or a gesture in my direction, he walked briskly down the summer house ramp and hurried across the garden towards the house.

I don't know how long I sat there. I could hear the television on the verandah, where most of the residents sat on long, warm evenings, and the infectious laughter of Avril, the nurse from the agency. Beyond the rose bushes, over there, across the lawn, people were gathered; substantial, familiar and alive. I didn't want to stay here, alone, with the dead. I rose slowly and cautiously, afraid to make a sudden movement which might remind Sam I was there, and jerk him into appearing or speaking to me; then panic took over and I leapt off the wooden platform on to the path, fled across the grass and burst on to the verandah.

Everybody hissed and shushed me irritably, as if they were hanging on to every word that Terry Wogan and his guests were saying, so that they could pass their O levels on it tomorrow. Every single person at The Haven was behaving abominably. I told them all to shut up and asked Avril for a couple of Codeines.

'Hang on a minute, Beattie. Can't you see I'm watching?'

'Can't you see I'm dying? Have you any idea what a migraine is?'

'Oh, come on then, you old nuisance. How come you ran across the garden like that if you're in such pain?' She glanced at me, got up, took my hand and led me into the surgery. 'Beattie!' she gasped. 'You look as if you've seen a ghost! You look awful! I'm sorry . . . I didn't realize . . . Here, sit down. Swallow these and stay there till I fetch you some tea.'

She drew the blinds, pulled two pillows out of the cupboard and put them behind my shoulders, then disappeared for a minute, returning with a cup of tea and two soggy biscuits. She massaged my neck and temples until I felt a little better.

'Listen, why don't you go off home? I'll see to the hot drinks and nobody looks as if they're going to die tonight – apart from you, of course.'

'Kitty's had a very tiring day. She might need an early night.'

'She's perfectly okay, holding hands with Alter in the kitchen, and gassing to Yetta and Rene. It's you who need an early night. Shall I phone Frank to come and fetch you?'

'No. I'll be all right once I'm out of this place. I'm off until Sunday afternoon. Say good night to the folks for me. I don't want to speak to any of them just now.'

I slipped out through the side door and drove home with the windows open. I felt completely well within a few minutes. Usually a blasting migraine lasts at least one whole day. It must be The Haven getting on my nerves. I thought of my day off tomorrow with relief.

Frank had prepared a lovely American salad for supper, and we ate it on the garden table under the tree. I told him about my horrible day, but of course it was a waste of time and energy. He's very limited when it comes to understanding what I go through at The Haven.

'You're just suffering from hurt pride. You're offended that you've been temporarily excluded from a group of people you feel close to. Their background and culture are different from yours; they treat the spiritual and supernatural as part of life, but a private part in which you're not involved. You can't live in their pockets all the time, and don't wallow in self-pity. In a minute, you'll be telling me how much you do for them and that you're taken for granted. Save me from those remarks, Beattie, please!'

I'm continually amazed and mortified at Frank's unpleasantly accurate predictions as to what I'm about to say.

'I wouldn't dream of saying anything of the kind! You're always wrong about me!' I snapped. 'How would you like to be left alone with an unhinged ghost? If they want to babble to Sam, that's their business as long as they don't drag me into their mumbo jumbo. I hate ghosts. I don't believe in them, anyway, and even if I did, I wouldn't want a confrontation. Alter's usually so thoughtful and chivalrous, but even he didn't consider my feelings. I was so frightened, Frank, stuck in the summer house with Kitty's dead husband . . .'

'Why were you afraid?' asked Frank gently. 'Sam couldn't possibly think of you with malice. On the contrary! You're the last person in the world who would rouse his anger and bitterness.'

I looked at him sharply to see whether he was mocking me. He wasn't.

'You don't understand, Frank. Sam's got a screw loose. He isn't all there. Anyway, I'm glad it's my day off tomorrow. I need a break from that madhouse.'

'You're not the only one!'

I stood on the hose-pipe and sprayed his bare chest and he returned the compliment more accurately, soaking my face and hair. We star-gazed until well after midnight and the witching hour held no fears for me. I hardly gave a thought to the carryings-on at The Haven until noon on Sunday, when duty called me back there.

I decided to act as if no one had behaved outrageously towards me, and to be my usual agreeable, sweet-tempered self. Everyone would then feel deeply ashamed, and I had no doubt that I would be swamped with apologies before the end of the afternoon. I worked out the whole delightful scene driving to work in the car. I could hear Yetta saying, 'Beattie, please forgive me for my unkindness and rudeness. I haven't enjoyed a moment's peace of mind since Friday evening.' And I would reply with quiet dignity and a pleasant smile, 'Why, dear, whatever do you mean? There's nothing to forgive.'

I popped on my overall and went into the kitchen to clear up the lunch-time mess. Naturally, I had no intention of asking any of them to help, but of course, if Yetta, Rene or Kitty wanted to offer to wash up or set the trolley, I'd probably relent. I made enough noise to wake the dead, banging the pans around and putting the plates into the sink with a crash. They knew I was here all right. I certainly wasn't prepared to shout hello to them as I usually did. Let them come and greet *me* first, for a change.

The weather was still hot and close. I propped open the kitchen door and listened. Not a sound. They were probably all sitting idling in the garden and didn't know I'd arrived. I decided to go out for a few moments to see; make out that I needed a breath of air before I got down to the chores. To my astonishment none of the folks were outside. They were in the sitting room pretending to be resting.

I said 'Good afternoon' politely and coldly, but no one responded. Yetta didn't even bother to open her eyes. A casual observer might have imagined that they were dozing, that there was an air of tranquillity in the room, but I knew better. Never had I felt such tension; such an atmosphere of taut expectation. I felt as if I had intruded on a strange secret, crept back to the kitchen and washed the dishes on my own.

I was glad when the front doorbell rang, heralding the arrival of visitors. Whoever it was would be bound to penetrate the oppressive silence in the sitting room. I dried my hands and ran to answer it. It was the abominable Cynthia, carrying Kitty's dress in a see-through bag. She floated in on a cloud of perfume, followed by her husband and his two brothers. The situation was quite unique. Never before had this collection arrived in one fell swoop. I dodged back into the kitchen and pushed open the hatch, which was never used for anything except a spy-hole. They clustered around Kitty and bent to kiss her.

'I sent a message that you were not to come here. Why have you come? Go away.'

'I won't tolerate this nonsense, Mother!' said John. 'Cynthia wore herself out taking you shopping. We've come to find out what all these silly, childish tantrums are about. Now then, we're busy people and have no time to waste. What's the matter? Don't be afraid to tell us. Is it something to do with that woman who works here? The one who was so rude to Cynthia on Friday? Has she been upsetting you? We'll have her out of here in ten minutes if she's the cause of all this. We won't have our mother made unhappy by an ignorant, uncouth charwoman.'

'He means Beattie,' said Yetta. 'Your ignorant, uncouth son is talking about our friend, Beattie.'

'It's impossible to talk in here,' said Arnold. 'Isn't there a private room?'

'We'll take her into the bedroom,' said Cynthia. 'Come along.'

'Don't touch me and don't speak to me!' screeched Kitty. 'Get out of my sight!'

'Don't you want to try on your dress?'

'No. What for? I'm not going anywhere in it.'

'Have you forgotten that it's your granddaughter's wedding in three weeks?' asked John, slowly and deliberately, as if he were speaking to a rather backward child.

'I have no granddaughter,' said Kitty dreadfully. 'And no children. I will not be attending your daughter's wedding. I shall be here, at The Haven, the day she gets married.'

They stood there, silent and horrified. My heart banged. Everyone sat like statues. It was Alter who broke the silence. He walked slowly across the room, stood in front of Kitty, bent down and took her hand. He spoke to her softly, in Yiddish. Yetta told me later what he'd said:

'Your late husband, Sam, was my friend. Your sons are his sons. He was as pleased with them as the Almighty was pleased with the Creation. If he was by your side, you would both go to this wedding. Explain what has happened to make you change your mind. Tell them. They don't understand.'

'Your father doesn't want me to go. He told me. I sat in that one's car, in the driveway of her house. She didn't invite me in. When she came back, she didn't speak to me. We drove back here and she didn't say one word. She stopped, but she didn't say, "I'm going into The Haven to fetch Beattie to help you out." She looked at me. For half a minute she looked at me with her nose wrinkled, her eyes cold, wishing me under the earth. She got out and slammed the door. Then my Sam came to me. He saw my sore feet; my sore heart, and he said, "For *this* you slaved and wore yourself out and for *this* I spent my manhood so that I am not here to look after you, to kiss your tears away. No more, darling. No more trying. Enough is enough. Did she take you into her house for a rest? Did the gracious bride condescend to greet you? How many times have you been invited into our sons' homes? Met their friends? Been included in their lives? Do they need you, want you, love you? They have withdrawn their attention and affection all these long years. Who needs people like them, or their wedding? Did we leave our children when the clock struck four? Are these our children, then, who leave you? No, darling! We have no children!" '

At that moment, shockingly, the clock struck four.

Time for the end of the visit. Time for me to bring in the tea trolley. No one moved. Kitty's sons stood, heads bowed. I wondered how they felt, listening to the words of their dead father, for though it was their mother's voice, the style, the language, was not hers.

'You heard your father,' she said. 'I have no family. Go away! Go home!'

Alter bent down and kissed her on both cheeks. 'All of a sudden you're not in a hurry,' he said, turning to face them, waving his arms at them derisively. 'I remember you when you were little boys with torn trousers, before you changed your names and puffed yourselves up. To me, you're Mister Nobodies. Come, Kitty. We'll walk in the garden.' He helped her to her feet and led her out through the verandah.

The cups and saucers rattled as I set them on the trolley, and when I pushed it into the sitting room, all the folks had settled themselves on the verandah, leaving Kitty's three sons and Cynthia alone, wretched and forlorn. In spite of myself, I was touched with pity for them. Sam, I thought, had been rather hard. I carried over a small table and set tea and biscuits in front of them and they thanked me in low voices.

I went through to the verandah and Yetta called over to me, greeting me in her old, fond, familiar way as if nothing unpleasant had occurred between us.

'Where's Alter and Kitty?' I asked, pretending that I didn't know; that I'd been concentrating on the mucky dishes during the recent drama.

'Probably in the summer house.'

'I'll take a tray out to them. They must be gasping for a cup of tea in this heat.'

'Leave them alone. They don't want me, you or anyone, and if they want tea, let them come and help themselves. We're also gasping.' She sounded angry and upset.

'That bunch in there,' I said, jerking my head towards the sitting room. 'What are they doing here? I thought Kitty gave strict orders that she didn't want to see them.'

'So?' said Yetta sharply. 'And what if she did? You

150

think we didn't know that they'd all come running? Where's your sense, Beattie? You think Kitty's friends would let her send her children away from her, you silly girl? Sometimes you behave like you were born yesterday. And don't make out to me that you didn't watch what was going on in there. Haven't I seen you listening and looking through the hatch a hundred times? Why should today be different? Are we going to have our tea today? Get Rene to help. I'm very tired.'

'I can manage. What's going to happen, Yetta? About the wedding, I mean.' I felt quite nervous mentioning it. Yetta was so unpredictable. 'Her sons are sitting in there, absolutely mortified. One of them has his handkerchief out, and Cynthia looks almost human. That dress she bought with Kitty is beautiful.'

'She'll wear the dress. Alter will see to that. She'll do anything he suggests.'

'Well, well! Fancy old Kitty disobeying her husband! Whatever next! Or has he thought things over in the last few minutes, and changed his tune? Of course, Time and Reason probably acquire entirely different dimensions in Limbo-Land, and who am I to comprehend the workings of a ghost's mind? I don't mix with them on a day to day basis like you lot, and it's not for me to venture an opinion. *I* don't know anything. I must be very careful what I say, but I'm sure *you* all know what you're on about and that you're not thinking of encouraging Kitty to do anything to bring quaint old Sam's wrath down on your heads. I hope you'll pardon me for voicing my anxiety and that Sam will forgive my impertinence!'

Yetta set down her cup and turned to me. In the fourteen months I had known her, through her personal grief and suffering, I had never seen tears in her eyes. Now they shone there, bright and glittering, and I could see that it was only the mighty strength of her will, which prevented them from spilling over.

'Yetta, darling Yetta, what's the matter?' I gasped, banging down the tea pot and holding her close.

151

'Nothing for you to make a song and dance about in front of everybody. Get on with your work.'

'Not until you tell me why you're so upset.'

'Later, later.'

'Meet me in the kitchen at five o'clock, then. Promise?'

'Promise.'

I could tell she just wanted to get rid of me, but I knew she'd be there. I tried to recall what I'd said that might have distressed her, but my conscience was clear. Something must have happened on my day off, and what with me not being around, she'd had no one to talk to about it. Perhaps she'd been deeply affected by the few cross words we'd exchanged on Friday and thought I'd be unable to forgive her. No matter that we had occasional disagreements, we were close friends and always confided in each other.

I fixed a tray for two and carried it across the lawn. It was such a beautiful day; warm, bright and still. This was the weather for weddings and cheerfulness; sprawling on the grass, talking, reading, snoozing, licking ice creams. A time for falling in love and enjoying just being alive in this too bright, too brief glorious spring. This was neither the time nor the place for embittered ghosts to appear and cause family feuds and unpleasantness among friends. I couldn't help remembering what a fool I'd been, when I'd fled from my own crazed imagination, across this lawn, on Friday. I'd soon chivvy Yetta out of her depression; buck her up and make her realize that I hadn't taken her seriously.

Alter and Kitty had the right idea. They were sitting close together, hand in hand, like of couple of young lovers, talking to one of Kitty's sons. God knows which one it was. I'd never sort out who was who, especially here, with the sun blinding me. He probably saw me coming, though, and disappeared from view, on to the overgrown path which bordered the back of the summer house, obviously wishing to avoid me. It struck me as a rather odd thing to do. The path was full of nettles and yet he must have come out to them that way, otherwise I would have seen him pass through the verandah while I was serving tea there, and talking to Yetta. I called out to them, but they were so absorbed, that they didn't notice me until I set the tray down on the wooden table in front of them.

'Tea-time!' I said gaily, making out that I'd forgotten all about their bad manners on Friday.

'Hello, Beattie! How kind! Thank you! I'll pour. Would you ask the children to come out here, please?' said Alter, smiling.

'Wasn't Arnold here just now?'

'No,' said Kitty. There was something mischievous about the look she gave me. The change in her was delightful. 'Just tell the boys we want to speak to them privately, without Cynthia. She can hang my dress up for me. I don't want it crushed.'

How firm and decisive she sounded! What had come over her?

I ran back to the house. Rene and Yetta had disappeared into the kitchen with the trolley. The three men were talking softly to one another in the sitting room. Cynthia wasn't there. She was probably fixing her face in the cloakroom.

'Excuse me. Your mother wants to see you.' They were three eminent, grey-haired men, all well into middle age, but for all that, most painfully vulnerable. 'Go on,' I said, smiling, 'I'm sure she didn't mean what she said. She always talks of you with such pride and love.'

'Where is she? Would you be good enough to show us, please?' said Arnold.

'Weren't you with them just now?'

'No. We've been waiting here.'

'One of you was there. I saw . . . Just a few minutes ago, your mother and Alter were talking to . . .' The back of my neck prickled. 'Which one of you was it?' I shouted.

'Madam,' said Selwyn, 'my brothers and I have been sitting here together, waiting for our mother to return to the house. Perhaps she was talking to the handyman or the gardener. Surely this is nothing to get so overwrought about. Perhaps you could take us to her now.'

They followed me silently through the verandah and across the lawn. Of course it wasn't one of them I'd seen! These men were overweight and moved ponderously. The sun had been in my eyes. Kitty's visitor had retreated quickly and gracefully; yet there'd been something – some resemblance . . .

We turned on to the main path and from there you could see the summer house about twenty yards beyond. Kitty's sons thanked me and hurried towards it, and I turned to go back, but of course, I didn't. Instead, I darted behind the shed and cut across the overgrown path. There were plenty of cracks and holes in the old weathered boards at the back of the summer house. I was just in time. John, Arnold and Selwyn came up the ramp and stood in front of Kitty and Alter like naughty schoolboys before the head teacher.

'Mother, please!' John actually knelt down and put his head on her lap. It would have been laughable if the gesture hadn't been so terribly moving. 'How can you say to us that you have no children, and that you won't come to your granddaughter's wedding?' The other two stood watching sheepishly.

She put her hand on John's head and stroked the grey hair. 'Yankel, Yankel,' she said, again and again, 'and now you come here, Solly! Abey! Kiss your mother. What's so bad about the names your father chose for you? Are they so terrible? Aren't they good enough for you?'

'Yes, Mamma,' said Selwyn shakily, 'but the girls – our wives – they felt we should change them.'

'And did they have to change you, too? Did they have to make you behave like them? Proud and selfish, and ashamed of your mother, and your father's memory? Do they know, then, what your mamma sold to buy you an education? Do they know it wasn't just needles and combs? Would that Cynthia be so haughty, with her face-lifts and fur coats and fancy, shmancy wedding plans for

154

her rude and idle daughter, if she knew where all the money came from?'

'Kitty!' said Alter sharply. 'Don't say any more. It's enough that your sons know and that they suffered far more than they gained from the sacrifices you and their father made. Leave it now! We must all learn to live with our mistakes. Sam, may his soul rest in peace, doesn't have to. Now! Tell the children your good news!'

'I spoke to your father just now. We discussed the wedding again, and he thinks I should go after all, as long as I don't have to go alone.'

'We'll all be there to look after you,' said Arnold. 'You know how much we love and care for you. We don't visit you as often as we'd like, because we're very busy people, and . . .'

'Busy people have no time for an old woman. I will come to the wedding with my husband who is not too busy. You want to see him? Here he is! Here!'

I turned and fled along the path and arrived at the house with my legs scratched and stung from the prickles and nettles which barred my way. I stumbled into the kitchen, calling for Yetta, my nerves completely unstrung. She was there, waiting for me, and I gasped out to her everything that had occurred and why I had fled.

'She's drumming up that damned ghost again! I'm going to tell Rabbi Ezra of her! It's not right! It's not healthy or decent, mixing with ghosts as if they were people!'

'Is it so wrong for Kitty to talk to Sam? Who else is going to support her a hundred per cent and give her the excuse of saying what she feels? Have you ever known her admit she made a mistake? How many times have you heard her say she's good to everybody and nobody's good to her? She's always been self-centred, vain and possessive. So what's she going to do when she has to face the fact that the children aren't perfect? *Her* children? *Her* family? She has to say that they don't belong to her. She couldn't do that by herself. Sam had to do it for her.'

'Are you telling me that she made it up about seeing him?'

'Who said anything about *seeing* him? He came to her and they spoke – that's all. When you're old, lonely and depressed, it's good to talk things over with someone from the past, who loved and understood you. I should know.'

'I'm telling you, Yetta, she asked her sons if they wanted to *see* him! Then she took hold of Alter's hand again, and said, "Here he is!" That's why I ran away.'

'She asked her sons if they wanted to see *who*?'

'*Him*! Her *husband*!'

She turned deathly pale, and then, to my grief and astonishment, the tears which I had forgotten about shone in her eyes again.

'Yetta! What's the matter? Tell me! Tell Beattie! Is it your heart? I'll call Goss.'

'I'm all right. It's the heat. Bring me a glass of water and a cold flannel.'

'I'll fetch Selwyn, Yetta. Or is it Arnold who's the heart surgeon?' I wiped her face and neck with the flannel.

'I don't need anyone. Stop fussing.'

'Why are you keeping me in the dark? Why did you have a turn just now, when I mentioned that damned spook? This business has upset you dreadfully, and I won't have it. I won't have Kitty and that crazy Sam making you ill and depressed! I'm waiting, Yetta. If you can't or won't explain, I'm going to call that Selwyn in here, to take care of you.'

'You think Kitty and Sam upset me, you silly girl!' she said scornfully. 'She wasn't talking about *Sam*! She was talking about *Alter* as her husband – her future husband, anyway. I might as well tell you. Why should I keep it a secret from you any longer? What does it matter now? I've always liked Alter. When I was a young widow, he was kindness itself to me. He and Golda always welcomed me to their home and helped me in every way they could. He was such a handsome man and such a gentleman!

'Since Golda's death, we've been very close. We're two lonely old people with nothing to lose, no one to hurt and affection and companionship to offer each other. But Alter felt it wouldn't be right for him to make a commitment so soon after losing Golda and we decided to wait a bit longer and not say anything to anybody. We thought it best to stay here and turn Alter's and Golda's flat into Alter's and Yetta's.

'Why are you looking at me like that?' she asked defiantly. 'Is it so strange; so wrong? I know what you're thinking! We see each other all the time; we talk; we sit together; go to the park, and we live in a place where we're looked after. So what else do I want? An old woman like me? Is it bad to want to put your arms round someone and feel his arms round you? To be together? You think because I've been alone for nearly fifty years, I don't remember what it's like to have a husband to love, to share a joke or a tear?

'What can Kitty share with him? She doesn't know how to share! That poor, poor Sam! He was weak and she made him ashamed of their poverty. She manipulated him and her sons and now she's manipulated Alter. All the weekend she's been crying to him about how lonely and neglected she is and that she's no husband to take care of her. That's why he's doing this – sacrificing himself to marry her and look after her. It's what he needs to do; what he has to do. He's a good man, Beattie. Too good. There's no fool like an old fool, though.' She pretended to wipe the sweat from her face. My head was spinning like a top.

'Darling, you've got it all wrong. Kitty was calling to Sam. Not Alter. He was sitting with her, holding her hand, that's all! She was going to produce Sam for her kids, like a conjurer. I told you. Alter isn't a complete lunatic. He wouldn't let Kitty nobble him – not when he's got *you*! He's a man of honour; of character.'

'You don't know her like I know her. She imposes on Alter's finer feelings all the time. She has to come first. It's her nature. And both you and she know very well that you can't make a dead person appear to the living. Talking to them's one thing; seeing them's another. Alter

knows he's free to do what he wants. We made no promises to each other.'

'I hate him!' I shouted. 'He's weak, dishonourable,
selfish and wicked, and so is Kitty. I hate them both!
They make sacrifices of other people, and try to make us
believe they're sacrificing themselves. It's not fair! It's not
right!'

'Shut up,' said Yetta. 'They're here. Behave yourself.'

I opened the hatch and saw Kitty hobble in on Alter's
arm, followed by the three stooges, just as Cynthia came
into the kitchen, without so much as a by your leave.

'Who's in charge here, please.'

'Matron.'

'Where can I find her?'

I reached up and took a postcard from the top of the
fridge and read out the address slowly and deliberately:
'Hotel Plaza, Room 304, Benidorm, Spain. She's there on
holiday, but if you need her urgently, I'm sure you can
get a flight. I believe Gatwick . . .'

'I suppose you find all this amusing. No doubt you
encouraged my mother-in-law in her ridiculous behaviour!
A woman in her eighties, ill and crippled, who can hardly
be considered capable of deciding anything for herself,
telling her sons she's going to marry a penniless, doddery
old stick who doesn't know what he's doing either. It's
disgusting! My *daughter* is getting married in three weeks.
Can you imagine what our friends will think when her
grandmother turns up with *her* bridegroom! Of course we
won't allow it. Thank you for helping to humiliate and
distress us.'

I longed to drag her down to the floor; to inquire mendaciously whether Angela wasn't too old and disgusting
to marry. But I was seized simultaneously by a flash of
inspirational power.

'Mrs Horton, please don't let's squabble. I assure you
that I had no idea of your mother-in-law's intentions to
marry until this afternoon. If Matron was here, I'm sure
she would discourage the plan as strenuously as you.
There are no facilities for a married couple on the ground

158

floor, and I don't think either Mr Freid or Mrs Horovitz realize that they'd have to live with you. They couldn't possibly cope without constant attendance. This sudden decision of theirs has obviously not been thought out. I'm sure it's just a reaction to the fact that she feels lonely and neglected and her friend is sorry for her. If she thought that there'd be lots of jaunts and outings and visits from her family from now on, she'd soon come round to your way of thinking. How have her sons taken the news?'

'They don't know what's hit them! They're terribly upset, but they think there's nothing they can do or say to dissuade her. They're weak; stupid! They've always been under her thumb! My sisters-in-law and myself have had trouble from her all our married lives! What are we going to do?' she wailed. 'None of us will have them to live with us! It's quite out of the question!'

'Of course it is!' I crooned. 'May I make a suggestion?'

'Well?'

'Why don't you arrange a family conference – now – in the guest room? It's quite private there, and you won't be interrupted. Just you, your husband, his brothers and their mother – and Mr Freid. Point out to them how difficult it will be to cope with the upheaval if they had to live with you. They'd both feel they were a burden and it wouldn't be fair on anyone. Ask why they can't remain just good friends and how nice it would be for her, if Mr Freid escorted her to your daughter's wedding on that basis, to take care of her on that special day. And if you mentioned that once Angela's off your hands, you and Mr Horton will have lots more time for outings; and if Mr Selwyn and Mr Arnold and their wives invite her over to their homes every other weekend, I'm sure she'd recover from her disappointment; and to tell you the truth, Mrs Horton, I think both of them will probably be secretly relieved. You're a very clever woman, and if you can make her think it's her idea to call off the engagement, it would be tactful and kind.'

I daren't look at Yetta. She didn't interrupt to remind me that a chair lift was going to be installed on the staircase next month, so that Alter's wife, whoever she might be, could sail up to their private quarters, and down again, without any problem.

'Go on,' I said gently. 'It's best to get all this settled once and for all.'

I eased her out of the kitchen, and led her over to the guest room. She collected the family and Alter, and they followed me in. I fetched a few extra chairs from the verandah and returned to the kitchen, where Yetta had started the washing-up. She looked cheerful and didn't seem in the least tired.

'You're a wicked girl, Beattie, and I'm no better. How am I going to live with myself?'

'I don't think you'll have to. We've probably saved that stupid Alter from a miserable life and Kitty will have her wretched family eating out of her hand. *My* conscience is clear. Now let's get a move on. I'm all behind with my work. I hope that from now on, Sam will leave us all alone.'

Yetta finished the washing-up while I had a short rest, to recover from the shock and emotional stress of the afternoon.

'Come in!' I trilled, in answer to a knock on the open kitchen door. It was Alter. He sat down on the stool and smiled at us ruefully.

'Women!' he said, in the way that men say 'women' when men are entirely to blame. 'I have just had a very narrow escape. Kitty, bless her silly heart, decided to give her sons a rocket, by calling on her husband while I was sitting by her, holding her hand. So they assumed *I* was the husband! I've only just this moment informed them that I'm already spoken for. They want me to escort her to her granddaughter's wedding and they're falling over themselves to be nice to her, making arrangements for visits and outings.'

'Spoken for, Alter?' I asked, cunning as a fox. His blue eyes twinkled and he looked so handsome and adorable, that I could quite easily have fallen in love with him myself.

'Well, Yetta? Shall we let Beattie in on our plans? I think it might be opportune, since Kitty is so unpredictable at the moment. We should make our intentions known and why should we wait any longer? We haven't exactly got all the time in the world. We're not eighteen.'

He stood up, walked over to where Yetta was standing next to me and put his arm round her waist. She nodded and smiled back at him with such tenderness that tears filled my eyes.

'I would like to introduce you to the lady who honours me by promising to be my wife. Nothing can make me prouder or happier.'

'Bless you, both,' I said, kissing them. 'When will the wedding be? I hope it won't clash with Angela's!'

'Perhaps the week after. What do you say, Yetta? Let's walk in the garden and discuss it.'

'Can you manage the suppers, Beattie? Shall I call Rene?'

'Get out of here, the pair of you. Go on! Scram!' I pretended to chase them. I sneaked on to the verandah to watch them walk across the lawn, arm in arm, towards the summer house. A couple of eighteen-year-olds!

Kitty and her family came out of the guest room.

'We'll be leaving now,' said Cynthia pleasantly, 'but we'll all be back during the week to have a look at Mother in her new outfit. Thank you for all you've done for her – for us. We're most grateful.'

They smiled and shook hands and Kitty and I waved them off from the front door.

'Kitty,' I said, 'have you got the strength and inclination to give us a hand with the damned supper? I'm about two hours behind. It's cauliflower cheese.'

'I don't know what you'd do without me, Beattie. Where's my pinnie?' She hobbled ahead of me into the kitchen, and grated the cheese while I washed the vegetables.

'Where's Yetta?'

'In the garden. She didn't have any visitors today.'

161

'Terrible!' sighed Kitty. 'Thank God, I've got a wonderful family. And Alter? Where's he?'

'Also in the garden. I think they're both in the summer house together.'

'Men!' said Kitty, in the way that women say 'men' when men are to blame. 'They never move themselves until you push them off balance! They think they've got all the time in the world. I'd never marry again. No one could take the place of my Sam, but Yetta doesn't feel deeply, like me. She's always needed someone to take care of her. I don't speak out about these matters, but I can tell you, Beattie, her Jack wasn't up to much. He used to visit me sometimes; you know, after work, while my poor husband was still at his bench, slaving for his children. Between you and me, that Jack was a bit of a handful. He fancied himself as one of the boys, always with an eye on a pretty girl – and more than an eye, if he got the chance. Alter was never like that. Never. A gentleman, through and through, but they're the ones who need a push. Yetta don't know how to push, so I did a bit of pushing for her. I'm good to everyone, but nobody's . . .'

'How did you push Alter?' I asked slyly. 'I don't follow you.'

She cackled so much and so infectiously, that I started to laugh too.

'They thought I wanted to marry Alter. Even Alter thought that! He turned as white as a sheet, Beattie! He didn't know what to say! My boys were nailed to the floor, and before Alter could say anything, Cynthia came running over, and Yankel told her I was getting married. Alter's such a gentleman! He didn't want to shame me in front of my family. He didn't know how to refuse me. But he needed a good fright; a bit of a shaking up. Yetta can't wait much longer. When you're our age, a month is a long time. I made him think *I* was after him. It brought him to heel. I'm a woman of the world, Beattie. I know these things. Yetta don't know from nothing. She don't understand men. Is my new dress hanging up?'

'Yes,' I said. 'Yes, darling. It's beautiful – and so are

162

you. I'm so glad you're going to the wedding! What made Sam change his mind?'

'Men don't know their own minds, Beattie. Even Sam, God rest his soul, still has to be guided by me. We both worked hard to give our sons a start in life, but I was the strong one who pushed them all the time. Sam used to say I was always right; always knew best. Of course, he was a little upset about the way they've been behaving lately, but no one will ever know what those boys meant to him. No one. He sacrificed himself for them. But it wasn't enough. I had to make sacrifices too. An expensive education for them was all he wanted in the world. Even I couldn't make him change his mind about that. Do you really think, after all we'd been through in our lives, he wouldn't want me to go to our granddaughter's wedding?'

'Of course he would, Kitty!' I smiled. 'It will be so nice for Alter, too, to go along with you.'

'Silly girl! I can't take Alter with me. My husband will be there.'

'Kitty!' I said sharply. 'Stop talking like that. Your husband's dead. You've got to accept that. Your place is with the living. You can't go to the wedding with Sam. He isn't here!'

'Who said I was going with him? I said he'll be there, that's all. Just because *they* couldn't see him doesn't mean that nobody can. He told me in the summer house that he'd be at the wedding to love and look after me. He was so close to me, I could have reached out and touched him.'

'Are you trying to tell me that you *saw* him? What does he look like then?'

'I think *you* know,' said Kitty, smiling. 'The image of my Abey.'

12

The Wicked Sister

On the first Friday of every month Matron went off duty for a long weekend, and since there always had to be a qualified nurse on the premises, capable of dealing with a medical emergency, Nurse Goss stayed in Matron's flat. Goss had a bee in her bonnet about being alone with the folks at night, and although she disliked me intensely, with just cause, she was grudgingly grateful to me for tactfully volunteering to sleep over in the guest room on the rare occasions when she was on her own. Matron would have taken a dim view of Goss, had she discovered this weakness in her, and it was silently yet sacredly agreed that I would never let on that I stayed overnight. It followed, of course, that she was unable to blab to Matron about anything in my behaviour which she disapproved of on these Friday evenings, although it didn't stop her carrying tittle-tattle at all other times.

With only seven residents at The Haven, no one was exactly overworking. However, I'd made myself indispensable, since I now did practically all the cooking. Mrs Jones had gradually cut her hours down because of continual ill health, and, as rumour would have it, because she'd found a nice little job on the side. On the first Friday of every month, I encouraged the residents to invite family or friends to the evening meal which I prepared. Clive and Debbie always came with little Gloria to see Yetta, and two members of Kitty's family attended regularly. Alter generally brought a friend home after the synagogue service, and Boris and Olga never missed. Sarah's middle-aged grandson came with his wife, both very upper-class, but charming and friendly, always bearing flowers, fruit and cakes for the residents; and I think for Sadie's elderly nephew and niece, our Friday night supper was a very happy social event. Only Rene never invited anyone. She had no family and maintained that she was very choosy about her friends, and didn't latch on to just anyone, like some people she could mention. I understood her dilemma and never pressed the point.

The Jewish Sabbath – or Shabbos, as it is called – begins at sunset on Friday and ends when you can see three stars in the sky on Saturday night. During the week, meals were served in the dining nook, which was really an extension of the huge kitchen, but on Shabbos, whether we had visitors or not, everyone ate in the sitting room. I would carry in the Formica-topped tables, bunging them next to each other to make one large surface, and the residents would get busy spreading the snow-white cloths and setting out the specially pretty napkins and the polished cutlery and glasses. The best of everything was served on Friday night: delicious, sweet red wine; soft plaited rolls; the traditional Jewish fare of cold, fried and boiled fish, which I'd learned to prepare exactly as the folks liked it. Plates of spicy cakes and fancy biscuits were served with tea after the meal and the shining brass candlesticks were set on the sideboard.

Each old lady had her own pair of candlesticks, and at sunset, when everyone was bright-eyed and bushy-tailed, dressed in their best clothes and bedecked in head-scarves, they would each light two candles, bless them with a short prayer, and after the last Amen, we would wish each other Good Shabbos. Then the folks would sit round the table, passing the time talking about their childhood while waiting for the visitors to arrive, and Alter and Boris to return from the synagogue. The atmosphere, so harmonious and peaceful, never failed to ease my heart and I knew it did the same for all the residents. Even Sarah and Rene were civil to each other.

I never tired of listening to the stories from their past. This was the night when their exhausted parents would rejoice in the day of rest with the family; when poverty, persecution and pogroms were forgotten. For the Jewish man is king at his table on Shabbos, and his wife is the queen – no matter what the hostile outside world thinks of them. On Friday night, it seemed that their families from the past came to join them, too, kindly and benign, and the wrinkled old faces in the candlelight were young and hopeful; little girls, with ribbons tied on their shining hair; Boris and Alter, lads with curling side-locks, singing Sabbath hymns, Yiddish lullabies and folksongs. Even though I was a stranger to their customs, I felt like a welcome and honoured guest at a family feast. All the residents' parents were born in Eastern Europe and spent their youth there, before being hounded out and emigrating to England. The traditions of life in the small villages of Lithuania and Poland continued in the ghettos of London's East End, and although their villages had been destroyed long since, along with the Jewish communities, the memories of those days had been passed on to the children and were more fresh and vibrant than yesterday.

After the special supper, while they sang the Grace after Meals, I loaded the dishwasher, set the trolley in preparation for tea and cakes, brushed the crumbs off the tablecloths and then listened through the hatch, to the old voices, mingling with the younger ones, singing, talking, laughing – and surprised myself with the singular joy and pleasure it gave me. If I stayed the night, my duties were always the same after the visitors had departed. The Deaths Announcements from the *Jewish Chronicle* had to be read aloud. For a long time I was under the impression that this was all part of the Friday night ritual, like lighting the candles and blessing the wine and bread, and therefore I did as I was told without question. But when I discovered that it was mere entertainment, I couldn't resist taunting the folks about the pleasure they derived from this gloomy pastime. Always, when I returned to the table, the newspaper was folded over neatly at the births, marriages and deaths.

'How long are we expected to wait?'

'Much she cares! She can read the news; she isn't cut off from the world.'

166

'Read! Read!'

'I haven't had my tea and cake yet.'

'Here! Stuff yourself! You can read and drink tea at the same time.'

'I'll start with the Hatches. "Avery – to Sandra and Jonathan on November second, a son, Dan. Brother for Samantha and Emma; another darling grandchild for . . ."'

'Who wants to know from babies? Stop wasting time!'

'The Matches, then. Aren't you interested in weddings?'

'No. Dispatches! Dispatches!'

'All right! All right! I'll just finish my cake.'

'You enjoy, Beattie. You enjoy filling your belly and tormenting old sick people. Now you'll be telling us you've got something better to do. We don't matter. You happen to earn a good living working in an old folk's Home, but a favour, a little kindness, you don't know nothing about.'

'I'll have you know, Kitty, that if I got paid for overtime and insults, I'd be a rich woman. Now, if you'll all stop yattering, I'll begin.'

After each announcement there would be an animated discussion about the departed soul and his or her relatives, and if one connection could be managed, there was a feeling of triumph. 'Remember Annie Shine who sold children's dresses in Morgan Street? Her sister was married to Menachim Abramsky.'

'The name of the person is Mark Andrews,' I said.

'So? He fancied himself an Englishman. Don't it say, "deeply mourned by his sister-in-law, Annie"?'

'It says, "September thirtieth, after much suffering, bravely borne, our darling Dad and Grandpa left us to be reunited with his sweetheart, Pearl. Deeply mourned by his daughter Freda, son-in-law, Irving, grandchildren Maurice and Sydney, great-grandchildren Jason, Melanie and Wayne. God bless, Granpy." That's the only entry. Nothing about anyone called Annie.'

'What! No entry from Annie and Percy Shine?'

167

'Maybe it'll be in next week.'

'Wasn't Annie's sister called Pearl?' said Sadie excitedly. She had a phenomenal memory, as long as the event to be recalled was more than sixty years ago. Anything more recent, like whether she'd had lunch or the name of her late husband, escaped her. She was tiny and bent, while Bubba, her best friend, was large and round. Knowing Bubba to be very deaf, Sadie kept her informed of anything her ears may have missed. At one time I made every effort to clear up misunderstandings, but only caused irritation and more confusion. Sadie was an absolute whizz when it came to identifying those departed souls listed in the obituary column. 'She lived in Brune House and helped Annie sometimes,' she said. 'A nice woman. Oy!'

Everyone remembered, of course. 'I wonder if Annie is still alive,' pondered Kitty. 'She wasn't such a chicken, but she dyed her hair red. She wasn't a day less than fifty when my Abey was a toddler.'

'In that case, she should be receiving a telegram from our dear Queen any day,' I said impatiently.

'All being well!'

'Who died? Who did you say died?' shouted Bubba right in my ear. I leaned over and tuned her hearing aid.

'Nobody – I mean, nobody you know. Maybe we'll strike lucky on the next one. Now are we all ready? "Apfel – Fanny. My darling wife, Fanny, fell asleep on September twenty-eighth. My angel for fifty-two wonderful years. The sweetest lady in the world. From my arms to the Almighty's. May her dear, sweet soul rest in everlasting peace. Her heart-broken husband, Phil, sons Saul and Leonard, daughters-in-law, Vera and Greta, grandchildren, relatives and friends."

'Next entry – "The staff of Philifan Ladies' Gowns, wish to express their sympathy and sorrow to Mr Phil Apfel, Saul, Vera, Leonard and Greta on the sad loss of a dear wife and mother." . . . And another: "Our deepest sympathy to Mr Philip Apfel on the death of his beloved wife. The Board of Management and members of Greenfield Lane Congregation." Greenfield Lane! Isn't that the synagogue you attend, Alter?'

Instead of the usual animated discussion, no one spoke a word. 'What's up?' I asked nervously. Everyone was looking at Rene. Even in the flickering candlelight I could see the flush on her face and neck and that her knobbly hands were clenched tight. All the others seemed to have been shocked into stupefied silence. I looked down at the entry again.

'Rene, is Fanny someone you know? A friend?'

'A friend?' she yelled, then said something in Yiddish. 'Would I curse a friend?'

'Rene,' said Alter gently. 'Fifty-two years is long enough for curses. Let her rest in peace.'

She raised her fists and banged them against her head with terrible violence. 'Never!' she screamed. 'Never!'

'O God!' I gasped. 'Rene, what's got into you?'

'Phil, Phil, Phil!' She rocked backwards and forwards, moaning and lamenting. I jumped up and poured out a glass of the wine with trembling hands and held it to her lips. She waved me aside. I gulped it down.

'Phil's alive,' I burbled. 'Will someone tell me what's going on?'

'You've only gone and told poor Rene that her sister is dead,' gloated Kitty, recovering her venomous tongue.

'Oh, no!' I whispered, horrified at my blunder. 'Alter, run and fetch Nurse Goss. She's watching telly in the staff room.'

I helped Goss to get Rene to lie down on her bed with a hot-water bottle. Goss sat with her and told me she'd call me if I was needed, and I hurried back to the buzz of excitement round the table.

'I didn't know,' I said shakily. 'I didn't know that Rene had any family alive. She's always telling me she's the last one left. What dreadful news. Didn't she get on with Fanny?'

'Fanny took her sweetheart away from her,' said Sadie. 'It was Rene's last chance. Fanny was still a young girl, a bad girl, and she could have found another young man.

169

Nu! She had to take from poor Rene. Where's my supper? I haven't had anything to eat since yesterday.'

They all started to nod and mutter about the wickedness of Fanny and how she had forced Rene to languish in a shameful single state. Even Sarah, who taunted Rene daily for being an old maid, let fly a mouthful of curses on the late Mrs Apfel. I felt very sorry for Rene but thoroughly exasperated by their attitude.

'For heaven's sake,' I snapped, 'if Phil and Fanny fell for each other, it doesn't mean they were wicked! They must have been madly in love, and perhaps very distressed about Rene's feelings. These things unfortunately happen in families and among friends. Haven't any of you heard about love and passion?'

Bubba was sitting right up against me and had managed to catch the gist of what was going on.

'Love and passion,' she sneered. 'You don't steal from a sister. You keep busy. You work at the sewing machine and you help Mother with the cooking and cleaning and you put the love and passion on the floor and stamp on it until your turn comes. Didn't your mamma teach you what's right? So you'd take away your sister's only chance? You should be ashamed of yourself, Beattie. I hope that bastard, Fanny, didn't know a moment's happiness with Rene's man!'

Most unusually for me, I lost my temper. 'None of you have got an ounce of imagination!' I shouted. 'Can't any of you remember the meaning of romantic young love? And for your information,' I screamed in Bubba's ear, 'they had fifty-two happy years together!'

'You hear what she's saying? You hear?' Bubba hollered, as if everyone else was deafer than she was. 'A donkey brays with more sense. You think that it's true, because a cheating, stinking gadabout writes it in the paper? What he says ain't worth twopence-ha'penny.'

I looked around at all the faces. Even Alter and Yetta were nodding in agreement.

'All their married life,' said Alter soberly, 'they must

170

have had Rene on their consciences. Well, Fanny is at peace at last. Now her husband will have to suffer alone.'

I stood up. 'There are at least fifty more entries in the dispatches, but I'm not reading any more,' I said spitefully. 'Why should I bother, if you don't believe in the sentiments of the bereaved?'

'Poor Rene; an old maid all her life because of that street woman, Fanny,' said Sarah.

'You're the one who always torments her! Did any of you know Fanny?'

'Know her? Who wants to know her? We know Rene – it's enough. Rene's parents lived in Hackney. You think we know the whole world?'

'You shouldn't malign a person you've never met – especially someone who's dead and can't defend herself. It's not right.'

'Is it right that she took Rene's bridegroom from under her nose? Is it right that Rene lost her chance?'

'It's not so terrible to remain unmarried. It's better than marrying someone who doesn't love you.'

'Love! Listen to her! Who's talking from love?'

'You're not a nice person, Sarah. I'm going to see how Rene is. Here, Alter, you read to them if you want.' I threw the paper over to him rudely.

'I can't see well enough in candlelight.'

'I'll put the light on.'

'No. We'll wait a few minutes. Don't sulk, Beattie. Don't spoil your pretty face.'

The old charmer was irresistible. I made a hideous grimace at all of them, and popped in to see Rene. She was sitting on her bed in her dressing gown. She appeared more composed and was talking to Nurse Goss.

'Fancy reading out Deaths,' said Goss. 'It's morbid, and look what a shock you gave Rene.'

'I'm sorry, Rene,' I said humbly, taking her hand. 'I can't tell you how sorry I am. May I offer you my condolences?'

'It's not your fault,' said Rene with unusual generosity. 'She was dead to me for years. How should you know

171

that I was cursed with a wicked sister – always jealous of me? I was my parents' favourite, and when Phil came to lodge with us, I was his favourite, too. She couldn't stand it, that he wanted to marry me and not her, so she schemed and plotted to take him away from me. I came home and showed her my wedding shoes; she looked at them; she looked at me. You know what she said?'

'No, Rene.'

' "Phil and I love each other. He wants me and I want only him. He'll never marry you. Please try to forgive me." That's what she said! I screamed, hit her with my shoes, but she sat like a ghost, staring at the wall. My mother, God rest her soul, pulled her round the room by her hair, cursing her, while Father ran to fetch the Rabbi and call Phil from the workshop. He looked at me as if he didn't know me no more. He went straight to Fanny and put his arms about her. You know what he said?'

'No, Rene.'

'He said, "I will marry her, and no one else, rabbi or no rabbi, permission or no permission; blessings or curses, I don't care. And if anyone lays a finger on her, I will burn the house down." She was a witch, Beattie. She cast a spell on my poor Phil. My father said, "You will marry her over my dead body. Take your things and yourself from my home!" Then Phil told Fanny to get her coat. Of course I tried to make peace. My poor Phil had no family to go to, and I implored my parents to let him stay. Fanny was the bad one who had cast her evil eye on Phil. They should throw her from the house and let her live on the street where she belonged. But the rabbi said, no, that they must not do! A daughter is a daughter. He would find other lodgings for Phil and we should all calm down and wait a few months. Then the slut told them she was expecting Phil's baby, so she was sent to my Auntie Landis and they got married from there. Of course, it was a lie. I always knew what a liar she was!'

'You mean she wasn't expecting a baby?' asked Goss.

'Phil wasn't like that!'

172

I was beginning to wonder what Phil *was* like, but daren't ask. 'Did your parents keep in touch with her?'

'I got sick. Every time her name was mentioned, I fainted,' boasted Rene. 'My health was ruined. My parents gave the rabbi strict orders that they were never to come to the house again.'

'Did you know where they lived?'

'Who cared where she lived? Phil was the best tailor in Hackney. He opened his own workshop, and the witch worked with him. He made a good living and after a year or two, they went to live in a fancy flat in Stamford Hill. They used to send money and presents to my parents and once a picture of the baby, but I threw it on the fire. Before Mother died, she would sometimes cry out for her, but she was very confused. Fanny tried to come to the funeral. I told my father he would have to bury me too, if she showed her face. He knew what was right. When my poor father was sick in the hospital, she found out and sneaked in to see him when my back was turned. She was always evil and sly. He died without ever forgiving her. She used to send me letters and messages, but I always threw them on the fire.'

'How dreadful!'

She misunderstood me.

'Dreadful! Wicked! Bad! She ruined my life!'

'Did Phil know it wasn't his baby?' asked Goss. For a few moments Rene stopped rocking and sat quite still.

'How should he know – an innocent, respectable boy? What did he know from a cat from the gutter? I want to go back into the sitting room, now. I want to be with my friends. I only had one cake.'

Nurse Goss walked her back slowly. Everyone greeted her with sympathy, warmth and affection. 'Rene, come and sit by us. Are you feeling better? That such a thing should happen to you! Terrible! Terrible!'

I made a fresh pot of tea, loaded the plates with buns, then called through the hatch to Alter to help me carry the trays.

'Alter,' I hissed. 'Mr Apfel is a member of your synagogue. Do you know him?'

'A man came this evening to say the Kaddish for his wife. It could be him.'

'Do you think he'll come again?'

'Naturally he'll come again. The Kaddish is a mourner's prayer. He must repeat the prayer at Synagogue every day for a year.'

'That means he lives round here.' I grabbed the telephone book and shuffled through the pages. 'Here! Apfel P., Number five, The Links. That's Millionaire's Row, alongside the golf course. If you cut across the park, it's not ten minutes' walk away! I wonder if Rene knows! I wonder if she took it in that he's a member of the local synagogue! My God! She's been living practically on top of her sister ever since she came to The Haven! How bizarre!'

'Best not say anything to her just now. She's had enough of a shock for one evening.'

'Do you think Fanny knew – and Phil? He must be rolling in money to live round here. They might even have *been* here – to one of the garden parties! They may have been just a few feet away from Rene without any of them knowing! How strange! How sad! Alter, maybe Fate is telling us that Phil and Rene should meet after all these years. What do you think?'

'Who knows what to think? Let us leave it in the hands of the Almighty.'

The folks were calling for their tea.

'If we left everything in the hands of the Almighty, they wouldn't get their tea tonight. For heaven's sake, Alter!' Sometimes he could be most exasperating.

'I'll offer my condolences to Mr Apfel at morning service, and introduce myself as his neighbour. Later on, I may mention to him that Rene lives here. The Almighty will guide me.'

We walked through with the trays. Nurse Goss was sitting at the table, joining in giving sympathy to Rene who seemed to be enjoying herself. I told Goss I needed a breath of fresh air and that I'd be back to help her get the folks to bed. I slipped on my coat, and went out into the dark, chilly air.

Number 5 was a beautiful bungalow set in enormous grounds. The driveway was lit up by lamps leading from the gate to the front door and a Mercedes was parked there. Mr Apfel had done well since the days when he lodged in an East-End tenement as a young immigrant lad, and fell in love with the wrong sister. Poor old Rene!

I helped to get the folks to bed, then joined Yetta and Alter in their flat for a Friday night tot of brandy. I mentioned to them that I'd seen the house; that poor Rene never had visitors, and that she might now want to become acquainted with her sister's family.

'After you went out, she told Alter she'd like to meet Phil again,' said Yetta.

'So she knows he's a member of the local synagogue?' I felt a little scared, but didn't know why.

'Rene don't miss anything, Beattie. She listens to the dispatches with her ears, eyes and nose.'

'She asked me to invite him in to The Haven after the service, for a drink,' said Alter carefully.

'Well then! The Almighty is pointing the way for you!'

'But she asked most particularly, that I shouldn't mention her name.'

'Maybe she wants to surprise him. There isn't much excitement in Rene's life. She gets one lousy letter a month from her bank and no personal visitors from one year to the next. There's no harm in her wanting to surprise her old flame.'

'Rene can be very spiteful,' said Yetta softly, 'but she did promise Alter that she wouldn't say anything bad about Fanny. She swore on her mother's grave.'

Alter sighed. 'Maybe it will help her to get over her bitterness. It has soured her life and sickened her soul.'

Rene and I suffer from the same disease, I thought to myself. I smiled at the two old people so dear to me; dearer since their marriage four months ago. They had both suffered pain, loneliness, bereavement and hardship,

175

but never the sickness of the soul that devoured Rene and me. Perhaps Alter had once, but he had recovered. What was their secret? Why couldn't I learn it?

'I'm like Rene,' I said, turning my head away from their bright faces.

'Nonsense, Beattie,' said Alter, refilling my glass, 'you're nothing like her.'

'And never will be,' said Yetta. 'Don't talk silly!'

They smiled at each other. Who was I to remind them about love? 'Maybe Phil and Rene . . . when he's recovered from Fanny's death, of course,' I added quickly. 'Wouldn't it be romantic?'

Yetta gave me one of her looks. I laughed; got up to go, and joined Nurse Goss in the staff room to watch the late night movie on Channel 4.

I didn't sleep well. The guest room was very comfortable, but I missed Frank, and the thought of Fanny, totally rejected by her family, haunted me. What was in those letters she had written to Rene? Had she begged for forgiveness; asked to be reinstated as a sister? Fanny was dead. No one would ever know. Would Phil be glad to see his sister-in-law after all these years?

Alter, Boris and Olga were due back from the Sabbath morning service at midday, and if the weather was reasonable, Yetta usually walked up to the seat, about thirty yards along the road, to meet them. It was a mild, bright morning and she trotted off. From where she sat, she could see me on the pavement, outside The Haven, and had a good view of the road as far as the main junction, which was hidden from me by the tree-lined curve. We arranged a signal, so that I'd know whether Alter was walking along with someone. I must have run out half a dozen times, until, at last, I saw Yetta waving her hanky in her right hand. Phil Apfel was with them! Maybe they were walking along with someone else though! Alter and the Skolnicks were very friendly; they often walked home with one or two other people! Perhaps their companion wasn't Mr Apfel. Rene was sitting on the bench in the

176

hall, a black scarf on her head. She appeared quite calm. What else?

What was it about her that made me afraid? The stillness! Her eyes gazed unblinkingly ahead fixed on an invisible object with horrid fascination.

'Rene,' I said softly, 'are you okay?' She didn't move or answer. 'Alter, Olga and Boris are coming. They've got someone with them.' I hoped fervently, vainly, that their companion was not Phil Apfel.

'It's Phil,' she said, in a voice that made me jump stupidly.

'He's not expecting to see you. He'll be in a low state. The shock might be too great for him. Why not join the folks on the verandah and let me or Alter tell him you live here, so he'll be prepared?'

'Was I prepared, when he ran off with my wicked sister?' she asked coldly. 'I am staying here.'

I shivered. 'He's an old man; a bereaved old man.'

'And I'm a bereaved old woman.'

'What are you staring at?'

'Her. Go and open the door.'

I peeped through the spy-hole in the front door. Yetta and Olga were walking up the drive, arm in arm, followed by Alter and Boris, on either side of the visitor. I turned back to Rene.

'Please, Rene, don't sit here in the hall.' I took her arm.

She elbowed me in the stomach. *'Open the door!'*

I opened it.

'Beattie, this is our neighbour, Mr Apfel. We've asked him to join us for a little refreshment.'

'Good Shabbos, Mr Apfel. We read of your sad loss in the *Jewish Chronicle* last night. I'm very sorry. I wish you long life.' Alter had taught me that this was the customary greeting one always gave Jewish people after the death of a close relative.

He clasped my hand. He was no taller than Alter, but broad-shouldered, strong and vigorous for his age. His brown eyes shone suddenly with unshed tears. I took his coat and hung it on the hall-stand while he removed his spectacles and wiped them on a snow-white handkerchief. His suit was elegantly and expensively tailored.

'Thank you. I can only stay a few minutes. My children are waiting for me at home, but I couldn't refuse such a kind invitation.'

Yetta and Olga disappeared into the cloakroom. I longed to follow them.

'Come through to the sitting room. Boris, will you pour the drinks please? Everything's ready on the sideboard.'

He gave me a mock salute and bustled off. Alter put his hand under Mr Apfel's elbow. My knees were like jelly. I forced myself to turn round. Rene was still sitting on the bench but now she was looking at Mr Apfel.

'Rene,' said Alter, 'this is Mr Apfel – Mr Philip Apfel. I believe you once knew each other.'

'Rene! I don't think so. The only Rene I ever knew was my wife's late sister.' He was a little confused, but who could blame him.

'Your late wife's sister,' I gabbled idiotically. 'Rene has been extremely distressed by the news of her death. Of course they hadn't seen each other for years, but nevertheless . . .'

'Poor Fanny!' sobbed Rene. 'My poor little sister! If only I'd known she was ill! If only . . . Oh, Phil, this is terrible, terrible!' There was a wariness, a watchfulness in her eyes, which were as dry as mine, no matter that she dabbed at them with the corner of the black head-scarf.

Mr Apfel's face had turned as white as paper. He swayed, then steadied himself with his hand resting against the wall. 'Who? Who is this?' He spoke in a scarcely audible, quavery old whisper, but Rene seemed to hear quite well.

'Remember me? Remember your Rene – the girl you left behind?' Even at this tense moment, it occurred to me how curious it was that I had known Rene ever since I started working at The Haven, but only now realized

178

how much I disliked her. Doctor Taylor had noticed, though. He'd recognized my aversion almost a year ago.

'Whisky, wine and cake in the sitting room!' Boris announced cheerily.

Rene hooked her skinny arm through Mr Apfel's and propelled him through the door. Yetta and Olga came out of the cloakroom and they and Alter followed. They tactfully joined all the other residents on the verandah while I showed Mr Apfel and Rene to a couple of easy chairs conveniently placed near the serving hatch, and put a tray next to them. I served the others quickly. I didn't want them traipsing in just yet, disturbing the reunion.

'I'm in the kitchen preparing lunch, Rene,' I called out. 'Bang on the hatch if you need anything.'

I stood as still as a mouse at the other side of the hatch, hoping against hope that they would talk in English and not Yiddish. He spoke without a trace of an accent, unaware that I could hear every word.

'Who could have told Fanny such a falsehood? Who could have been so wicked; so callous as to tell her that her only sister had passed away! Who? Why? Why? I was in Philadelphia with Saul – a business trip – and when we returned, she was most unwell. The shock of hearing that she had lost you – her only sister – grieved her terribly. She never fully recovered. She became so agitated when I tried to talk about it – about you – that I thought it best not to mention the matter again. If only we'd known you were alive and well, I would have made every effort to bring you into our family again. Perhaps my poor Fanny would have rallied. It's too late for her. Too late.'

'Never mind, Phil. Don't upset yourself. She was always very good to me; very charitable. Only last week I received a little money present from her. She always felt she should try to give me something regularly, to make up for what she took away.'

'What are you talking about?' he spoke sharply; shouted. 'Fanny gave you money last week? That's impossible! I've just told you that she thought you were . . . you were no longer alive. This must be very difficult for you Rene, but Fanny was under the impression that . . .'

'I don't like to speak ill of the dead. I'm not made like that. Poor Fanny! I wrote to her; told her I was moving into this Old Age Home and that I was alone; all alone in the world. All I had was her, and I asked if I could visit since we lived so close; see her happy family and make my peace with her. You know what she wrote to me? You want to know what she said?'

'What? When was this?'

'Three years ago. Was that when she made up the story that I was dead? Oh, dear! Oh, dear me! Fancy her telling you that, when I lived so near to her! Wasn't that wicked? My poor Phil! Fanny always found it so hard to tell the truth. She told you lies, Phil; she told you many lies. But I mustn't speak ill of the dead. She was always very generous. She sent me extra money every month as long as I kept away from her. What could I do? I don't go where I'm not wanted.'

'O Fanny! What does it all mean? O God! What does it matter? What does anything matter, now!' I heard him weeping; blowing his nose.

'Doesn't it matter that she lied to you all her life?' said Rene suddenly and terribly.

'Speak of my wife with respect, please. Otherwise, refrain from mentioning her name. Whatever Fanny said to you or about you, there were good reasons.'

'I knew her for what she was. She was a liar. Poor Fanny. She couldn't help herself.'

'I knew you for what *you* were. Thank God I found out in time.' He stood up.

'And did you know *her* for what she was?' Her voice rose in a horrible shriek.

'I knew her as my beloved wife and the mother of my children. Miss! Miss!' he shouted; I came running into the sitting room. 'Would you kindly fetch my coat?'

'Of *all* your children?' Rene sneered. 'Even the eldest, who runs your business for you?'

When I returned with the coat, he was standing in front

of Rene, his face ghastly with pain and hatred. He seemed unaware of me.

'My poor Fanny! My poor, silly little Fanny, allowing you to torment her all these years, and not telling me of it. God took the wrong sister!'

'You did! *You* took the wrong sister!'

'Mr Apfel – your coat. Rene, get the hell out of here,' I snarled at her like a mad dog.

She didn't flinch.

'The arrangements will continue, then?' she asked him.

'Yes.'

'Through my bank. I'll send you the details. You hear, Beattie? You're our witness.'

He was buttoning up his coat. Suddenly he seemed to lose control of himself and grabbed her roughly by the shoulders. 'You wicked woman. You wicked old woman!'

I pulled Rene away from him.

'Saul – your wonderful son, Saul!' she sneered. 'She wrote to me; begged me not to tell. Please, Rene, please! Phil's so proud of him, and the boy worships his father. His father!' She turned away and walked on to the verandah.

I went to the front door with Mr Apfel, then fearful that he might be too upset to get home safely by himself, I slipped on my coat and followed him down the drive. He waved me away, but I continued to walk along with him. He was weeping. As we turned into the park, he stood for a moment, holding his handkerchief against his mouth.

'Whoever thought up this meeting – this joke – wasn't very clever, or very kind.'

'It was Rene. She asked Mr Freid to invite you, and made him promise not to mention her name. We thought she wanted to give you a pleasant surprise. Please believe me.'

'Yes,' he said. 'Yes. I believe you.' We walked along in silence for a minute. 'I'm afraid I didn't catch your name.'

'Beatrice Dwek. I work at The Haven as a general help.'

'Mrs Dwek, my late wife sent money to her sister regularly. For some reason, she didn't tell me, although, of course, I would not have objected. I wish to continue the arrangement and would consider it a favour if you would ask Rene how and where the allowance should be paid. I shall not be seeing her again. This is a personal and private matter and I'd be grateful if you would keep it to yourself.'

'Of course.'

'Thank you. I'll telephone you in due course.'

'Are your children and grandchildren staying with you?' I asked.

'My younger son, Leonard, was here, but he and his family left after the funeral. They'll be down again next weekend. But Saul, Vera and my granddaughter, Lucy, live quite close and are staying with me for a few more days. They'll be wondering where I am. Thank God I have a wonderful family. They meant all the world to my wife.'

We walked along in silence. Despair and wretchedness hung about him like a garment. I couldn't bear it. 'Please, Mr Apfel, may I say something to you about what happened just before? Just a word? Don't let anything Rene said exacerbate your grief. She's a bitter, destructive, lonely old woman and is jealous because her sister had such a happy life with you.'

'I don't understand,' he said. 'The pain she caused my wife hasn't ended with her death. She can cause Saul – me – all of us – great distress.'

'But I do understand. I understand everything.' He stopped; looked at me painfully. His eyes were sharp, intelligent, searching.

'None of us is perfect; we all make mistakes,' he said softly. 'Fanny made a mistake a long, long time ago. She came from an unforgiving family. Did she think that I was unforgiving too? Why didn't she tell me that Rene was torturing her; threatening her all these years? That was Fanny's big mistake.'

'And now you're going to continue it?'

'What can I do? Saul knows nothing.'

182

'Zeida! Zeida!' I looked over his shoulder. A young girl was running across the golf course. He hadn't heard or seen her. Zeida was the Yiddish word for Grandfather. A couple of other girls joined her, and she slowed down, and walked along with them. I was gripped by a strange, inspirational power.

'Is that your granddaughter?' He turned to look. 'The girl on the left in the green jacket?'

He waved, smiled, turned back to me.

'You know her, Mrs Dwek?'

'No. I've never seen her before, but she's so like you. So exactly like you.'

No one had ever scrutinized me more closely. I didn't flinch.

'This is Lucy, my son, Saul's daughter.' We smiled at each other. Her two companions shouted a greeting and walked off.

'Zeida, where've you been? Mum and Dad thought you'd got lost.'

'Unmistakable, Mr Apfel,' I said very softly as we shook hands.

'I *was* lost, darling. Just for a few minutes – I had a lot on my mind.' She put her arm round him. 'Then Mrs Dwek came along and put me right.'

For a few moments I watched them walking along the footpath, hand in hand. I hadn't told Nurse Goss I was going out, and the folks would be waiting for their Shabbos lunch. I turned and ran back to The Haven, and as usual was met by complaints.

'Sorry, folks. Why not have another drink? I'll have the grub on the table in ten minutes flat. Alter, here a minute! How's Rene?' I said, crowding the table with plates and cutlery.

'Much, much better, thank God. She's been telling Yetta and Olga how glad she is to have seen Phil after all these years, and that she's forgiven her sister, Fanny. All the old bitterness has gone because of that meeting. But as for your romantic ideas – I'm sorry to disappoint you, Beattie! She doesn't want to see Mr Apfel again. The

Almighty has helped her to come to terms with her problems at last. He always shows us the right way.'

Rene and Yetta came over to help set out the bread rolls and napkins.

'Nurse Goss was looking for you,' said Rene. 'I told her you'd walked home with Phil. She wanted to know what he was like. Well, I told her like I'm telling you, that I'm glad I didn't marry him. He isn't the sort of man I thought he was. Poor Fanny!

'You've been out a long time,' she added suspiciously.

'To tell you the truth, Rene, we got a bit lost by the golf course, but then the Almighty turned up and showed me the way.'

13

The Thaw

Towards the end of February there was a slight thaw; a touch of warmth in the iron-cold air. It had been a long, hard winter. Sarah had some errands to do, so I succumbed to her nagging and cursing, padded her up with two hot-water bottles and a mountain of blankets and shawls, and pushed her down the road to Waitrose's. On the way home, I questioned her maliciously about her purchases.

'What do you want with a bottle of vinegar and two bags of cooking salt? And why buy matches when you don't smoke, or sanitary towels when you don't . . . when you don't even remember what they're for? I hope that the check-out girl didn't think I was related to you.'

'May you lie deep in the earth,' answered Sarah.

It started to snow – a drizzly, watery snow – and I pulled the waterproof cover over her and balanced the huge umbrella on top of her head, and she remained dry and cosy, while I got drenched. The weather wasn't doing my frozen shoulder a bit of good; nor was pushing the wheelchair up the hill. As we rounded the bend I saw the Rolls parked behind my car outside The Haven. I was so astonished that I must have involuntarily jerked my muscles and a dreadful pain shot through my neck and down to my elbow. The owner was unmistakable; the ostentatious number plate – GOT 1 – still in place. I swung the chair sharply to the left, and cut down the narrow track which led to the play-park, and sat on a swing conveniently situated under a dripping tree. I found a crumpled cigarette in my overall pocket.

'Could I trouble you for a light, please, Sarah?' I asked humbly. She raked around in her rag-bag and struck a match expertly with her one hand. I managed to make contact at the third attempt.

'What you shaking for? You seen a ghost?'

'Yes,' I said.

'You see a ghost an hour before you die. All my brothers and sisters saw ghosts before they died. "I seen a ghost, Sarah!" Each one of 'em said that, then died an hour later.'

I swung to and fro, smoking, trying to control my agitation; to examine the reason for it. What was he doing at The Haven? Why had he come? I ground my cigarette into the wet gravel and shoved the chair through the slush, back on to the pavement.

'Tell Goss you've got the chills and could do with a tot of brandy to revive you. I'm going mad with this damned pain in my shoulder.'

'And who gave you leave to take a frail old lady out in the snow?' yelled Nurse Goss, as I settled Sarah in her armchair and placed her lunatic purchases within easy reach, on the swivel table. There's something about the way she says 'and' when she thinks she's got one over me, that drives me into a frenzy.

'Perhaps you'll be good enough to fetch the brandy,' I answered calmly.

'Quick! Brandy!' croaked Sarah. 'I saw a ghost!'

I managed to swallow it while Sarah sent Goss for a heart tablet, then she got to work, filling a pre-war stocking with salt, which she first spread out on a burning hot oven tray I brought at her behest. She used a teaspoon so as not to waste a grain. When Goss returned, she told her in picturesque detail what she could do with the heart pill. You can't call Sarah a frail old lady and hope to get away with it. I went into the kitchen again and brought her a jug of boiling water. I didn't bother to ask her what she wanted it for. I had enough on my mind.

'And the buzzer's been going non-stop. Just wait until Matron hears . . .'

'Hears what?' I asked, sharp as a jagged lump of ice. 'That Sarah needed to get out for a breath of fresh air

186

after being cooped up for three solid months? That she had urgent shopping to do? That she was warm and dry and cheerful during the entire time we were out? It's coming back in here and seeing *you* that gives her the shivers! I can think of two – no, three – little items of news that Matron would be agog to hear, about your . . . but I wouldn't stoop to such behaviour.'

I had no idea what I was talking about, but I know from experience that every one of us has something to hide. For a painful moment, I wondered if Professor Gottleib had forgotten himself and had said something to Matron. Betrayed me. Goss was looking at me with a peculiar expression on her face: fear and suspicion, with a dash of hatred for extra flavour. I pushed my fingers through my sopping hair, braced my good shoulder and knocked at the office door.

'It's me, Matron! Beatrice Dwek!' I called idiotically. He would almost certainly be in there with her, and perhaps he, too, needed a few moments' warning to enable him to hide any sign of recognition. Instead of her usual, exasperated 'Come *in!*' she responded with a flirtatious 'Hel*lo* there!' which was singularly nauseating. She was alone.

'Our Honorary Medical Officer, Professor Gottleib, is here. I gather you're acquainted with him, Beatrice!' she lilted archly. 'I was most surprised when he asked after you. He mentioned that he and your husband worked on a project together, concerned with the brain-waves in chronically depressed patients. You never told me. I wonder why that should be! After all, he is a most eminent and well-known personality! Fancy your husband . . . ! Does he mix with him socially?'

She really had sunk low, even for her. Of course I knew what the loathesome snob was on about. How could a worthless old drudge like me be married to a PhD, who mixed with the likes of Professor Gottleib? She made me sick. My contempt for her grew, as hers for me diminished. I couldn't resist giving her a poke in the eye.

'Unfortunately, yes,' I said. 'They drink together at

Dirty Doreen's at least once a fortnight. There's nothing eminent or distinguished about him when Frank drags him home, half cut, and he's worse than Doctor Taylor when it comes to an easily available woman.' For a few moments I toyed with the question of who liked me best: Nurse Goss or Matron, alias Mistress Taylor. It needed pondering over. 'What was it you wanted to see me about?'

'Drop everything you're doing – or rather, not doing – and prepare the guest room. A very difficult and disturbed patient is expected, arriving from Sandy Banks with a student of Professor Gottleib's. Apart from her mental instability, she is well, strong and active, but needs rest and quiet, and it would therefore be preferable if you had as little to do with her as possible. There will be no need for you to make her an excuse for neglecting your work. I want a table set in the staff room for them, and a tray prepared for two – for Professor Gottleib and myself – the silver service, if it isn't in too disgusting a state. Bring it to my flat five minutes after you hear the buzzer, instead of three quarters of an hour. And close the guest room door when you vacuum. Professor Gottleib drove straight here from his clinic and is resting in my sitting room.'

The guest room is on the ground floor, next to the garden door. I keep it clean and aired and the bed there is always made up. There's a radio and a small telly with a bedside control panel, a couple of chintzy armchairs, a wardrobe, bookshelf, chest of drawers and a coffee table – and even a private shower room. The windows open out on to the verandah and the walls are primrose yellow. There's a picture hanging there of a rural snow scene, by a Victorian artist I've never heard of. I love that picture. It is brimming with life and gaiety and humour, and every character in it seems to be telling his own story. When I go in to flick a damp cloth around for ten minutes every week, I usually spend nine of them leaning against the back of one of the chairs, looking at *Winter in the Country*. I sleep in the guest room on the occasional Friday night, when Goss is on duty by herself, but it is never used by permanent residents of The Haven; it is exclusively for people who need looking after on a temporary or emergency basis. Perhaps the family have gone on holiday, or a devoted daughter is cracking up. Sometimes a guest arrives quite suddenly, when the husband or wife – the more vigorous partner, as a rule – has been admitted to hospital or has died. The guest room is a sad room, no matter how merrily the people in the snow shout and caper.

I trundled in with the vacuum cleaner and a handful of rags. Even if I left the door open, Professor Gottleib couldn't possibly hear the racket from as far away as Matron's flat. It was typical of her carping, commonplace little mind to hand out ridiculous orders. Professor Gottleib was stretched out on the bed, his head propped on his hand. He made signs for me to shush and close the door behind me, then he unfolded himself and stood up.

'Well, Beattie?' he said, taking the dusters away from me and shaking hands.

'Very well, Professor Gottleib,' I smiled. 'Not all cakes and ale exactly, but at least the table isn't groaning exclusively with gloom and desolation. Two steps forward; one step back. It must be five or six months since we last met, but I often think of you. I read all your articles, and every time I see you on the telly, or hear you on the radio, I get the urge to write and tell you how much I value your opinions – and to thank you for all you did for me. But I never wrote. I never said "thank you". I'm glad to have the opportunity of doing so now. How are *you*?'

'Two steps forward, three steps back – on a good day. You don't attend group therapy any more, either, do you? And I thought we'd agreed to see each other every three months, in spite of your discharge.'

'I decided it was time to go it alone, Professor Gottleib,' I said.

He nodded, but said nothing for a few moments.

'But that's not why I'm here. Don't worry! I was most discreet and circumspect with the matron as to how we knew each other, and explained about Frank being a one-time colleague and an old friend. She showed me in here as I wanted to see where my patient would be staying; then she said you'd be coming in to clean up. She invited me to rest in her flat, but I decided to wait here for you. She has a most oppressive personality – a stupid woman, I think. How have you managed to stick it out with her?'

'I must have been hooked by the time Matron Tinker left. I keep hoping she'll be back one day, when she's completely recovered. This one's a totally different kettle of fish, but there's something to be said for confronting real, honest-to-goodness mutual dislike. It keeps the claws sharp and the streak of malice strong and bright. I had a good time telling her a few unwholesome lies about you just before. I hope you don't mind.'

I told him how I'd maligned him, and why. He laughed and promised to back me up. Professor Gottleib was so balanced; so confident. He didn't give a damn what people thought of him.

'I heard from the Welfare Board that Matron Dixon has applied for and been accepted for a post in Nottingham starting in September. Are you in touch with Miss Tinker?'

'Yes! We talk on the telephone practically every week. Oh, you don't know what it would mean to the residents to have her back again!'

'So you'd recommend her, eh, Beattie?'

'Very highly!'

'Then let me have her address and telephone number some time this afternoon. How long have you been working here? Two years?'

'Yes. Two whole years! I don't know how I would manage without them – the residents, I mean. They've become my friends; my allies; my family . . .'

'Your children?' asked Professor Gottleib.

'No,' I said. 'Old people die.'

'And children don't?'

I ignored him.

'It's hard when it happens. Sometimes it's so dreadful that I feel I'll never get over it. But I do.'

'How? How do you get over it?'

'I write,' I said, 'about my experiences here at The Haven. Incidents that have touched me concerning the old people, and the share that I have in their lives – or have had. I've discovered it helps me to come to terms with what's inevitable. Afterwards, I'm ready to carry on again.'

'And the experience that brought us together? That brought you here? Have you written about that?' I shook my head, picked up a duster and flicked it at the window sill.

'You've not come here to listen to the further outpourings of Beatrice Dwek, Professor Gottleib,' I said. 'Your cup runneth over with them. I've got to fix this room for your patient. She'll be here soon.'

'I want the room left as it is. Stop waving that venomous rag about, and sit down. There's a buzzing in my ears. Can you hear it, too?'

'It's Matron with her finger on the call button. She'll be coming in here, looking for me. I'll leave you to rest in peace, but I think she'll want you to join her for coffee and sandwiches in five minutes. Make if fifteen if you can. I haven't got anything ready.'

I had my hand on the door handle when she burst in, cracking the vacuum cleaner with the door. It could quite easily have been my foot. She really was quite unbalanced in her behaviour towards me.

'Do you realize,' she shrieked, 'that Professor Gottleib and I have important and private matters to discuss, and that the coffee and tray have not been prepared?'

Never in a million years did I ever dream that I would ever feel compassion for that detestable woman; yet I did. Too late, she saw him lolling on the guest room bed, and turned first putty-grey, and then brick-red.

'I never drink coffee, thank you. I'm surprised Mrs Dwek hasn't informed you of my preferences.' He turned to me, smiling. 'Haven't you and Frank known me long enough, Beattie? Scotch and soda, if you please, Matron. I'm sure petty cash will reimburse you,' he added, coldly

191

and outrageously. 'And surely you don't seriously think that I would discuss a patient to the exclusion of my colleague, and the staff who will be assisting you in her care? Let's assemble after I have interviewed Miss Margolis. I wonder, would you mind . . . ? I'd rather like to continue a conversation with my old friend, here; in this case, a personal and private one.'

He held the door for her and she scuttled out. He stretched out again, neither gleeful nor sorry for her humiliation. Cool. Professional. The tonic he gave me had a curiously bitter taste. Professor Gottleib hadn't changed.

He gestured towards the armchair and I took the cigarette and light he offered.

'It's fortuitous, as it happens, that you're here, Beattie. I want to talk to you about this patient of mine.'

'I'm the menial here. It isn't protocol.'

'Behave like a menial, then, and don't presume to tell me what is and what is not protocol. The matron's going to insist that someone remains on duty while she and her staff are closeted with me in her office. We don't have to be very astute to guess who that someone will be. Now be quiet, and show some servility.' He moved to the other armchair and sat facing me. 'Early this morning, Bertha Margolis, an unmarried lady in her sixties, hitherto of impeccable character, attacked her lifelong friend and companion, violently and brutally, while staying at the Sandy Banks Holiday and Cultural Centre. They had travelled from their home in Israel to attend a series of lectures on the plight of Soviet prisoners, and they were due to give a talk to the gathering, on their personal experiences, towards the end of next week. Last night, guests sleeping in the adjacent room were roused by the commotion, and the victim, Miss Rosa Kagan, is recovering in the sick bay there. She is very badly bruised and suffering from shock, yet despite her injuries, and the fact that Miss Margolis was forcibly restrained from continuing to beat her, Rosa insists that she started the fight by provoking her friend beyond human endurance.

'The organizer of the symposium is a personal friend

of mine, and because of the peculiar and bizarre circumstances, he sought my advice. I suggested that Miss Margolis be persuaded to come here for a few days, so that I can try to assess the situation, and, I hope, help her. Ah! Our whisky at long last! Only one glass? Fetch another one, please.'

He stood up and walked around the room until Nurse Goss returned, then dismissed her with a curt 'thank you', poured the drinks and handed me one.

'Do you know what sparked off the attack?' he continued, as if there had been no interruption. 'Due to some error in the allocation of rooms, the two friends had to share – something they've never done during the many years they've lived together – and Rosa couldn't sleep because of Miss Margolis's loud snoring. She has a broken nose which affects her breathing. After enduring a sleepless night, she apparently complained to Miss Margolis, who then turned on her violently. Ever since, so I gather, Miss Margolis has been calm, entirely without interest or curiosity as to the welfare of her friend, and has expressed no sorrow, no remorse and no explanation for . . .'

. . . 'Beatrice Dwek; the jury has found you Not Guilty of the attempted murder of Edmund James Prescott. However, it is little short of a miracle that he survived your frenzied attack on him, and you might well have been standing before this Court on a very grave charge. Due to the tragic circumstances which motivated this savage assault, and after listening to the evidence of Professor Gottleib, I direct that you undergo treatment on his recommendation, until such time as he considers you to be . . .'

I should never have carried the vacuum cleaner with one hand. I must have wrenched a muscle in my frozen shoulder, and a sickening, clawing pain shot through it. I stood up and leaned against the back of the chair, trying to focus on *Winter in the Country*, working my way into it; longing to be part of its carefree gaiety and merriment.

'Excuse me for interrupting you, Professor Gottleib,' I said. 'I must go in search of my pain-killers. This shoulder is giving me hell today. It's probably due to shoving vacuum cleaners and wheelchairs around. Miss Margolis couldn't be in better hands. I should know.'

I walked to the door, but he was there first, blocking my way. A shameful, not unpleasant thought flashed through my mind that he was going to kiss me and a hot, pre-menopausal flush suffused my face and neck. He held my head between his hands and looked at me with passionless appraisal.

'The pain-killers will not help you, Beatrice Dwek,' he said softly, 'because it is not *your* shoulder which torments you. You carried the vacuum cleaner in your left hand, and yet the pain is in the right scapula.' His hand stroked my upper arm, then moved to my neck. His fingers felt like icicles. 'And what is this stiffness; this tension here? Have you a panacea for that, too? We've travelled a long way together, Beattie, but there's still considerable mileage to cover.'

I removed his hands and backed away from him. I hated the words he used, and felt that I would faint with the pain.

'The shoulder is *mine!*' I said harshly. 'I strained it and the joints around it are swollen and inflamed. My painkillers, my *extremely effective* pain-killers, are in my friend's bag, and if I don't go now, and swallow a few, and then get on with my work, I'll lose my job as well as the use of my arm!'

He stood aside, and I hurried into the sitting room.

Sarah had filled two stockings with hot salt and tied them together like giant sausages. She'd soaked the sanitary towels in hot water and vinegar and strung them into a chain. She was as mad as a hatter.

'My pain-killers are in your bag, Sarah. May I take them out?'

'I threw them down the toilet, fool. I know better from pills and doctors. I make poultices. I just made them hot again. Kneel down, or you won't be able to move tomorrow.'

'You wicked old devil! I'd like to wring your scraggy

194

neck!' I hissed at her, but I did as I was told, mindful of the pimple I once had on my chin, and suffered her capable fingers to poke around my shoulder. She instructed me to place the chain of pads across my chest, like the Order of the Garter, then tied the stocking-sausage round my neck, bringing the ends up in a half-throttle. I pulled my overall back on, and ran to answer the front doorbell for Miss Margolis and her escort – my old enemy, Velvet. If they wondered why they were assailed by an overpowering smell of vinegar, or bemused by my stocking-scarf, nothing showed on their faces. Velvet smiled and tactfully made out we'd never met before. He introduced Miss Margolis to me, and she held out her hand.

'I'm Beattie, the dogsbody. I'm very pleased to meet you. Do come in. I'll take you through to Matron.'

'Would you mind showing me the bathroom first?'

I directed Velvet to the office and Miss Margolis followed me, asking good-humouredly whether I cleaned the floor with vinegar. She had a strong foreign accent, but spoke with ease and fluency. I told her it was my new perfume, and why I was wearing it.

'It was a popular remedy for aches and pains in the village where I grew up. You'll feel much better in two or three weeks.'

I handed her a clean towel and told her I'd take her suitcase to her room, then come back for her.

'Don't go. I won't be a moment.'

She disappeared into one of the cubicles, and I looked in the mirror, adjusting Sarah's contraption. The front of my overall was already stained and wet. Miss Margolis joined me and washed her face and hands, then opened her handbag and drew out a comb. Her thick-lensed spectacles lay on the shelf above the wash-basin, and I knew she couldn't see me watching her slyly. Her face was lined, but the flesh was firm, the skin clear, and her eyes were a deep, glorious grey. Her hair was thick, dark and naturally wavy, shot with one streak of white. She pulled the comb through it carelessly, without vanity or affectation, as if the fact that she had once been beautiful had long been forgotten or ignored. The catastrophic slant of her nose marred the symmetry of her features, but when she replaced her glasses, they almost succeeded in camouflaging it. We smiled at each other through the mirror, and then she turned to me, pulling up the collar of her jacket as if she was about to go out again, into the cold. I remembered how icy her hand felt when we'd been introduced.

'You'll soon be warm,' I said. 'The heating at The Haven is always turned up to boiling point, and your room is very pleasant and comfortable – the nicest in the house.'

'Will I be sharing with anyone?'

'No. Everyone here has her own room. I'll take you now, if you like. We can get to it through the side door.'

We went into the hall. I picked up the suitcase. She tried to help me, but I still had one strong arm and we made it, unobserved, to the guest room. I showed her the bell-pull, and where to hang her clothes.

'I know Professor Gottleib is anxious to talk to you. I'd better go and tell him where you are. Here's the whisky we didn't manage to finish. Would you like a drink to warm you up until I fetch you something more substantial?'

'No, No, thank you, Beattie. May I call you that? Bertha's my first name. Give me two or three minutes – to adjust to my surroundings.'

'I'll tell Professor Gottleib to dawdle.'

She took a step towards me and held out her hand as if wanting to detain me.

'Just pull the bell twice if you need me.'

To my amazement, she took hold of it and did just that, then stood looking away from me, her hands hanging by her sides. I had never seen anyone so forlorn or so desolate. I was already halfway out of the door, but I came back, closed it behind me, and took her hands in mine. They were still cold, and I felt I touched a wound, so grievous and so palpable, that the anguish of it infected me, and rose in my throat and eyes, as if unaccountably, I recognized a need greater than my own.

'I was once all alone, just like you,' I said. 'Bewildered, frightened and cold. My feelings and actions didn't belong to me. I was a total stranger to myself. I thought I was the only person in the world experiencing this horror, and no one could possibly rescue me from it. But Professor Gottleib did. He helped me through the most dreadful period of my life, and because of him I began to understand why – what I was feeling – and to recover the person who used to be me. I'm on your side, Bertha,' I babbled foolishly. 'Always. And so is Professor Gottleib. I talk too much. I'm sorry. I'll see you later – or tomorrow.'

'I look forward to hearing you talk too much,' she smiled.

Professor Gottleib was standing outside the guest room, probably eavesdropping, but I felt strangely elated and didn't bother to rap his knuckles. I spent the rest of the afternoon being at everyone's beck and call and preparing the suppers. Professor Gottleib stayed with Bertha in the guest room for ages, then he and Velvet had a conference with Matron and Nurse Goss in the staff room. I was on the point of banging on the door to inform them that I had a home to go to, when Goss emerged and said she'd take over. Matron wanted to see me.

'Ah, Beatrice!' said Matron winningly. 'We wish to speak to you about your duties tomorrow.'

'I'm sorry. I'm already late, and I don't have a cook or a skivvy at home. Perhaps you could speak to me about my duties during duty-time – tomorrow.'

She looked daggers at me, but Professor Gottleib stood up before she could say anything.

'We won't keep you,' he said. 'I've told Matron to arrange for temporary help for a few days, so that you're free to keep Miss Margolis company if and when she wants it. She seems to have taken a liking to you, and we want her to be as happy and as relaxed as possible.'

I was so surprised and pleased that I almost smiled, but I caught myself just in time.

'I suggest, Matron, that you ask for two people from the agency. One pair of hands can't cope with what I do here,' I added sourly. 'I'll see you tomorrow, then.'

Of course the place was in chaos when I arrived next morning. No one had turned up to replace me and Goss and Matron were seeing to the breakfasts. I felt most gratified and remembered not to put my overall on or to interfere with their work. I told the folks where to direct their complaints, and that from now on they might learn to appreciate me.

'Since your Miss Margolis doesn't want to mix with the residents, perhaps you'll deign to take a tray into her,' Goss sneered.

'Certainly,' I piled on enough for two and took it to the guest room. Miss Margolis was listening to a music programme and looking at *Winter in the Country*. She looked tired and drawn and obviously hadn't slept well.

'Do you mind if I join you for breakfast?' I asked.

'Please do. Have you the time?'

'Lots of time.' We set everything out on the table. 'I love that picture,' I said, pouring the coffee. 'Especially that kid's scarf with the dropped stitches. His mother probably had the same knitting troubles as my mother. I had one just like it. And the atmosphere is so carefree; so happy.'

'It's a little too romantic for my taste. Have you ever experienced such idyllic pleasure?'

'I'm not sure,' I smiled. 'But the artist makes me believe that I've known winters like that one – when I was young, tobogganing and snowballing with my friends; wearing my raggy blue scarf. Don't you have memories like that, too, Bertha?'

She didn't answer, and I realized I had said something hurtful and tactless. I felt my face redden and we drank our coffee in uncomfortable silence, until I heard her sigh.

'I'm a bitter old woman, Beattie; not wistful, like you. I spent eight years of my youth in a Siberian prison camp – a salutary, totally effective experience for avoiding nostalgia and wishful thinking. Or so I believed,' she added softly. She took off her glasses and bent her head, holding the broken bridge of her nose.

'Eight years!' I gasped. 'Why?'

'For sawing up a fallen telegraph pole – with my friend, Rosa. We and our neighbours had no firewood, and the cold was unimaginable. The law of the land was somewhat capricious. We served our sentences together, and survived – unlike our families who were lost during the war. Not a living soul cared what became of us, but we had each other.'

I tried to swallow my mouthful of toast, but the lump in my throat blocked the way. I held my napkin against my mouth.

'It all happened a long time ago,' said Miss Margolis. 'It's all over; buried in the past. We were among the lucky ones to receive exit visas to Israel fifteen years ago. We made a new life for ourselves; interesting and useful lives, I think. Work we enjoyed; a delightful home in a city we love. What about you? Do you have a family?'

'No.'

'You live alone?'

'I thought you meant do I have children. I live with my husband, Frank, and we have a little grandchild who lives in Brighton – about sixty miles away.'

'A grandchild, but no children?'

'We had a daughter, Gloria. She was killed.'

'How terrible. I'm sorry. I'm very, very sorry. Was her death the cause of the breakdown you told me about? Was that why you had treatment from Professor Gottleib?'

'I don't want to burden you with my troubles,' I said, as briskly as possible.

Miss Margolis looked at me so accurately with her short-sighted, beautiful grey eyes, that I felt that the blur she saw was compensated fully by what she saw within.

'It's just that you have your own preoccupations,' I mumbled.

'I wonder how many times you have said that, Beattie. I wonder how many times you have burdened people with your silence and exclusion; pushed them away from you with the same hackneyed, false reasoning. Please don't do that to me. Please don't push me away, when I need a friend so badly. You told me yesterday that you were on my side. I took that to mean we *were* friends, and that you understood I was on your side, too.'

'Yes,' I said. 'Yes. It's just that . . . I think Professor Gottleib is due in a few minutes, and I'm probably needed in the kitchen. Won't you try some of this marmalade, and have another cup of coffee?'

I fussed about, handing her the rolls, pouring the coffee, feeling deflated and miserable when I had expected to be cheerful; comforting; in charge; exuding trust-worthiness, understanding and confidence. She seemed to droop, as forlorn and as isolated as ever. I told her.

I told her how Edmund Prescott had turned up on my doorstep, a week after he had killed Gloria; carrying a bunch of flowers; weeping; begging forgiveness for what he had done. Expecting it. Expecting to be admitted into our home; to be comforted and forgiven so he could get on with his life, after he had deprived Gloria of hers.

I stood in front of him on the step. I made him tell me exactly how he had opened his car door without looking; without seeing Gloria coming up, alongside, on her bike. I asked him what it felt like, to have pushed my daughter under the lorry. What it felt like, to be a murderer. He said he didn't know. He wasn't a murderer.

I snatched the bunch of flowers, and pushed them into his hateful face, then shoved him backwards down the front steps. He missed his footing and fell on to the path and I stood over him, shrieking that I would find out for myself what it felt like to kill someone.

I meant to kick him to death, but I was wearing my slippers, and even though blood was oozing from his head, he tried to get up. A piece of old gas-pipe had been standing against my dustbin for weeks, but it seemed to me that it had just been placed there for the purpose. I smashed at his right arm and shoulder – the arm that had pushed open the door of the car.

'I'll kill you, you killer! I'll kill you!'

But I didn't. I fractured his scapula. But the police knew I meant to kill him. I told them so. I told them the truth.

'No you didn't,' said Miss Margolis. 'You told them a lie.'

'No,' I said.

'Why didn't you hit him over the head? Why didn't you smash his skull?'

'I wanted him to feel the arm go first. The dustmen jumped over the fence and snatched the gas-pipe before I could finish him off. They'd been promising to take it away for me. They got their timing all wrong.'

I started to laugh. I was laughing so much that I didn't care about Professor Gottleib coming through the verandah window. I just felt a draught; a sort of squeamish shudder.

'He's permanently disabled. He can't drive a car again, and will always suffer pain, I'm glad to say.'

'Just to put the record straight, Miss Margolis, I feel I must tell you that Mr Prescott's shoulder is completely healed, and although he is able to drive a car, he has chosen not to,' said Professor Gottleib calmly. 'Beattie is correct in saying that he will always suffer pain, but that is nothing to do with the injuries she inflicted. Are you still comfortable about my colleague sitting in with us for our session? Good. He'll be here in a few minutes.'

I managed to stop laughing at last. The notion of the dust-men taking the gas-pipe, as promised, struck me as very amusing, although Miss Margolis and Professor Gottleib didn't seem tickled by it. I got up to collect the breakfast dishes and picked up the tray, but I felt so shaky, I had to put it down again. Professor Gottleib led me back to the armchair and Miss Margolis knelt down next to me, chafing my hands. Hers felt much warmer than mine.

'Please stay, Beattie,' she said. She turned to Professor Gottleib. 'I would like my friend to be present.'

'By all means,' he said.

Velvet came in, carrying a chair from the verandah, and

201

placed his recorder on the bedside table. Miss Margolis lay down on her bed. Professor Gottleib sat on the other armchair and I looked at *Winter in the Country*. I looked at it all the time, while Miss Margolis spoke about the labour camp.

She told us how she and Rosa shared everything they had and took care of each other. One day, Rosa was taken violently ill with gastro-enteritis, but nevertheless she was forced to join the working party. The prisoners had been chopping down fir trees, and were loading the timber on to huge sledges. Rosa leaned against the pile of timber for a few minutes, doubled up with pain, while Bertha tried to cover for her, but Rosa was noticed, and brutally pushed and shoved by the bully in charge. Bertha told the guard that she would do her friend's work, as she was very ill, and she should be allowed to go back to the camp for the day. Without any warning whatsoever, the guard hit her full in the face with a truncheon, and broke her nose. Blood poured down her face and she could hardly breathe, and the guard asked if she was still prepared to do Rosa's work. She saw her friend lying in the snow, vomiting. Yes. Rosa was taken back to their hut and Bertha worked in the forest until the second roll call.

For the remainder of her prison term she was only able to breathe through her mouth, and prisoners and guards alike jeered at her and mocked her, calling her the grunting pig with the broken snout, who kept them awake at night – but she had her friend, Rosa, always there, supporting her. They never parted, even after their release, and were on the same emigration quota which left for Israel fifteen years ago. Bertha had several operations there, but remained permanently disfigured. At Sandy Banks, Rosa called her a grunting pig with a broken snout.

'The rest you know,' she said.

No one said a word. I was afraid to clear my throat; even to swallow, in case I broke the silence. I looked at the girl slipping on the ice, caught in the arms of her sweetheart, her little button boots waving in the air, ankles and petticoat revealed; the elderly couple stepping along cautiously, holding on to each other, watching the young lovers wistfully. Remembering. Two little girls screaming with joy, being chased by harum-scarum lads, one of their snowballs hurtling through the air; a split second later, it would knock off the old man's hat. Rosa, crouched against the frozen timber, sweating and sick with fever and pain. Bertha's nose, pouring with blood, staining the snow. And I heard the insult; the horrible, unforgivable insult; knowing that Bertha heard it too. It drowned the laughter of *Winter in the Country* and exploded in the silence.

'Your first quarrel?' asked Professor Gottleib with gross tactlessness, making me jump. 'I hope it will not be the last,' he went on, not waiting for an answer. 'Rosa is here. Her distress is so acute that my friend was afraid for her health, and at her insistence drove her to London early this morning, and brought her to The Haven an hour ago. She cares for nothing but the hope of seeing you, in order to beg your forgiveness. She is bewildered and horrified by what she said to you. I have rarely seen anyone more desperate; in so much pain. The injuries you inflicted are negligible in comparison. They will heal in two or three weeks.' He got up. 'We'll leave you now, Miss Margolis. You need time to yourself to consider what you wish to do. Take as long as you like.'

Velvet turned off the recorder, opened the door quietly and left the room. Professor Gottleib helped me to my feet and steered me towards the window which opened on to the verandah. He picked up a shawl lying there and placed it solicitously around my shoulders, then led me out into the garden.

'We must look after that frozen shoulder,' he said, taking my arm. 'How is it?'

I really disliked the easy way he detached himself from the painful scene we had just witnessed, and launched, without preamble, into the mundane.

'Much better, thank you,' I said coldly.

'Good. What is the name of your pain-killers?'

'Salt and vinegar,' I answered spitefully. 'A well-known cure for aches and pains in Eastern Europe. Surely you've

203

heard of it,' I sneered. 'It's working miracles for me, and that's only since yesterday afternoon.'

'A chip on the shoulder – soaked in salt and vinegar! Well! Well! It sounds edible – if incredible!'

I ignored his feeble attempt at humour, considering his remarks to be the height of bad taste. We walked along the gravel path in silence. The lawn sparkled wet and green under the marvellous sun, only a few patches of dirty snow remaining, but the ice still lay thick and solid on the roof of the little summer house, ahead of us. I thought I heard the guest room bell ring twice, and stopped; turned to go back.

'Bertha's ringing for me.'

'No she isn't. The bell isn't for you. Mind your own business. Come along.'

'Miss Margolis *is* my business!' I snapped. 'I don't like the idea of her being left alone.'

'Then set your mind at rest. Your friend, Velvet, is probably just at this moment showing Rosa into the guest room.'

I felt so shocked, so strangely overcome, that I had to lean against the summer house staring at him in disbelief.

'What!' I gasped. 'How can Bertha bear to look at her again? Do you mean to tell me she's going to forgive her for what she said? How can she?'

'How can Rosa ever forgive herself?' said Professor Gottleib, fielding my question with one of his own. It was an old, mean trick of his. 'What a long, hard winter she has ahead of her! One simply has to wait for a thaw. It can happen quite suddenly. A ray of sunlight; a slight shift in the temperature and the ice in the soul shifts, begins to melt – the process of self-forgiveness is underway. Not Guilty. Well, Beattie?'

A chip of ice fell on to my shawl and bounced off my shoulder. Professor Gottleib pulled me away, and we stood on the lawn, looking up at the sloping roof, as a great, glassy sheet slid slowly towards the edge. The sun shone down on it, shearing it irresistibly with reflected light beams; the brightness stinging my eyes and sending tears pouring down my face like warm rain. A choking, heaving mass of unbearable grief cracked in my chest and tore through my lungs, escaping, racking my whole body with insatiable weeping. He held my head in his arms as the ice crashed down.

'The thaw, Beatrice Dwek,' said Professor Gottleib. 'It's arrived. Once it's begun, there's no stopping it. It's been a long, hard winter.'

14

The Change

'Frank, have you noticed anything different about me?'

'You've put on a bit of weight, but so do most women of your age – and everyone does, after a holiday! A man could still span your waist with his hands, as long as he was built like an octopus. Look! Here's where I fastened my belt before we went away, and now I can't get anywhere near it without doing serious damage. We'll try going on a gentle diet – tomorrow. Pass the strudel.'

Ever since we came back from holiday, I've felt a change in me. It's quite hopeless and entirely unrewarding to discuss anything mystical with Frank. If there isn't a protein, a mineral or an enzyme involved, he panics, and when he panics, he tends to reduce violent inner turbulence, heightened awareness and subtle variation of mood, to the weather or the menopause. Occasionally he resorts to weak-minded flattery, remarking that women are much more intuitive, more finely tuned to atmospheric change, than men, who tend to be unaware of nuances in the psyche or anywhere else.

'Have you noticed anything else?'

'Yes. You haven't smoked since we got home; not in my presence, anyway. Three months, isn't it? I'm proud of you, Beattie. We'll be able to go on a world cruise next year, now you've stopped burning all the money.'

'I'm serious,' I said. 'I wish *you'd* try to be. I'm not talking about giving up smoking or getting fat. Something important, but elusive, is happening to me *within my soul*. It's as if a mischievous spirit had brushed against me carelessly, telling me half a secret which is of enormous significance, and I'm looking for the rest of it. I've felt

206

like this before, but I can't remember where or when. Am I making myself clear?'

'As a mountain stream. Would it count as a betrayal if you told me your spirit's half-secret so that we can work out the remainder and get to bed tonight?'

'I wish you wouldn't patronize me, Frank!' I said irritably. 'I don't *know* what it is, and if I did know, I wouldn't tell you, as all you can do is scoff!'

He stood behind my chair and massaged my shoulders. 'We've both changed. I'll never, never forget our holiday. I felt as if we were eighteen again, and on our honeymoon. We're bound to take a different view of the familiar and mundane and feel disoriented for a time.'

'For a time? We've been home three months! I've left my heart and soul behind, like the poet who saw those mountains in Peru, and never recovered from the experience.'

'You left your troubles behind, too, Beattie,' Frank reminded me. 'I haven't seen you looking so well and relaxed for ages. This is the first real peace of mind we've experienced since Gloria died. Try not to examine all your thoughts and feelings in such microscopic detail.' He bent down and kissed me. 'The holiday's over, but not the honeymoon. Come on. Let's turn in. I'll clear up the pots in the morning.'

'What I'm saying . . .'

'Won't it keep till later?'

'What I'm saying,' I said later, 'is . . . Oh, what the hell! I could murder a cup of tea, sweetheart. Bring in the rest of the strudel as well. We can't start a diet until it's eaten up and done with.'

He brought in a tray and we drank our tea and stuffed ourselves with the remains of my mother's baking, then huddled up together under the duvet and watched the rain slanting past the windows. August in London! The poor tourists! It seemed as if it was only yesterday we were swimming in the Red Sea and walking in the moonlight in summer clothes. We'd spent the whole of April in Israel, half the time as guests of our friends, Bertha and Rosa.

We stayed in their flat overlooking Jerusalem and almost every day we were taken out to places I had hitherto only dreamed of or read about. I loved the contrasts; the noise; the silence; the wildness; the space and grandeur of desert and mountain; the indescribable beauty of the sunrise and sunset; the wonderful variation of people, traditions and language. The way Frank and I shared all our new experiences, marvelling together; talking, laughing, holding hands as if we were a girl and boy again. We never seemed to feel tired; we were never bored. Bertha and Rosa and their friends fascinated us with their knowledge and stories and experiences. Before we went to bed, Frank and I would sit on the balcony in the moonlight with our arms round each other. We'd been so happy.

We toured for the last two weeks of our stay, ending up with a few days by the Red Sea, swimming, boating and snorkelling, and I found time to write in my notebook, sprawled on the beach, while Frank read or snoozed.

'What was the most memorable day of our holiday for you, Frank?'

'The trek through the wilderness on the donkeys with Oz and Uri to see the clinic and being entertained by Abdul in his tent. I felt we went back in time. I think part of *me* is still there, too. Oz told me that Abdul's tribal way of life hasn't changed for about two thousand years, and when the clinic was opened most of the patients came out of curiosity. They'd never seen an ordinary door and didn't know how to open it. And I don't think I'll ever forget Abdul's hospitality. What an experience *that* was!'

'Oh, yes! It was fine for you, supping and gorging yourselves with all the men, while I had to stay with his wives and kids who couldn't understand a word I was saying and never stopped laughing at me, because I couldn't sit cross-legged like them and didn't have fifteen children! While I was being humiliated, I could hear you being vastly entertained. Of course, you had Oz and Uri to translate for you while I had to make do with sign language. I meant to ask you what Abdul said that made you laugh so much. I know it was about me. I heard you say "wife" when you answered him.'

'I don't remember that.'

'Frank Dwek, you're lying! You think I can't see that grin on your face! What lewd remark did that randy old Bedouin make about me? You're not going to sleep until you tell me the truth!'

'Will you shut up, then, if I tell you?'

'Yes.'

'Promise?'

'I promise,' I lied.

'He asked why I didn't take another young wife who could give me sons. I told him it wasn't our custom, and that I was satisfied with the wife I had. He insisted that this was not possible and that he would find a wife for me who could bear sons. Oz warned me that it was impolite to refuse, so I thanked him, and told him I'd been very ill as a young man and no woman, however young and fertile, could give me sons. He got very upset, and offered Oz and Uri a reward if they would cure me at the clinic. He suggested – in erotic detail – a "cure" himself, so Uri had to explain to him the difference between impotence and infertility. The conversation became rather basic, incoherent, bawdy and full of Eastern promise. Good night.'

'And you found – find that amusing? When a man talks disrespectfully about your wife, you laugh like a hyena? How ungallant you are! And Uri and Oz are no better. I really thought they liked and respected me.'

'Of course they did! You know they thought the world of you. But once inside Abdul's tent, we, his guests, had to adjust. We weren't eating cucumber sandwiches and drinking tea with your friend, Miss Whatshername.'

'More's the pity. I hope you remember what a hangover you had.'

'God only knows what his wives mixed in the liquor. No wonder he needs four of them to keep up with him, if he drinks that marvellous stuff every evening! We must write and ask him for the recipe. It had a camel's kick in it.'

'No; not quite. I watched them brew it up in the women's quarters. Camel's sperm and goat's wee-wee. That's why I stuck to coffee. What's the difference between a Western promise and an Eastern promise?'

'Eastern ones are less reliable – but much more agreeable. We've got to be up for work in a minute. Let's get some sleep.'

'Even work's different,' I said. 'The folks – Yetta, Sarah . . . all of them – they sense a change in me. I don't know what or why.'

'Try asking them – and buy a refill pack for your notebook tomorrow. You always sort out your thoughts best on paper and it's the only way I'll get any peace. You haven't written a thing since we came home.'

'Are you actually taking an interest in my writing, Frank? Am I really hearing this?'

'Of course I'm interested! It stops you talking!'

I listened to him pretending to be asleep, then sat up and turned on my bedside light and looked down at his face. My Frank! After all these years, still making light of a subject that had caused him so much personal grief. He caught mumps when he was nineteen, just weeks after I became pregnant with Gloria, and developed serious complications which left him unable to father more children. I'd been frantic about him, and didn't care about anything, just as long as he got well again. Our baby was on the way, and we could always adopt another one if we wanted a bigger family! But the waiting list was so long, and childless couples were given priority. When we became childless ourselves, we had other things on our minds, and I'd have been too old and too batty, anyway, to be considered a worthy parent.

'If Abdul offered *me* a change, plus troops of kids, I would have told him what to do with his hospitality,' I said. I got out of bed and stood by the window, looking at the sodden trees in the avenue. 'Gloria,' I said. 'Gloria! What's the matter with your crazy old mum? *You* know, don't you?' I felt her so close to me, I couldn't help smiling at my reflection in the window.

'Beattie! Come back to bed! What's got into you?'

'I can't sleep.'

'Do you think . . . don't fly off the handle, but do you think it would be a good idea to have a chat with Professor Gottleib? A lot of women have problems adjusting to the Change, especially when it starts rather early: the body's chemistry . . .'

'I don't need *him* any more. *He's* the one riding on three wheels, if you ask me. Can't you do better than talk about chemistry or make ridiculous suggestions?'

'Then perhaps you should see the doctor.'

'Why? I feel perfectly well. Frank,' I said, softening, 'don't worry. I'm not about to have another breakdown, I promise you. I'll sort myself out.' I climbed back into bed and rested my head on his shoulder. 'Stop talking, will you? I'd like to get some sleep.'

'Yetta,' I said, the next day at The Haven. 'Is there something wrong?'

'Not with me,' she answered sourly.

'With me, then?'

'How should I know. I'm not a doctor.'

'You're my friend,' I said. 'Doesn't that count for anything?'

'It does to me.'

'Then why . . . ?'

'Beattie,' said Yetta, 'how long have I known you? How long since you came to work here? Two and a half years nearly?' I nodded. 'All this time we've been friends and shared our troubles. Even my Alter, the best husband in the world, doesn't know from the things you spoke to me about. He understands how close we've always been. You come back from holiday, and straight away I felt the sunshine even though it was cold and raining outside. I'd never seen you so happy; so well. I saw the change in you the first minute. We all did. Then only last week Alter mentioned what it was and I knew he was right. Naturally

I was puzzled. How could it be? I didn't say one word of what was going on in my mind to Alter, but I thought maybe you would confide in me like you always did. But no. You don't say anything, so why should I ask? Maybe my friend, Beattie, doesn't trust me any more. After two and a half years of . . .'

'Yetta,' I said, 'I trust you like always, but I don't know exactly how to explain what's happened to me. I've tried to discuss it with Frank, but he thinks I'm finding it hard to settle after the holiday and that I'm going through a phase. So tell me, Yetta. What is it? You can't be more puzzled than I am!'

'You mean Frank doesn't know? You must tell him, Beattie. You're a brave girl, and he loves you. Of course he'll be angry and hurt and upset, but he'll get over it. He isn't perfect, either. We all make mistakes.'

I leaned back in the armchair. It was cosy in Yetta's and Alter's little flat. They were so happy together, and now Yetta was going senile; losing her mind, just like Golda, his first wife.

'Drink your tea,' she said. 'Try not to worry. You've got to think of the baby, remember. You're not so young any more.'

'What baby, darling?' I said gently. The cup rattled on the saucer, and I had to put it down on the table.

'Don't talk to me as if I was a senile old woman. If you don't want to trust me, say so. It's time we went down to make the coffee. Come on. Don't get lazy!'

'WHAT BABY?'

'Beattie!' gasped Yetta. 'You don't *know*?'

'Know *what*?'

'Sit down. They can wait for their coffee a few more minutes. You're going to have a baby. You're pregnant.'

I burst out laughing. 'O, God! What are you going to say next,' I gasped. 'Married life is making you broody! I'm going through the change, Yetta, and I've been eating like a pig, so I've put on weight. Frank and I can't produce a kitten between the pair of us, let alone a baby. Don't you remember what I told you about him? Yetta, you sly old devil! Of course you remember! So you thought I'd been carrying on with someone else and got myself in the club? I've a good mind to wash your mouth out with soap. Alter's having a bad influence on you! Come on! They'll be screaming for my blood downstairs, let alone for a cup of coffee. Just wait till I tell Frank about this!'

I ran downstairs, while Yetta followed more slowly on the chair lift. I wondered if all the folks were thinking on the same lines. I couldn't stop smiling. Even Matron couldn't wipe the grin off my face, and I didn't take a scrap of notice when she looked at her watch and tut-tutted. She sat at the kitchen table, talking to Cook, so Yetta kept out of the way. When I rattled into the sitting room with the trolley, all the folks were busy with the occupational therapist. Bubba's grandson Clive was married to Yetta's granddaughter Debbie, who was expecting another baby, and the two of them were making enough little jackets and bootees to clothe an army of midgets.

'I hope some of these are for Baby Dwek,' I whispered to Yetta. 'I haven't got any hand-me-downs, remember! Alter, could you make a doll like this one for *my* little stranger?' I said mischievously, handing him his coffee and biscuits.

'This *is* for your baby,' he smiled. 'But don't say anything to him or her. I want it to be a surprise. I hope it is not too early to congratulate you, Beattie. Your baby and Debbie's should arrive about the same time, and it will be a double joy for us.'

Things had gone too far. 'Alter,' I said quietly. 'I'm not pregnant. You and Yetta are mistaken. I shouldn't have made fun of you. I'm sorry.'

'I don't think you can keep this secret for much longer, Beattie. It was I who told Yetta. But of course we won't say anything to anyone. I suppose you'll be leaving The Haven in a few months. We'll miss you so much.'

'I won't be leaving, Alter,' I said curtly. 'Frank and I can't have more children. We knew that when Gloria was on the way. But you learn to accept these things after a time. I'm sure you and Golda would have liked a family, too.'

I collected the coffee cups and took the trolley back to the kitchen. For some reason, tears blinded my eyes, but I dashed them away and got on with the washing up. It didn't seem funny any more. I wouldn't say anything to Frank. He might not think it very amusing, either.

'Beattie.'

'Alter! You startled me!' I dried my hands on the towel and he put his hand on my shoulder.

'Beattie,' he said again. 'Would you do something for your old Alter?'

'Of course.'

'Ask Doctor Taylor to check you over. He's due this afternoon.'

'I'll see my own doctor – when I feel ill, and not before. I'm not having a baby, Alter. Please don't go on about it. There are medical reasons which make it impossible. I can't go into details. I've put on a bit of weight, that's all. It happens at my time of life.'

'My Golda was pregnant four times, but she could never carry a child beyond the first three months. I used to watch her so carefully at these times. It was a great grief and disappointment to us that we weren't blessed with children. The last time it happened, she was forty-seven. She also thought it was the change of life. But I knew. It was our last chance. I begged her to see the doctor, but she wouldn't. Like you, she thought I had made a mistake. Did I ever think that I would have a grandchild; great-grandchildren to share with Yetta? Miracles happen, Beattie.'

'It's wonderful that you have a share in Yetta's family,' I said, giving him a hug. 'Wonderful for them, too, to have a grandfather and great-grandfather as thoughtful, as kind and as wise as you. But that's good fortune. Miracles don't happen, and even if they do, they don't happen to me.'

'Yes. To you. Humour an old man, and speak to Doctor Taylor.'

214

'All right then! But I'm going to feel such a fool. I'll have to blame it all on you.'

'I hope he won't misunderstand you,' he chuckled.

I gave the folks their lunch and kept some over for Doctor Taylor, as usual. He came straight into the kitchen. I hadn't seen him since before I went on holiday. A locum had been attending the folks at The Haven as he'd been off on some course or other, to do with a particular branch of his medicine.

'What's cooking, Beattie?' he called, bustling in and rubbing his hands. 'You look ravishing when you smile like that. What have you been up to?'

I pulled my face into a scowl. 'You really should have your eyes tested. Sit down at the table. You make me nervous, pacing around. It's nice to see you haven't deserted us completely. Did you enjoy the course?'

'Very much. When I qualified, alternative medicine was on a par with witchcraft, but I've always had an interest in it.'

'You can't mix with Sarah and remain unconvinced of its efficaciousness. Do you mind if I ask you a medical question – alone those lines?'

'As long as it's short and simple.'

'Is it possible for an infertile man to regain his fertility after years and years?'

'It depends on the cause,' said Doctor Taylor. 'I've heard of this happening, but usually it's because the diagnosis was wrong in the first place. A man may have a very low sperm count, due to illness, but under close clinical supervision, conception can be accomplished sometimes. May I ask why you're interested?'

I felt very embarrassed. Frank wouldn't want him to know his personal business. They'd met a couple of times, and had thoroughly disliked each other.

'I was just curious.'

'Fair enough.' He finished his soup and I served the next course. 'Now ask me what you really want to know. Anything you say to me is in the strictest confidence,

Beattie. I hope you'll remember that. I'm at your service as a friend as well as a doctor.'

'I've started this conversation the wrong way round,' I said. 'One of the old women here has put on weight, and the others think she's pregnant. I promised Mr Freid I'd tell you about it.'

He looked at me quizzically, and with such pleasure and kindness, that I felt myself blushing like a girl.

'Bring her to the surgery at, say, three thirty. I'll have got rid of Nurse Goss by then. What's for afters?'

'You eat too quickly. Don't you ever suffer from indigestion?'

'Never. Do you?'

'No.'

'Not even when you were pregnant?'

'I can't remember. It was a long time ago.'

'Don't you ever think about that time?'

'Oh, yes! Frank was terribly ill and I thought he was going to die. I was only eighteen, but I remember how anxious; how distraught I .. . .'

'But can't you recall the details of your pregnancy?'

'No. Not really. Why should I?'

'It might be a useful exercise to try. Hello, Nurse Goss! I'm ready, if you are. Thanks for the grub, Beattie. See you later.'

He followed Nurse Goss out of the kitchen, leaving me alone with my thoughts. They whirled around in my head; wild imaginings shot with some blessed hope which I couldn't control. Could Yetta and Alter be right? *They* believed in alternative medicine. All the old folks at The Haven did, although they didn't use that name exactly. Could Frank have recovered without either of us knowing? How was it possible, after all these years? After all the tests he'd undergone without success? 'We've got Gloria, Frank! Don't worry any more!'

I got on with my work, zombie-like, and at half past three knocked at the surgery door. My mouth felt parched and I was shaking like a leaf.

'Come in, old woman! Take your clothes off and put this sheet round you. How old are you? Eighty-five?'

'Forty-three.'

'When was your last period?'

'Three and a half months ago. Frank and I went to Israel in April, and the change seems to have unsettled me. I suppose the body's time-clock responded likewise. Frank things I'm going through the Change.'

'It's a bit early for that, but of course it's not uncommon. How many times have you been pregnant?' he asked, after poking and pressing and listening as if I was an antique radio set.

'Just the once.'

'And how long ago was that?'

'Nearly twenty-four years. I'm a grandmother.'

'And you and your husband have had a regular sex life.'

'I hope this isn't just idle curiosity on your part,' I snapped. The whole business was an embarrassment to me. This man wasn't my doctor, and I shouldn't have asked him to examine me.

'Would you answer my question, please?'

'I'm sorry,' I mumbled. 'I'm finding all this very difficult. After our daughter was killed, I lost interest in that side of our marriage.'

'And before she was killed?'

'I suppose so.'

'But you never got pregnant again?'

'No. I told you. I've only been pregnant once.'

'Twice,' smiled Doctor Taylor. He covered me with the sheet and popped a pillow under my head. 'Just stay where you are for a few minutes. It's not the Change, Beattie. Not the sort of change you had in mind, anyway! You're into your fourth month. Congratulations! I'm delighted to be the one to tell you such good news. I hope *you* think it's good news! I don't want you to worry, but at your age it would be sensible to take certain precautions. I want you to make an appointment to see your own doctor as soon as possible; say, tomorrow, so that you can be monitored at regular intervals, but I see no reason why you shouldn't give birth to a healthy baby, as long as you take reasonable care and keep fit and well. I'll just check your blood pressure. There, there! I can see this news has come as a shock to you. It's good to cry sometimes. Take your time. Are you worried about anything? About your husband's reaction?'

I tried to speak, but each time I burst into tears. Doctor Taylor held my hand and dried my eyes. I felt so full of joy; so superbly, wonderfully happy, yet so confused, that I wondered whether I was dreaming. He helped me to sit up, then took out the brandy bottle from the surgery cupboard and poured a good measure into two medicine glasses. He sat down next to me on the examination table.

'To you, to Frank and to this forthcoming happy event,' he said, patting my stomach. I pulled myself together at last, and took a sip.

'Are you *sure*, Doctor Taylor? Are you *absolutely* sure?'

He nodded, smiling. 'Are you absolutely sure about the answer to *my* question?'

'You ask too many. Which one?'

'The last one.'

'I've forgotten what it was.'

'Well, here's another one. What were you doing in April?' He sounded quite exasperated.

'We were on holiday.' I started to laugh hysterically.

'And you had . . . you had a holiday romance?'

'Yes! A change of scene works wonders for one!'

'This may not be as hilariously funny as you seem to think,' he said soberly. 'You asked me a question at lunch-time and it was and is patently obvious to me that Frank was the subject of your query. Is *he* aware of his problem?'

'Of course!'

'Then you'll have to tell him he was mistaken. Would you like me to speak to him first? I really don't want you to be upset just now.'

'Upset! Why should I be upset? Is something wrong?' I shivered.

He took hold of my hand again, and held it in his. 'Beattie,' he said gently, 'if Frank believes he can't be the father, he may not be as pleased as you are. Do you follow me?'

'It's all right,' I smiled. 'It really is. Frank will be as delighted as I am. You see, he had treatment quite recently, but it somehow slipped my mind. I think it slipped his, too! One of these days, I'll explain, but not just now, if you don't mind. Thank you for everything, Doctor Taylor. Is it okay if I get dressed now?'

'Yes. Don't forget to see your doctor tomorrow, and if you ever need to ask me anything, remember I'm here every Tuesday!'

I pulled on my clothes and kissed him on the cheek, which was a mistake, but I didn't care. After I'd extricated myself from his not too brotherly embrace, I rushed off to catch up on my work. The rest of the afternoon passed in a euphoria of joy. I gave Alter and Yetta the thumbs-up sign and they both came over to hug me. I looked around me through a blur of tears and it seemed to me that they were all smiling at me – even Sarah. My family. My friends. My therapists. My Haven. Tinker was coming back in two weeks and I knew they wouldn't fail her, either.

Frank was cooking supper when I arrived home. I went into the living room and poured out two glasses of sherry.

'Frank!' I called. 'Could you turn down the oven and come here for a minute! I want to ask you something important. Have you noticed a change in me?'

'Oh, God!' he groaned. 'Not again!'

'All right,' I said. 'I promise this is the very last time I'll ask you. Take your sherry and make a toast – the same one that Abdul made before he gave you that stuff to drink.'

'Beattie,' he said irritably, 'give it a rest, will you!'

'Humour an old woman, Frank. He said, "This will give you sons!" Am I right?'

'Something like that.' He took a sip. 'Come on, old woman. Take your coat off and set the table. Supper in five minutes.'

'There's something much better than supper in the

219

oven, sweetheart! In five months' time it'll be cooked to perfection!' I took his hand and pressed it on the front of my coat. For a few moments he stood quite still. I looked into his face. He looked pale; wretched.

'Beattie,' he said gently. 'Let's make an appointment for you to see the doctor tomorrow. You've put on a bit of weight, that's all. Don't let your imagination run away with you. Don't hope for miracles. I know how much you wanted another child. How much we both did. But it wasn't to be. It isn't to be. Perhaps we should have talked about it more, but you know how I avoid painful subjects. I'm sorry. I'll try to change.' Poor Frank! After all, he was a scientist and didn't understand.

'I've made an appointment to see the doctor. I telephoned from work. You're right. I should see him. I know I've put on weight and I won't let my imagination run riot or hope for miracles any more. I don't have to. There's no need, because the miracle's happened. Alter told me this morning. I didn't believe in them either until Doctor Taylor mentioned alternative medicine and examined me, and told me I was four months pregnant. Then I understood, of course!'

I took his hand and pressed it on the front of my coat again. For a few moments he stood quite still. I looked into his face. I had never seen such pure joy – except perhaps once – a long, long time ago, when he was a boy of nineteen.

'Are you sure? Oh, Beattie, are you *absolutely* sure?'
'Absolutely.'
'But how? When? I don't understand!'
'If only you'd listen to me, Frank,' I said. 'Ever since we visited Abdul in his tent, I've noticed a change in you.'